INSPECTOR HADLEY

THE DIPLOMAT MURDERS

by

PETER CHILD

Benbow Publications

© Copyright 2011 by Peter Child

Peter Child has asserted his right under the Copyright, Designs and Patents Act, 1988 to be identified as the author of this work.

All rights reserved. No part of this publication may be reproduced, stored in a retrieval system, or transmitted in any form or by any means, electronic, mechanical photocopying, recording or otherwise without the prior permission of the copyright holder.

Published in 2011 by Benbow Publications

British Library
Cataloguing in Publication Data.

ISBN: 978-1-908760-01-2

Printed by Lightning Source UK Ltd
Chapter House
Pitfield
Kiln Farm
Milton Keynes
MK11 3LW

First Edition

OTHER TITLES BY THE AUTHOR

ERIC THE ROMANTIC
ERIC AND THE DIVORCEE

THE MICHEL RONAY SERIES:

MARSEILLE TAXI
AUGUST IN GRAMBOIS
CHRISTMAS IN MARSEILLE
CATASTROPHE IN LE TOUQUET
RETURN TO MARSEILLE

THE INSPECTOR HADLEY SERIES:

THE TAVISTOCK SQUARE MURDERS
THE GOLD BULLION MURDERS
THE TOWER OF LONDON MURDERS
THE AMERICAN MURDERS
THE DIAMOND MURDERS
THE ROYAL RUSSIAN MURDERS
THE SATAN MURDERS
THE MEDICAL MURDERS
THE WESTMINSTER MURDERS
THE GIGOLO MURDERS
THE HOLY GRAIL MURDERS

NON-FICTION

NOTES FOR GOOD DRIVERS
NOTES FOR COMPANY DRIVERS
VEHICLE PAINTER'S NOTES
VEHICLE FINE FINISHING
VEHICLE FABRICATIONS IN GRP

ACKNOWLEDGEMENTS

Once again, I wish to gratefully acknowledge the help and assistance given to me by Sue Gresham and to thank Wendy Tobitt for the splendid cover presentation. Without these talented and patient ladies this book would not have been possible.

Peter Child

INTRODUCTION

In June 1882 Sergei Brasov, a Rumanian Diplomat, is murdered in Hyde Park whilst waiting to meet his mistress, Natasha Galati, wife of the Embassy Secretary Antone Galati. Inspector Hadley and Sergeant Cooper are assigned to the case and are told to proceed carefully when questioning Diplomatic staff. Events move at a breathtaking pace as two more Diplomats are murdered and from then on Hadley and Cooper face a roller coaster ride of uncertainty to find the assassin before he strikes again.

Characters and events portrayed in this book are fictional.

CHAPTER 1

It was just before three o'clock on a bright sunny afternoon in June 1882 when the Diplomat, Sergei Brasov left his office at the Rumanian Embassy in Sussex Gardens, crossed the Bayswater Road and entered Hyde Park through the Victoria Gate. He was on his way to meet his beautiful mistress Natasha Galati, wife of the Embassy Secretary Antone Galati. Galati was a much older man and more interested in Balkan politics than his young wife who, after years of neglect, looked elsewhere for her emotional needs. It was love at first sight when Brasov arrived in London the previous Christmas and met Natasha at an Embassy function. The affair had been consummated at The Piccadilly Hotel in January and since then they met regularly after Natasha finished her Wednesday shopping in the West End. It was their practice to meet by the Serpentine Lake in Hyde Park then stroll along to the Hotel for their afternoon pleasures before returning separately to the Embassy.

Brasov sat on the usual seat at their meeting place overlooking the Lake and glanced at his fob watch, wondering how long it would be before Natasha arrived. An unseen assassin moved quietly from the trees behind the seat, looked about and approached Brasov before quickly thrusting a thin bladed stiletto up through the slats on the back of the seat into his victim's body. The single stab wound pierced Brasov's heart and he died instantly without a murmur. The killer audaciously pulled Brasov's hat down over his eyes, as if he were asleep and quickly left the scene.

Minutes later Natasha arrived and smiled when she saw her lover waiting. 'Sorry I'm a little late, darling, but the shops were so busy today,' she said as she sat down beside him. When he did not reply she looked at him and asked 'Sergei… are you sleepy?' She slowly lifted his hat from his ashen face and whispered 'Sergei?' but his wild staring eyes made her scream with horror as she realised he was dead.

Inspector James Hadley had just returned from a week's leave in Bognor Regis with his wife, Alice and their two children. It was the family's favourite seaside town and Hadley had taken them there for a complete rest after he had finished investigating the gruelling case of the Holy Grail murders. Hadley's assistant, Sergeant Robert Cooper, had also been on leave and taken his young wife, Doris, to Eastbourne for a well earned holiday to rest and recover his strength after being wounded during the Grail investigation.

The detectives arrived back in their office at Scotland Yard on the Monday and were greeted by their affable clerk, George, who had a pot of tea waiting for them to start the week. After discussing with George the merits of their enjoyable holidays, they attended to accumulated paperwork, wrote reports and replied to requests from the Crown Prosecution Office for details of pending cases.

On the following Wednesday Big Ben was striking four o'clock when the news came through that a Diplomat had been murdered in Hyde Park, Chief Inspector Howard Bell immediately sent for Hadley.

When the Inspector entered the Chief's office, Bell waved him to sit in the creaking chair and asked 'had a good holiday?'

'Yes thank you, sir, it was…'

'Good, I'm glad you're back… there's been a murder in Hyde Park and I want you to start the investigation immediately,' interrupted Bell.

'Right, sir, is it…'

'The victim is a Diplomat and when I inform the Commissioner in a minute, I want to tell him that you're already on the case, Hadley.'

'Very good, sir.'

'There will be hell to pay when the Home Secretary knows about the killing.'

'Why is that, sir?'

'Well apparently this Johnny Foreigner was a Rumanian… from the bloody Balkans, Hadley!'

'Really sir?'

'Yes… it could mean turmoil and disorder on our London Streets!'

'I don't see how…'

'Hadley, don't you read the papers?'

'I've been on leave, sir, besides I don't believe everything...'

'Well you'd better believe the fact that these East European Foreigners are intent on destroying themselves and everybody around them... God only knows why we let any of them in!'

'Quite so, sir.'

'Now there's a complication with this investigation which will prove very difficult for us, Hadley.'

'And what's that, sir?'

'It's the Diplomatic Immunity aspect which will inevitably hamper our inquiries,' replied Bell.

'Well I'm sure we'll overcome any difficulties, sir.'

'I'm glad to hear you say it, Hadley, but I'm not so confident.'

Hadley ignored the comment and asked 'were there any witnesses, sir?'

'Apparently a passerby saw a screaming woman running from the Park...'

'Do you think she was the killer, sir?'

'I've no idea... that's for you to discover!'

'Yes of course, sir.'

'The Police were alerted at Paddington and Inspector Baxter attended the scene with his Sergeant but when they arrived they were surprised to see the corpse being carried away on a stretcher by four men...'

'Good heavens, sir.'

'And when they were stopped by Baxter, these unruly foreigners told him that they were from the Rumanian Embassy and as the murdered man was one of their Diplomats they were taking the body back there...'

'But they can't do that, sir!' interrupted Hadley.

'Well they did.'

'Who alerted them to the murder, sir?'

'We don't know... but it was possibly the screaming woman,' replied Bell.

'What action did Inspector Baxter take then, sir?'

'He accompanied them to their Embassy in Sussex Gardens and when he was refused admittance he returned to the station and telegraphed me,' replied Bell.

'Good grief, sir.'

'Exactly, Inspector, so get over to Paddington, talk to Baxter and any witnesses, then see if you can find this screaming woman while I go up and inform the Commissioner.'

'Yes, sir.'

'God knows where this will all end,' said Bell with a sigh and a shake of his head.

Within ten minutes Hadley and Cooper were in a Police coach being driven at speed through the busy traffic towards Paddington Green station. Hadley told Cooper all he knew about the case and the Sergeant looked quite bemused.

'They took the body back to their Embassy, sir?' he asked in disbelief.

'Yes they did.'

'Didn't Inspector Baxter try to stop them, sir?'

'I'm sure he did, but they must have claimed Diplomatic Immunity, so he had no alternative but to stand back and report the incident, Sergeant.'

'Well, this could be a very tricky investigation, sir.'

'Indeed it could,' replied Hadley as the coach turned into the yard at Paddington Green Police station.

When the detectives entered Baxter's office he looked up from his desk, smiled at Hadley and said 'good afternoon, Jim.'

'Afternoon, Peter.'

'I'm glad to see you. The Chief Inspector telegraphed that you were on your way and would be taking over the investigation and I must say I'm very relieved,' said Baxter as he waved them to sit.

'I'm sure you are, Peter.'

'I didn't fancy getting involved in such a difficult case when I've so much else to attend to these days.'

'I know the feeling... we've only just finished the investigation into the Grail murders.'

'Yes I know and of course the Press didn't help, making such a great palaver out of it,' said Baxter.

'Ah... they know that sordid details sell newspapers,' said Hadley with a smile.

'And the more sordid the better it seems!'

'Quite so, now tell me about this incident, Peter.'

4

'Right… a gentleman came into the station at three fifteen and reported to my Duty Sergeant that a man was found dead on a seat in Hyde Park. It appeared he'd been stabbed and a woman was seen running away towards the Victoria Gate. I hurried over with Sergeant Edwards and was surprised to find four men carrying the body through the Park, so I identified myself and told them that this was a Police investigation.'

'What happened next?'

'I instructed them to leave the body immediately but one of them said the deceased was a Diplomat from the Rumanian Embassy and they were taking the corpse there. I challenged this but the man claimed Diplomatic Immunity and they carried on walking. I remained with them and attempted to enter the Embassy to speak to a higher authority but was forcibly barred from doing so.'

'Good grief.'

'So I came back here and immediately telegraphed the Yard.'

'Hmm, this is not going to be easy… what about the woman? Any sign of her?'

'No, Jim, she's disappeared.'

'Any other witnesses?'

'Yes, a nanny pushing a pram says she thought she saw the woman sitting on the seat with the victim but can't be sure and the gentleman who reported the incident says he only heard the woman scream before she ran off,' replied Baxter.

'Not a lot to go on then,' said Hadley gloomily.

'I'm afraid not, Jim.'

'Are the two witnesses still here?'

'No, Jim, they've given statements, which really don't amount to much, but we have their addresses if you want to speak to them,' replied Baxter.

'Yes I think I will after I get the Commissioner to ask the Home Secretary to send a telegraph through to the Embassy.'

'Blimey Jim, that will take some doing!'

'Everything is possible when a murder has been committed, Peter,' said Hadley with a smile.

The detectives hurried back to the Yard and Hadley immediately went up to Bell's office.

After explaining what he wanted to the bemused Chief, Bell shook his head and said 'it's totally out of the question, Hadley… and that's absolutely final!'

'Sir, with respect… we have to get the body released for a post mortem and I need to question the Embassy staff if we're to have a snowball in hell's chance of catching the killer,' said Hadley forcefully. Bell leaned back in his chair and gazed at the ceiling for inspiration whilst Hadley waited patiently in silence for the reply. After a few moments the Chief looked at him and said 'on second thoughts, although I don't agree, you'd better explain what you want to the Commissioner… but I must warn you to watch your step because when I told him about the incident, he was not a happy man!'

'I will be careful, sir.'

When the detectives entered the Commissioner's office it was obvious that the great one was not in a good mood as his side whiskers were twitching more than usual. He glanced up from his desk at both officers and remained in stony faced silence as Bell said hesitantly 'Inspector Hadley would like to make a request, sir.'

'Would he now,' replied the Commissioner in a menacing half whisper.

Hadley took a deep breath and said 'yes, sir, I'd like you to ask the Home Secretary to send a telegraph to the Rumanian Ambassador requesting that he releases the body of the murdered Diplomat for a post mortem examination and allow me to question the Embassy staff.'

'And that, Hadley, would probably cause a diplomatic incident at the highest level leading to the possible breakdown of relations with England's only ally in the Balkans!' thundered the Commissioner.

'Well I can't see how it can be avoided if I am to apprehend the murderer, sir,' said Hadley.

'You go too far, Inspector!' roared the Commissioner whilst Bell tut-tutted and shook his head in despair.

'But, sir, with respect…' began Hadley.

'Listen to me, Inspector, since Rumania declared its independence from Russia five years ago there has been nothing but unrest in the Balkans, made worse when Prince Battenburg became the ruler of Bulgaria three years ago!' interrupted the Commissioner.

'I am sure that is so, sir, but...'

'There are no 'buts' with regard to Rumania, our only ally in Eastern Europe at the moment, Hadley!' said the Commissioner angrily.

'Well sir, if that's the case then I cannot see my way forward in the investigation,' said Hadley and there followed a deathly silence before Brackley entered the office and announced 'sir, the Home Secretary is here to see you.' The Commissioner stood up immediately as Sir George West swept into the office and nodded at them.

'Good afternoon, Commissioner... Chief Inspector... Inspector.'

'Good afternoon, sir,' they chorused.

'Now what's this I hear about the murder of a Rumanian Diplomat in Hyde Park?' asked Sir George.

'I'm afraid it's true, sir... I was just on my way to officially report it to you' replied the Commissioner, blushing slightly.

'Well this could cause problems if the assassin turns out to be from one of the other Balkan countries,' said Sir George.

'I'm sure, sir.'

'They'll be fighting one another in some crazy vendetta!' said Sir George firmly.

'Perish the thought, sir.'

'Indeed... but you know what these hot blooded Eastern Europeans are like.'

'Yes I do, sir, they don't have our calm approach to adversity.'

'Very true, Commissioner, so if we fail to stop this now with a quick arrest and conviction we could have more killings to deal with.'

'I'm sure you are right, sir and we will make every effort to stop any escalation of violence.'

'Indeed you must, now what progress have you made so far in apprehending the killer?'

'Inspector Hadley has begun the investigations sir, and he was about to give me his report ...'

'Good, let's hear it then, Inspector,' interrupted Sir George and

Hadley gulped.

'Well, sir, there's not a great deal to report at the moment…' Hadley began.

'But surely you must have discovered something, Inspector, I'm on my way to the House to inform the Prime Minister and I can hardly tell him that we've nothing to report,' interrupted Sir George and the Commissioner looked anxious.

Hadley gave a succinct account of what had happened and when he finished he asked Sir George if he would consider sending a message to the Rumanian Ambassador requesting his assistance. The Commissioner and Bell looked horrified but breathed a sigh of relief when Sir George replied 'I think I must do that in all conscience, Inspector, we must ensure that we have the victim's body and are free to question the Embassy staff… after all it is in their own interest. We cannot have our ability to uphold the law in this country compromised by fatuous claims of Diplomatic Immunity by foreigners.'

'Quite so, sir,' beamed the Commissioner and Bell nodded.

'As soon as I return from seeing the Prime Minister in the Commons, I will send a telegraph to the Ambassador requesting his help, so I suggest that you, Chief Inspector Bell, go with Hadley to the Embassy and wait until the body is released then send it to the Marylebone for a post mortem examination,' said Sir George.

'Very good, sir,' replied Bell.

'And tell the Embassy Secretary when you wish to start interviewing his staff.'

'I will, sir.'

'If I remember correctly his name is Galati, he's a bit of an old fire brand so watch how you go with him,' said Sir George.

'Of course, sir.'

'We must be diplomatic with these foreigners to achieve the results we want without ruffling their feathers too much.'

'Quite so, sir,' replied Bell and the Commissioner smiled.

'Well, I'll leave you gentlemen to get on with your duties while I inform the PM about this tragedy,' said Sir George before he nodded at them and hurried from the office.

The Commissioner sank back down in his seat, sighed and said 'whatever you do, Chief Inspector, make sure you don't cause any problems with these Rumanians.'

'I will be very careful, sir.'

'I'm relieved to hear it,' said the Commissioner with another sigh.

After they had left the Commissioner's office and were descending the stairs, Bell said 'telegraph Doctor Evans at the Marylebone and tell him to organise an ambulance to meet us at the Embassy for the Diplomat's corpse.'

'Yes, sir.'

'And Hadley, make sure he understands the urgency of this investigation... I want to see his report into the cause of death as soon as possible,' said Bell as they reached the landing outside his office.

'Very good, sir.'

'We'll leave in half an hour, so that should give Sir George enough time to get back from the Commons and telegraph the Ambassador before we set off.'

After telegraphing Doctor Evans, Hadley returned to his office and asked George to make a pot of tea while he told Cooper what had transpired.

'So it looks like a late night again, sir,' said Cooper gloomily.

'I'm afraid so, Sergeant.'

'Well that's a pity... I'd promised my wife that I'd take her to the music hall tonight.'

'I'm sure there will be many other times, Sergeant,' said Hadley with a smile as George brought in the tea.

Big Ben was striking seven o'clock when the detectives left the Yard in a closed Police coach and made their way through the busy traffic towards the Rumanian Embassy in Sussex Gardens. On the journey nothing was said but Bell looked apprehensive and Hadley had deep forebodings about the investigation, which he knew could prove to be very difficult.

CHAPTER 2

The ambulance from the Marylebone Hospital was already outside the Embassy when the Police coach arrived. Hadley made himself known to the attendants and briefed them on the situation whilst Bell and Cooper climbed the steps and waited at the front door of the building. When Hadley joined them, he gave a nod to Cooper, who rang the bell.

'Let me do all the talking, Hadley,' said Bell.

'As you wish, sir,' said Hadley in a resigned tone.

'Well as I'm the senior officer it's better that the questions come from me because you know how touchy these foreigners can be about status,' said Bell as the door was opened by a swarthy looking man. The Chief held up his warrant card and said pompously 'I'm Chief Inspector Howard Bell from Scotland Yard and this is Inspector Hadley and Sergeant Cooper... I believe we are expected.' The man nodded, stood back and held the door open for them to enter the hallway.

'Please stay here,' said the man in a thick accent before he disappeared up a flight of stairs. The spacious hallway was dark and had an air of gloomy decadence about it which gave a poor impression of the Embassy. Hanging on the dark green walls were several pictures of decrepit old statesmen which did not give the onlooker much confidence in the government of Rumania.

Within a few minutes the man returned and said 'Secretary Galati will see you now, please follow me.' He led the detectives up the stairs and along a corridor to the end, where he opened double doors for them to enter a large office. Antone Galati stood up from behind his glass topped desk and gave a courteous nod.

'Good evening, Secretary Galati, I'm Chief Inspector Howard Bell and this is Inspector Hadley and Sergeant Cooper.'

'Good evening, gentlemen,' said Galati in a thick accent.

'I believe that our Home Secretary, Sir George West, sent a message to your Ambassador regarding our visit,' said Bell.

'Yes he has, Chief Inspector.'

'Well I'm sure you know that it is in connection with the dreadful incident that took place in Hyde Park this afternoon.'

'Yes I know,' replied Galati in an unemotional tone.

'On direct orders from Sir George we have come to recover the body of your murdered Diplomat and arrange a convenient time for interviewing your Embassy staff, sir,' said Bell and Galati's expression remained impassive.

'Please sit down, gentlemen,' said Galati as he waved them to seats in front of his desk. Hadley looked at the ageing Rumanian and suspected that he had a cruel, uncaring streak within him. Galati's eyes were hard and unblinking and his pallid face was topped with thick grey hair giving an appearance of cold ruthlessness, which Hadley surmised was necessary in a man dealing with difficult political situations in the Balkans.

Galati cleared his throat and said 'Ambassador Sulina has instructed me to release the body of our murdered Diplomat, Sergei Brasov, for your examination... but we want a copy of the coroner's report and the body returned for burial in Rumania.'

'Yes of course, sir.'

'And It will not be necessary to question our staff because we know who the killer is,' said Galati. There was a moment of shocked silence before Bell asked 'and who is that, sir?'

'We don't know his name but he is a Bulgarian assassin,' replied Galati firmly.

'And why would he wish to murder Diplomat Brasov, sir?'

'It is a long and complicated story, Chief Inspector, but in essence the Bulgarian government suspected that Brasov was a spy in Sofiya and when he was posted to London a few months ago, we believed they would attempt to murder him here so they would not be connected and blamed for his death,' replied Galati. Hadley knew immediately that the investigation would be cloaked by a web of deceit and confrontations with the Eastern European Diplomatic community would ensue. If he was going to apprehend the killer he needed help from the Home Secretary every step of the way and that was not going to be easy.

'We shall follow up every line of inquiry, wherever it leads us, sir, but we still need to question your staff, just to clear our routine investigations you understand,' said Bell with a smile.

Galati sighed and replied 'if you wish Chief Inspector, but you will be wasting your time, I assure you.'

'Well as it's our time, sir, you can have no objection can you?'

'No,' replied Galati with a shrug of his shoulders.

'Who discovered the body and informed the Embassy, sir?' asked Hadley. Galati looked at him and hesitated for a moment before he replied 'actually it was my wife who found Brasov... she was returning through Hyde Park from a shopping trip, Inspector.'

'Did she say if she saw the killer, sir?'

'No, she didn't... and she was far too distressed to say much.'

'I'd like to have a few words with your wife if I may, sir.'

'That's out of the question, Inspector... she is in a state of shock. She has been attended by our Doctor and is now resting,' replied Galati.

'Then perhaps tomorrow, sir?' persisted Hadley and Bell glared at him.

'Only if the Doctor says she is well enough, Inspector.'

'Of course, sir, now may we speak to the members of staff who brought the body in from the Park?' asked Hadley.

'If you must, but I warn you their English is not good so I will translate your questions,' replied Galati and Hadley was immediately suspicious.

'Thank you, sir.'

Galati turned round and pushed a bell-button in the wall behind him. Within a few minutes the swarthy man appeared and Galati spoke quickly in Rumanian. The man nodded and left the office.

'There were four of my security men who went to the park this afternoon, Chief Inspector...'

'We know, sir, our Inspector Baxter reported that fact to the Yard and he was taken aback when your men refused to co-operate with him,' interrupted Bell.

'Well I regret any misunderstanding, but as I said, their English is not good,' said Galati with a smile.

'And Inspector Baxter also reported that he was barred from entering your Embassy to speak to someone in authority!' said Bell as the door opened and four men entered. Galati ignored Bell's comments and spoke quickly to them and when he finished they all nodded.

'So what questions do you wish to ask, Chief Inspector?' asked Galati with a smile as Cooper took out his notebook.

'I would like to know their names and what duties they perform,' replied Bell. Galati looked uncomfortable and replied 'surely you only wish to know what occurred in Hyde Park, anything else is irrelevant.'

'On the contrary, sir, everything is relevant in a murder inquiry... so please give us their names,' said Bell firmly.

Galati sighed and replied 'our chief of security is Vlad Bacau and the others are Simeria, Vaslu and Arud.' Each man nodded as Galati relayed their names and Cooper made notes.

'Would you ask them if they saw the killer or anything untoward, sir?' asked Bell, Galati translated and they shook their heads.

'Can any of them give a clue, however small, as to why your Diplomat was murdered?' asked Bell and Galati translated. The men looked at Bacau for a lead and he replied at length. The detectives waited for the translation and were disappointed when Galati said 'they know nothing, Chief Inspector.'

Hadley waited for a moment before asking 'which one of you spoke to Inspector Baxter?' Galati looked anxious and was about to say something when Bacau replied in perfect English 'it was me, sir.'

'Ah, I thought so... now Mr Bacau would you like to tell us why you claimed diplomatic immunity in reply to a challenge by a Police Officer in the middle of Hyde Park while carrying the body of a murdered man?' Hadley demanded and Galati looked horrified.

'I was ordered to, sir,' replied Bacau.

'Who by?' asked Hadley but before Bacau could reply Galati said firmly 'enough of this questioning!'

'Please let him answer sir,' said Bell calmly and Galati looked angrily at Bacau, who hesitated before replying 'our Ambassador, sir.' There followed a moments silence and Hadley glanced at Bell who raised his eyebrows.

'Well I think we've heard enough this evening, so Mr Galati would you kindly release the body of your Diplomat so it can be examined by our pathologist at the Marylebone Hospital?' said Bell. Galati looked relieved and replied 'yes of course.' He then spoke rapidly in Rumanian to Bacau who nodded and left the office with his assistants.

'The body will be brought to the front door, Chief Inspector,' said Galati.

'Thank you for your co-operation, sir.'

'You're welcome, Chief Inspector.'

'Inspector Hadley will be back tomorrow to question other members of your staff and of course your wife... if she is well enough,' said Bell with a smile and Galati looked decidedly uncomfortable but just nodded.

The detectives were escorted downstairs to the hallway where the body of Brasov lay on a stretcher under a sheet and Bacau was standing by the door.

'Sergeant, let the ambulance men know we're ready to get the victim away to the morgue now,' said Hadley.

'Right, sir,' replied Cooper and after he left the hallway, Bacau said to Hadley 'I must speak to you away from here, sir.'

Hadley glanced at him and, sensing the man's anxiety, replied 'then come to my office at Scotland Yard as soon as you can.'

'I will be there at noon tomorrow, sir,' said Bacau with a nod before he hurried away down a corridor. Hadley glanced at Bell, raised his eyebrows and said 'that may prove interesting, sir.'

'Possibly,' replied Bell as the attendants entered the hallway with Cooper, lifted up the stretcher and removed it out to the ambulance. The detectives left the Embassy and stood watching the ambulance as it trotted off towards the Marylebone. Bell turned to Hadley and said 'now we've got the body safely away, let's get back to the Yard and write up a report for the Commissioner before we go home tonight.'

'Very good, sir.'

'I think this investigation is going to get very tricky from now on with these damned foreigners, so the more we have written down to cover ourselves, the better, Hadley.'

'Yes I agree, sir.'

As soon as they arrived back at the Yard they began writing reports and it was after nine o'clock when Hadley took his hand written notes up to Bell.

'Jenkins will get it all typed up for the Commissioner first thing tomorrow, Hadley.'

'Thank you, sir.'

'And I'm sure he'll want to talk to us about the case so stay in your office in the morning,' said Bell.

'Very good, sir.'

Hadley said 'goodnight' to the Chief and returned to his office where Cooper was tidying his desk before leaving.

'Well, what a day it's been, sir.'

'Yes indeed... and I'm sure that tomorrow will be just as busy,' replied Hadley.

'Are you leaving now, sir?'

'In a minute, Sergeant, after I've sorted a few things out... but you get off home.'

'Right, sir... goodnight.'

'Goodnight,' replied Hadley just as a messenger arrived with a telegraph. He handed it to Hadley and said 'I was told to take this to Chief Inspector Bell... but he's left for the night so I've brought it to you, sir.'

'Thank you.'

Cooper waited in the doorway as Hadley opened the brown envelope and read the message.

'Oh dear God, no,' whispered Hadley.

'What is it, sir?'

'It's from Inspector Palmer... he says a Diplomat has been a murdered in Whitechapel, he was with one of the street girls!'

'Bloody hell sir!'

'Precisely, Sergeant... let's get over there as quick as we can!'

The Police coach was driven at speed through the dark streets to Whitechapel station and Hadley's mind was in a whirl with questions. Had the same killer struck again? Was he a Bulgarian assassin in the pay of the government? Did Vlad Bacau know who this man was? Hadley wrestled with many un-answered questions before the coach turned into the yard at Whitechapel. The desk Sergeant in reception instantly recognised the detectives and said to Hadley 'good evening, sir... I expect you've come about the murder of the Diplomat in Church Alley?'

'I have, Sergeant.'

'Very good, sir... Inspector Palmer and Sergeant Morris are in the interview room talking to the witnesses.'

'Thank you, Sergeant,' said Hadley before he hurried down the corridor.

Jack Palmer looked up and smiled when the detectives entered the room and said 'blimey Jim, that was quick!'

'You should know by now Jack that I never waste any time,' replied Hadley with a grin as he glanced at the three women seated at the table. He knew them all very well and smiled saying 'hello ladies.'

'Oh Jim, we're so glad you're here,' said Agnes Cartwright, a woman whom Hadley had known for many years from his days as young Constable patrolling the foggy streets of Whitechapel. He had been attracted to the abused woman after he first arrested her brute of a husband for drunken affray. A few years later, after a fight on the dockside, Cartwright had met his end by drowning in the Thames. Agnes became a streetwalker after failed relationships with several unscrupulous men.

'Too blimmin right,' added Florrie Dean, who was Agnes's constant companion on the streets. At that moment Molly Barnet began to cry and Agnes put her arm around the young woman and Palmer said 'you're safe with us now, Molly.'

'I know guvnor, but it was 'orrible... just blimmin 'orrible,' she said as the tears coursed down her pale cheeks.

'I know it's upsetting for you but just tell us again so Inspector Hadley hears what happened, Molly,' said Palmer gently as Hadley sat down opposite the tearful woman. They waited whilst she composed herself and when she was ready, said 'he was one of my nice regular's, so to speak, he'd meet me in the Ten Bells most Wednesday's... he'd buy me a gin and talk about his family before we came out and did the business...' She stopped to wipe her eyes with a handkerchief.

'Please go on, Molly,' said Palmer calmly.

'Well I'd gone into the pub where he was waiting for me, he was such a gentle fella and took his time you know,' she said and Agnes nodded, adding 'there's precious few of them about these days.'

'Too blimmin true' said Florrie.

'So what happened next, Molly?' asked Hadley gently.

'We had a drink and a chat, then we went outside and down to Church Alley where we did it in one of the shop doorways...' she faltered and began to cry again. Palmer glanced at Hadley who raised his eyebrows.

'Go on, Molly,' said Palmer.

'Well, I felt him finish and suddenly I saw this bloke in a bowler hat standing behind him… then my fella grunted and clung on to me blimmin tight before he let go and fell down… as Gawd's my judge I didn't know what had happened to him, then this other bloke ran off!'

'Did you get a good look at him?' asked Hadley.

'No, guvnor, it took me awhile to realise my fella was dead… but when I saw all the blood on the step, I called out for help and a Bobby came… then Agnes and Florrie,' replied Molly before she started to cry once more.

'Thank you, Molly,' said Palmer as Agnes comforted the distressed woman.

'Where's the body now, Jack?' asked Hadley.

'After it was brought back here and searched for identification I had it taken to the Marylebone, Jim,' replied Palmer.

'How was he killed?'

'It looked like a single stab wound to the back,' replied Palmer.

'Doctor Evans will be busy because that's the second one today,' said Hadley.

'A second murder, Jim?'

'Yes… and the victim was another Diplomat.'

'Blimey!' exclaimed Palmer and the women looked anxious on hearing that.

'When I got your telegraph you sent to the Chief, I rushed over because a Rumanian was killed in Hyde Park this afternoon and I think the murders are probably linked,' said Hadley.

'Well this fella was a Bulgarian named Igor Plovdiv and his papers said he was a Diplomat at their Embassy,' said Palmer.

'Now we've got real trouble, Jack,' said Hadley.

'Why?'

'Because when we went to the Rumanian Embassy this evening to retrieve the body, the Secretary told us that he suspected the Bulgarian's for the murder of their man,' replied Hadley.

'Good God Almighty!'

'Have you been in touch with the Bulgarian Embassy and told them?'

'No Jim… I was leaving that little job to the Chief and the Commissioner,' replied Palmer.

'In the present circumstances I think that is very wise, Jack.'

'What now, Jim?'

'I think we should arrange for Molly to stay in protective custody until we find the killer because he may come after her if he thinks she can identify him,' replied Hadley. On hearing that Molly cried out 'oh my Gawd, the bloody bloke will do me in if he finds me and no mistake!'

'We'll not let any harm come to you, Molly,' said Hadley.

'Of course not,' added Palmer.

'You'll be much safer in here with all the young Bobbies than out on the streets,' said Agnes as she squeezed the tearful Molly.

'Can I stay with her for company, guvnor?' asked Florrie with wide blue eyes. Hadley glanced at Palmer who grinned and replied 'just for the night, Florrie.'

'Oh thank you, guvnor, I'll be ever so good... I promise,' said Florrie.

'Then mind you are... because I don't want you distracting my officers from their duties,' said Palmer in mock seriousness and Hadley grinned. Florrie was very attractive blonde who had been forced to sell herself on the streets of Whitechapel after being dismissed from her position as a house maid. She had been found by her Mistress half naked with the Master, amongst the pastries in the pantry. Florrie gave a 'special' service to refined gentlemen, which was appreciated by all her regulars who came down from their West End clubs to receive her close attention.

Palmer asked Sergeant Morris to make arrangements for the women to share a cell then organise some food and tea for them. When they had left the room, Hadley said 'I think it's too late to do anything tonight, Jack so I'll inform the Chief first thing tomorrow and get him to put the diplomatic wheels in motion to advise the Bulgarian Embassy through the Commissioner and the Home Secretary.'

'Thank you, Jim... it will be a weight off my mind I can tell you.'

'Let me have everything you found on the body.'

'Right you are.'

Hadley and Cooper left the station with Agnes and escorted her down to her lodgings in Gypsy Lane. When they said 'goodnight', she kissed them both and thanked them for all their help. The detectives hurried up the Lane to Thames Street where Cooper hailed a passing Hansom cab to take them to Hadley's home in Camden. As the cab rattled over the cobbled streets, Hadley remained deep in thought and Cooper knew not to disturb his Inspector when he was thinking about the case. Eventually the cab turned into Plender Street and when it stopped outside his house, Hadley said 'Sergeant, I believe we have before us an investigation that could destroy our careers if we are not very careful.'

'Really, sir?'

'Yes... I'm sure that powerful wheels within wheels at the highest level will attempt to thwart us... goodnight.'

'Goodnight, sir.'

CHAPTER 3

The next morning Hadley arrived in his office just after seven thirty and began sorting through the belongings of Igor Plovdiv. George arrived soon after and said in a surprised tone 'good morning, sir… you're an early bird today if I may say so.'

'Indeed I am, George… it's because we had another Diplomat murdered last night.'

'Good heavens, sir… what is the world coming to?'

'I often wonder, George.'

'Was he another Rumanian, sir?'

'No, this one was a Bulgarian.'

'Blimey sir, that'll put the cat amongst the pigeons!'

'That's just what I'm afraid of, George.'

'They'll blame one another, sir, these foreigners always do… you mark my words!'

'I'm sure they will if there is any link between the victims.'

'I'd better go and put the kettle on because I think you and the Sergeant will need fortifying before you start work today, sir.'

'Very true, George' said Hadley with a grin as Cooper entered the office.

Big Ben was striking eight o'clock when Hadley ascended the stairs to the Chief's office. He was not looking forward to the difficulties that lay ahead and he knew that Bell would only add to the complications. The Chief looked up from his desk and scowled at Hadley when he wished him 'good morning, sir.'

'What is it now, Hadley?'

'Sir…'

'You know I don't like being disturbed first thing when there is so much paperwork that requires my attention,' interrupted Bell testily.

'I'm fully aware of that sir, but I have to report that a Bulgarian Diplomat was murdered in Whitechapel last night when he…'

'Good God Almighty!' interrupted Bell but Hadley continued '…when he was with a streetwalker known to us as Molly Barnet,' and Bell's jaw dropped.

'Did she kill him?'

'No, sir…'

'She'll hang if she did!'

'She didn't do it, sir.'

'How was he killed?'

'It appears he was stabbed in the back by an assailant when he was with the woman, sir.'

'And what was a Bulgarian Diplomat doing at night in Whitechapel for God's sake?' asked Bell and Hadley was surprised at the Chief's naivety.

'He was indulging in casual sexual pleasures, sir.'

'My God… whatever next with these blasted foreigners?'

'I don't know…'

'So he was with this Barnet woman when he was killed.'

'Yes, sir, and according to her they met regularly in the Ten Bells pub before attending to the business…'

'You make it sound so bloody sordid, Hadley.'

'Well, that's because it is, sir, with little honest work available for these poor women they have great difficulty in just feeding themselves and their children, so it's no wonder they are forced into prostitution.'

'You sound as if you're sympathetic to these dreadful gutter snipes.'

'I am, sir, because they are constantly abused and usually the only way out of their sad predicament is their untimely death,' said Hadley firmly and there followed a few moments of silence.

'Did this Barnet woman see the assailant, Hadley?'

'Yes, sir, but she only caught a fleeting glimpse of the man when he stabbed the Diplomat and cannot give a good description.'

'Pity… now has the Bulgarian Embassy been informed yet?'

'No sir, I thought that unpleasant duty best be left to you and the Commissioner.'

Bell sighed and said 'yes, I suppose so… you'd better come with me to see the Commissioner now, Hadley.'

'Very good, sir.'

Mr Brackley looked anxious when Bell asked him to inform the Commissioner that they wished to speak to him on an urgent matter.

'He does not like to be disturbed first thing when he's attending to his paperwork, Chief Inspector,' said Brackley.

'I'm fully aware of that, Mr Brackley, but this is a very important matter that requires his immediate attention,' replied Bell firmly.

'Very well, but on your own head be it,' said Brackley with a sigh before he left his desk and entered the Commissioner's office.

Within moments he returned and they were admitted to the spacious office overlooking the Thames.

The Commissioner glanced up from the paperwork on his desk and said 'this had better be really important, Chief Inspector, because I am very busy.'

'I'm afraid it is, sir.'

'Well... what is it?'

'Another Diplomat has been murdered...'

'What!' interrupted the great one loudly as his side whiskers bristled more than usual.

'He was attached to the Bulgarian Embassy, sir.'

'Good God Almighty! Whatever is going on Chief Inspector?'

'I really don't know, sir.'

'Has the Embassy been informed yet?'

'No, sir, we thought it best that you attend to that.'

'Did you now?'

'Yes, sir,' replied Bell and the Commissioner shook his head slowly before saying 'give me all the facts.'

Hadley gave a succinct account of what had happened and when he finished the Commissioner said 'both of you get over to the Embassy and advise the Secretary while I inform Sir George of this latest tragedy.'

'Yes, sir.'

'If we're not very careful we could have major diplomatic incidents on our hands and knowing the current unrest in the Balkans that would be disastrous for us,' said the Commissioner.

Half an hour later the Chief Inspector, Hadley and Cooper were in a Police coach headed towards the Bulgarian Embassy in the Bayswater Road.

'This could prove to be even more difficult than the Rumanian murder, Hadley.'

'I'm sure of that, sir, and only after I've made more inquiries there can we hope to get a clearer picture of what's been going on.'

'Yes and I trust that Madam Galati will give us a lead, as well as that fella Bacau when he comes to see you at midday,' said Bell. Hadley nodded and they remained silent for the rest of the journey until the coach pulled up outside the Embassy.

'Let me do all the talking, Hadley,' said Bell before he opened the coach door and stepped down.

'Yes, sir.'

After Cooper rang the bell they waited on the steps of the Embassy for some minutes. Eventually the door was opened by a tall, swarthy looking man who gave a nod and said 'yes?'

'I am Chief Inspector Howard Bell of Scotland Yard... this is Inspector Hadley and Sergeant Cooper, we wish to see your Secretary immediately on a very important matter.'

'He only sees people by appointment,' replied the man as he started to close the door.

'You're obviously foreign and don't understand English my good man...,' began Bell.

'I understand perfectly and I say again, Secretary Varnia will only see people by appointment, so I suggest that you write in for one... good morning, sir,' interrupted the man firmly before he began to close the door.

Hadley looked hard at the man and said 'your Diplomat, Igor Plovdiv, was murdered in Whitechapel last night, so kindly pop along and give that information to Secretary Varnia if you would, while we go back to the Yard and get on with more important business... good morning.' He then turned away and descended the steps leaving Bell speechless and the man open mouthed. He had just reached the bottom step when the man called out in an anxious tone 'please... please come in, sir... I will inform Secretary Varnia that you're here and wish to see him.' Hadley turned, smiled and said 'thank you,' before climbing the steps and entering the hallway followed by a shocked Chief Inspector and a grinning Sergeant.

The man left them and they waited for only a few minutes before he returned saying 'Secretary Isma Varnia will see you now, gentlemen, please follow me.' They were lead upstairs to the office of the Secretary and announced to the Bulgarian as he stood up behind his ornate desk. Hadley looked at the pale faced, thick set man with a mop of black hair and wondered if he was capable of organising a political murder and decided that he was.

'I'm told that our Diplomat Plovdiv has been murdered… is this true?' asked Varnia.

'Yes, sir, and on the direct orders of the Commissioner of the Metropolitan Police I have to inform you officially that Igor Plovdiv was murdered late last night in Whitechapel,' replied Bell.

'This is a catastrophe!' exclaimed Varnia.

'It is, sir.'

'What have you done about apprehending the person responsible for this monstrous crime?'

'We have launched a major investigation which is ongoing as we speak, sir,' replied Bell.

'In other words you have no idea who killed him!'

'Sir, we are making …'

'Don't bandy words with me, Chief Inspector… how did he die?'

'He was fatally stabbed, sir.'

'It was probably a murderous Hungarian assassin who killed him… I must inform our Ambassador immediately… please wait here until I return,' said Varnia before he hurried from the office.

Bell glanced at Hadley and said 'you see how these hot headed foreigners react to adversity?'

'Yes I do, sir, but it is understandable in the circumstances.'

'I'm not so sure about that… and this is going to more difficult than I thought if they start blaming each other, Hadley.'

'I fear they will, sir.'

'May God deliver us from bloody foreigners!' said Bell loudly as Varnia entered the office.

'Your comments about foreigners are unwelcome Chief Inspector!'

'I'm sorry, sir…,' stammered Bell as his face coloured to a rosy pink.

'Our Ambassador Tolbukhin wishes to see you immediately, so come with me please,' said Varnia firmly. They followed the Secretary down the corridor to double doors at the end and into the spacious office of the Ambassador.

Tolbukhin was a tall, distinguished man with receding grey hair and he looked anxious as Varnia announced the detectives.

'I understand that Igor Plovdiv has been murdered... is this really true?' asked Tolbukhin.

'I'm afraid so, Your Excellency,' replied Bell.

'This is a terrible tragedy for us all who knew him.'

'I am sure it is, Your Excellency.'

'Do you know who killed him, Chief Inspector?'

'No, but we have a witness who was with him at the time and may give us a lead...'

'Who was this witness?' interrupted Tolbukhin.

Bell hesitated for a moment then replied 'she is a woman known to us as Molly Barnet.'

'Ah, so she is not Hungarian then,' said Tolbukhin in a relieved tone.

'No, sir, she's a...'

'A common prostitute.'

'Yes, I'm afraid so, Your Excellency.'

'No matter, Chief Inspector, a man's natural needs must be met.'

'May I ask why you appear to be relieved that the witness was not Hungarian, Your Excellency?' asked Hadley and Bell gave him a disapproving glance. Tolbukhin remained silent for a few moments before replying 'the political situation in the Balkans is finely balanced, Inspector, and after Prince Alexander of Rattenburg became our national leader three years ago, we have had serious doubts about the intentions of our neighbours, especially Hungary.'

'Why is that, sir?' asked Hadley.

'It is far too complicated to explain in simple terms, Inspector.'

'Well, if we are to apprehend the killer, any suspicions that you may have as to who was responsible will give us a valuable lead, sir,' said Hadley. Tolbukhin remained silent for a few moments and it was obvious he was carefully contemplating his answer.

'If you know anything relevant, sir, I urge you to share it with us,' prompted Hadley.

'Very well, I suggest that you begin making discreet inquiries about Vadim Osijek, he's the Secretary at the Hungarian Embassy,' replied Tolbukhin.

'On what grounds, Your Excellency?' asked Bell.

'We have reason to believe that he is using his security men for methods of political intimidation… and I would not be surprised if that became somewhat extreme in some cases… I can say nothing more, Chief Inspector,' replied Tolbukhin.

'So I take it that you suspect a Hungarian assassin for the murder of Plovdiv, Your Excellency?' asked Bell.

'I believe it is a strong possibility.'

'Then we will report your concerns to the Commissioner and follow up lines of inquiry into the conduct of Secretary Osijek and his men,' said Bell.

'Very good, Chief Inspector, meanwhile I will order our own inquiry into this senseless murder of our well respected Diplomat,' said Tolbukhin.

'As you wish, Your Excellency, but please don't make the mistake of taking the law into your own hands,' said Bell firmly.

'I hear what you say, Chief Inspector and will respect the rule of law.'

'Thank you Your Excellency.'

'Now where is the body of Igor Plovdiv?'

'It has been taken to the Marylebone Hospital for post mortem examination by our Pathologist, Your Excellency,' replied Bell.

'Would you like Secretary Varnia to officially identify the body?'

'Yes, that would be very helpful,' replied Bell.

'Very well, he will be along this afternoon, Chief Inspector… now would you please leave us to attend to the sad business of informing his family and friends in Sofiya?'   'Of course, Your Excellency,' said Bell with a nod. The detectives were escorted down to the front door by Secretary Varnia, who remained silent, just wishing them 'good day' as they left the Embassy.

'Well, what do you make of all that, Hadley?' asked Bell as the coach hurried back to the Yard.

'Quite frankly I'm very alarmed, sir, the thought of these Bulgarian security people running around London on missions of a dubious nature with murderous revenge on their minds may do nothing but divert our attention away from our investigations,' replied Hadley.

'I agree entirely and who knows where it will all end?'

'Exactly so, sir.'

'I will inform the Commissioner of this foreign threat to our law and order as soon as we get back to the Yard,' said Bell.

'Thank you, sir, I believe it is the right thing to do and he may wish to advise the Home Secretary.'

'Without a doubt, Hadley.'

'And I think we're going to need help from Sir George sooner rather than later, sir.'

'I'm sure of it. Now while I start inquiries into this Hungarian lot, what are you planning to do next?'

'After we've dropped you sir, I'm going to question Mrs Galati at the Rumanian Embassy,' replied Hadley.

'Very good, but make sure you're back by noon to see this Bacau fella, he may be able to shine some light on our darkness,' said Bell.

'Yes, of course, sir.'

Big Ben was striking ten o'clock when the coach pulled into the Yard and stopped as Bell left it and hurried into the building. Hadley looked at his fob watch, checked the time as the coach started out on the journey to the Rumanian Embassy and said to Cooper 'I'm afraid we won't have much time to question Mrs Galati, Sergeant.'

'I don't think you'll need it, sir, because she may have very little to say and speed is of the essence in this case.'

'You could be right, Sergeant, and I've a feeling that if we don't act quickly we'll have more murders on our hands,' said Hadley gloomily as he gazed out at the passing traffic.

'Indeed, sir... but hopefully Mrs Galati can give us a positive lead to the killer of Brasov if she saw him at the crime scene.'

'Possibly... but I expect that it is more likely Mr Vlad Bacau will provide worthwhile information for us, Sergeant.'

They remained silent until the coach pulled up outside the Rumanian Embassy. After the detectives were admitted to the building they were shown up to Secretary Galati's office and announced.

'Good morning, Inspector... Sergeant,' said Galati with a smile before he waved them to sit.

'Good morning, sir,' replied Hadley and Cooper nodded.

'Have you some important news for me?' asked Galati.

'I'm afraid not, sir, may I remind you that we've come to have a few words with your wife,' replied Hadley.

'Oh, then you've had a wasted journey I'm afraid,' said Galati and Hadley's suspicions were aroused.

'Really, sir?'

'Yes, I sent her away this morning to stay with friends in the country... she's very distressed at the moment, so our Doctor thought that for the good of her health, a quiet rest away from London was advisable,' replied Galati with a smile.

'When is your wife due to return, sir?'

'I've no idea, Inspector, perhaps in a week or so... but it does depend on how she feels,' replied Galati.

'Is it possible that we may speak to her at the country retreat, sir?'

'It's quite of out of the question, Inspector, Doctor Schubert insists that my wife must not be disturbed... you may ask him yourself if you wish.'

'That won't be necessary, sir, so we'll be on our way now,' said Hadley.

'Very well, Inspector... I know you've a killer to catch so I won't detain you... thank you for calling this morning.'

'Not at all, sir,' replied Hadley as he stood up to leave.

'And do let me know if I can be of any more help, Inspector,' said Galati as he rang the bell for them to be shown out.

After ordering the driver to take them to the Marylebone Hospital at speed, Hadley said to Cooper 'he's more cunning than a wagon load of monkeys!'

'Yes he is, sir... and it is so obvious!'

Doctor Edward Evans, the senior Police Pathologist, looked up from his desk as the detectives entered his office.

'Ah, good morning, Jim... Sergeant, I wondered how long it would be before you appeared,' said Evans with a smile.

'Morning Doctor,' replied Hadley.

'I expect you've come to view the latest deceased unfortunates who now grace my marble slabs?'

'We have, Doctor.'

28

'It's obvious that they are Eastern European... they're too dark and handsome to be English, Jim,' said Evans.

'Well their good looks didn't save them from the killer's knife,' said Hadley.

'That's very true.' replied Evans before he led the way out into the white tiled mortuary. The Doctor drew back the sheet covering Brasov and they gazed down at his handsome, serene features.

'This is Sergei Brasov, the Rumanian,' said Evans.

'You're right, Doctor, he is good looking for a foreigner.'

'Yes... now he died from a single stab wound to his back and to the left of his spine, upwards through the rib cage to his heart... his death was instantaneous.' said Evans.

'Were there any other injuries, Doctor?'

'No, Jim.'

'And what about Plovdiv?'

'He was also killed by a single stab wound to the heart... again through the back and I would say with some certainty that the same person killed them both with the same weapon, a thin bladed stiletto,' replied Evans.

'That's very interesting,' said Hadley.

'Whoever murdered them was ruthlessly efficient in their method and they certainly knew what they were doing.'

'Then I think that points towards a professional assassin as the killer, Doctor.'

'I would say so, Jim.'

'Thank you, Doctor, now as the Commissioner is involved in this investigation I suggest that you prepare your report and let me have it as soon as possible,' said Hadley.

'I will have it finished by this afternoon and send it over for your attention.'

'Thank you, Doctor... now Sergeant, let's get back to the office and wait for Mr Vlad Bacau to arrive!'

CHAPTER 4

Vlad Bacau arrived just before noon and was immediately shown up to Hadley's office by the Duty Sergeant. The Rumanian looked anxious when Hadley invited him to sit as Cooper drew up a chair and took out his notebook.

Hadley smiled and said 'I want to assure you that whatever you tell us will be treated in the strictest confidence, Mr Bacau.'

'Thank you Inspector.'

'I'm sure the cruel murder of Sergei Brasov has upset you and everyone else at the Embassy.'

'Indeed it has... but it was not entirely un-expected,' said Bacau.

'I see... now please take your time and tell us why his murder was expected and exactly what else is causing you concern,' said Hadley. Bacau nodded and remained silent for a few moments gathering his thoughts.

'What I am about to tell you is difficult for me, but I am determined to give you every assistance to catch the killer and bring him to face your English justice, Inspector.'

'Thank you, sir, that is appreciated so do please continue.'

'I must be direct and tell you that Madam Galati and Brasov were having an affair and I believe that one of her previous lovers followed Brasov and murdered him by the Serpentine.'

'Why should the assailant wish to kill him in broad daylight in such a public place?'

'Mindless, blind jealous revenge, Inspector, because that is where Brasov met Madam Galati every Wednesday before going to the Piccadilly Hotel to continue with this dangerous liaison.'

'Do you know who the killer is?'

'It could be any one of a number of men who have had intimate relationships with Madam Galati,' replied Bacau - Hadley was taken slightly aback.

'And of course as head of security at the Embassy you would know about Madam Galati's behaviour.'

'Yes Inspector, my people followed her everywhere and reported her behaviour directly to me.'

'Does Secretary Galati know of his wife's infidelity?'

'Yes... and he tolerated her reckless affairs...which I believe, rules him out as a suspect.'

'Possibly, sir... now can you give us the names of these men?'

'Yes, they are all Diplomats of various ranks who were at Embassy's in Sofiya where Madam Galati first met them,' replied Bacau. Hadley's heart sank on hearing that and he glanced at Cooper who raised his eyebrows.

'Are they all in London at the moment, sir?' asked Hadley after he had composed himself.

'I believe that most of them are here, Inspector.'

'Then please give us their names and the Embassy's where we can find them,' said Hadley.

'Very well, there's Rossi Hatvan... he's a Hungarian, then Mikhail Kamenka is a Russian, Cristos Korinthiakosis, a Greek and Igor Plovdiv, he's Bulgarian.'

'Did you know that Igor Plovdiv was murdered in Whitechapel last night?' asked Hadley. Bacau looked shocked and shook his head saying 'no... no, I didn't, Inspector, how was he killed?'

'He was stabbed, sir, in the same manner as Sergei Brasov,' replied Hadley.

'In that case I am sure that one of these other men is definitely the murderer,' said Bacau with conviction.

'It does seem likely, sir.'

'Then you must arrest them, Inspector!'

'That will be done all in good time, sir, but only after we've made our inquiries at the Embassy's.'

'Listen to me Inspector... you must act quickly because this jealous killer may strike again and escape back to his country... then you'll never catch him!'

'I assure you, sir that we will act swiftly to bring the killer to justice,' replied Hadley in a firm tone.

'I do hope so.'

Cooper escorted Vlad Bacau from the office and down to reception just before one o'clock. Hadley sat back in his chair pondering what he should do after he informed the Chief Inspector of the latest revelations.

When he had come to a conclusion he called out 'George...'

'Yes, sir?' replied the clerk from his adjacent office.

'I think a pot of tea and some sandwiches from the canteen would not go amiss.'

'Very good, sir… cheese and pickle or ham and mustard?' asked George as Cooper returned.

'I'll let the Sergeant choose.'

'Right, sir.'

After George had left the office with Cooper's choice, Hadley asked 'well, what did you make of all that, Sergeant?'

'It appears that there is an unbelievable boiling pot of jealous emotions surrounding Madam Galati which led to the murder of Brasov, sir.'

'I'm sure you're right.'

'And our investigation will be complicated by the fact that all the suspects are foreign Diplomats, sir,' replied Cooper.

'Exactly so, Sergeant.'

'It'll be hard for us to investigate without help from the Commissioner and Sir George, sir.'

'That's very true… and when I tell the Chief what Bacau has told us he'll go mad,' said Hadley.

'I'm sure he will, sir.'

Over lunch the detectives planned visits to the Embassy's to start making inquiries. When Hadley had decided on the priorities he went up to the Chief's office with the details and the list of Madam Galati's lovers.

Bell looked up from his desk and asked, 'how did you get on with this Rumanian fella?'

'He gave us the names of four suspects, sir,' replied Hadley as he placed the buff file on the desk.

'Did he by God!' exclaimed Bell enthusiastically.

'Yes, sir.'

'Good… let's get them arrested and see what transpires when we question them closely.'

'That will be difficult, sir, because they're all Diplomats.'

'Oh bloody hell!'

'Quite so, sir, and one of them is Plovdiv.'

'But he's dead.'

'He is, sir, but Bacau didn't know that when he gave me the list,' said Hadley as Bell opened the file and glanced at the names.

'It's so tiresome with these foreigners having such un-pronounceable names, Hadley.'

'It is, sir.'

'So why does Bacau think one of this lot murdered Brasov?'

'According to him the motive was mindless jealousy because they were all having an intimate relationship with Madam Galati, sir.'

'Good God... all at the same time, Hadley?' asked Bell in amazement.

'I'm not sure, sir.'

'Well if they were, then her bedroom must have been busier than the waiting room at Kings Cross station!'

'Probably, sir.'

'So what do you plan to do next, Hadley?'

'With assistance from the Commissioner and possibly Sir George, call at the various Embassy's listed and speak to the named Diplomats, sir, to see if they can provide alibi's for the time of the murders of Brasov and Plovdiv,' replied Hadley.

'I don't like the sound of this, it's getting far too complicated and the ramifications could be disastrous if we get it wrong, Hadley.'

'I'm well aware of that, sir.'

'I'm glad you are, now I'll go up to see the Commissioner with this and I'll send for you if he wishes to see you, Hadley.'

'Very good, sir,' replied Hadley and as he was about to leave Mr Brackley entered. The assistant glanced at them in turn and said 'the Commissioner would like to see you Chief Inspector... and you Inspector.'

'Do you know what it's about, Mr Brackley?' asked Bell.

'I'm not sure, sir, but the Commissioner has just returned from an urgent meeting with Sir George at the Home Office, so I believe it is with regard to the outcome of that discussion,' replied Brackley.

Bell raised his eyebrows, sighed and said, 'we'll come immediately.'

The Commissioner was standing at the window looking out at the myriad of boats passing by on the Thames when they entered the office. Bell cleared his throat and asked haltingly 'you wanted to see us, sir?' The great one replied 'yes, Chief Inspector' but did not turn round which un-nerved Bell while Hadley clasped his hands behind his back waiting for the inevitable verbal eruption. The detectives waited for what seemed an age before the Commissioner turned, faced them and said calmly 'gentlemen, I have been at a meeting with Sir George and he has instructed me to proceed with our investigations into the murders of these two Diplomats quickly and without hindrance from their Ambassador's claiming diplomatic immunity.'

'That's very welcome news, sir,' said Hadley enthusiastically.

'Indeed it is and it follows a meeting that Sir George had with Sir Jason Thornley, our Foreign Office Minister. It appears that the 1815 Vienna Convention on diplomatic rights does not cover murder or other serious crimes, which leave us free to pursue the killer without hindrance,' said the Commissioner.

'Thank heavens for that, sir,' said Bell with relief.

'Apparently Sir Jason had an unexpected visit this morning from the Bulgarian Ambassador and a relative of Prince Alexander Battenburg, a strident, difficult lady called Princess Helena Aida Radomir... I gather it was heated exchange where the Princess demanded immediate action to arrest the killer of Igor Plovdiv, whom she knew personally.'

'Goodness gracious me, sir,' said Bell.

'It seems that Sir Jason was not amused and referring to the Vienna Convention informed the Ambassador that he would brook no interference from anyone seeking diplomatic immunity from our murder investigations.'

'So from now on its full steam ahead, sir,' said Hadley with a smile.

'It is indeed, so go to it gentlemen, keep me well briefed with your reports and arrest this killer.'

'Yes, sir,' they chorused and Bell added, 'we already have a list of four suspects given to us by an informant working in the Rumanian Embassy, sir.'

'Good work, so bring them in and start the questioning... let's see if we can get a confession followed by a quick court appearance then a hanging... that'll please the powers that be and calm the nerves of the Diplomats,' beamed the Commissioner.

'I must sound a note of caution, sir...'

'What's that, Hadley?'

'The suspects are all Diplomats, sir.'

'Well, that should not deter you, as Sir Jason said, they can no longer hide behind their diplomatic immunity, which leaves you free to follow your lines of inquiry wherever they may lead you, Hadley,' said the Commissioner.

'As long as I am clear to proceed, sir.'

'You are, Hadley. Do whatever you must to arrest this maniac!'

'Very good, sir.'

'Now get on with it, gentlemen' said the Commissioner in a brusque tone, they nodded and left the office greatly relieved. As they descended the stairs to Bell's office he said 'I'll leave you and Cooper to begin the initial inquiries at the Embassy's, Hadley... I'll follow on... if it's necessary.'

'Very good, sir,' replied Hadley as they reached the landing below.

'Keep me informed so I may brief the Commissioner,' said Bell before he disappeared into his office.

Within half an hour the detectives were in a coach heading for the Hungarian Embassy in Portman Square to interview Rossi Hatvan, the first on the list of lovers. On the journey Hadley briefed Cooper on the fast moving events and said finally 'when we've finished with these three, I think we'll call at the Bulgarian Embassy and get the address of this Princess who caused ructions at the Foreign Office this morning as she may be able to throw some light on the murder of Plovdiv, Sergeant.'

'That will be an interesting meeting, sir, without a doubt,' replied Cooper with a grin as the coach pulled up outside the Hungarian Embassy.

After Hadley identified themselves to the doorman they were admitted to the Embassy and asked to wait in the hallway whilst Secretary Rossi Hatvan was advised that they wished to see him. Within minutes they were shown upstairs to a spacious office where a tall, distinguished man stood up from his desk when they were announced.

'Good afternoon, gentlemen... how may I help you?' asked Hatvan as he waved them to sit.

'Good afternoon, sir, and thank you for seeing us so promptly,' said Hadley with a smile as he sat on the plush seat before looking hard at the elegant Hungarian. He could see why Madam Galati would have been attracted to him as one of her lovers. Hatvan was very handsome with dark wavy hair, tinged with grey at the temples, a neat moustache and piercing blue eyes.

'Not at all, Inspector… now what can I do for you?'

'I need to speak to you about a delicate and personal matter, sir.'

'That concerns me, Inspector?'

'Yes, sir.'

'I'm very intrigued, please continue,' said Hatvan with a smile.

'I have reason to believe, sir, that you were closely and intimately involved with Madam Galati…' Hadley began and on hearing her name, Hatvan's composure immediately changed and he interrupted 'I have nothing whatsoever to do with that woman, Inspector!'

'Sir, I am conducting a murder investigation into the unlawful killings of two Diplomats, namely Sergei Brasov, a Rumanian and Igor Plovdiv, a Bulgarian, both of whom knew Madam Galati…'

'Yes I've just heard… but what's that got to do with me, Inspector?' interrupted Hatvan angrily.

'It is my duty, on direct orders from the Commissioner of the Metropolitan Police and Sir George West, the Home Secretary, to question every gentleman who had contact with Madam Galati in order to eliminate them from our list of suspects, sir,' replied Hadley.

'Surely you don't consider me a suspect?'

'We only wish to eliminate you from our inquiries, sir, so can you tell me where you were on Wednesday afternoon and late last night, sir?'

'I find that question very intrusive, Inspector and therefore most offensive… I will remind you that I am a Diplomat!'

'Indeed you are, sir, but offensive and intrusive or not… I must press you…where were you yesterday afternoon and late last night?' persisted Hadley firmly and Hatvan sighed then shrugged his shoulders.

'From two o'clock until nearly four, I was in a meeting with our Ambassador, Jan Mezotur, afterwards I attended to letters that arrived in the diplomatic bag from our Ministry in Budapest until about seven o'clock, Inspector.'

'And where were you late last night, sir?'

'I went to a dinner party with my wife at the American Embassy in Grosvenor Square and we left at about midnight... ask anyone who was there, Inspector,' replied Hatvan smugly.

'I will do, sir, now did you leave the party at any time during the evening?'

'No certainly not!'

'Thank you, sir, that will be all for the time being.'

'For the time being... what's that supposed to mean?' demanded Hatvan.

'It means that I may wish to speak to you again as the investigation progresses into the murders of the Diplomats, sir... good day,' replied Hadley before he stood up and left the office with Cooper leaving Hatvan open mouthed.

The detectives proceeded to the Russian Embassy in Connaught Square and were admitted promptly. When Hadley asked to see Mikhail Kamenka he was informed that the Diplomat was at an important meeting with the Ambassador and could not be disturbed. Hadley said that he would call back later to see if Kamenka was free and left no message for the Russian.

The coach hurried through the heavy traffic to the Greek Embassy in South Audley Street where they were told that Cristos Korinthiakos was on leave for the rest of the week and staying with friends in the country. When Hadley asked for the address, it was refused and he was told that the Diplomat would be returning on Sunday to resume his duties.

As the coach made its way to the Bulgarian Embassy Hadley said 'I wouldn't be at all surprised to learn that Madam Galati and her Greek lover were enjoying themselves at the same comfy hideaway in the country, Sergeant.'

'Neither would I, sir.'

'These foreign Diplomats are an unbelievable lot.'

'They are indeed, sir.'

At the Bulgarian Embassy they were shown up to Secretary

Varnia's office immediately and he looked apprehensive when they entered.

'Good afternoon, gentlemen, how can I help you this time?' asked Varnia.

'Good afternoon, sir, we've come to ask you for the address of Princess Radomir, who accompanied your Ambassador to the meeting with our Foreign Minister this morning,' said Hadley.

'Ah, yes, she is a relative of our Prince Alexander and a very important lady you know,' said Varnia with a smile.

'So we understand, sir.'

'Why do you want her address, Inspector?'

'I've just a few questions for her sir, regarding Igor Plovdiv.'

'Well I'm sure she knows nothing.'

'That may be so, sir, but we are duty bound to follow up every line of inquiry in a murder investigation.'

Varnia sighed and produced a small leather bound book from the drawer in his desk, opened it and after glancing at a page, said 'Princess Helena lives at 10 Berkeley Square when she is in London, Inspector.'

'Thank you, sir.'

Hadley discussed the case and his proposed line of questioning with Cooper on the journey to Berkeley Square. He looked at his fob watch as the coach pulled up outside the house, it was just after four o'clock.

'If the interview goes well we may be invited for afternoon tea, Sergeant.'

'With dainties and cucumber sandwiches... if it goes well, sir... but somehow I doubt it,' said Cooper with a grin as he followed Hadley out of the coach.

CHAPTER 5

A maid opened the door and after glancing at them in turn asked Hadley, 'yes, sir?'

'I'm Inspector Hadley and this is Sergeant Cooper, we're Police Officers from Scotland Yard... we wish to see Princess Helena Radomir, please.'

The maid hesitated for a moment then said, 'you'd better come in, sir,' before she stepped back for them to enter the plush hallway.

'Thank you, miss.'

'Please wait while I inform her Highness that you are here and wish to see her, sir,' she said before bobbing a curtsy and hurrying upstairs. The detectives looked around the spacious hall and admired the elegant décor. There were half tables against the wall, surmounted by ornate oval mirrors with soft drapes on either side, tied back with elegant bows and portraits of distinguished looking men in military uniforms hung on the walls.

'I wonder what she is like, sir?' whispered Cooper.

'Well according to the Commissioner, Sir George and Sir Jason Thornley, she's a strident, forceful and demanding woman,' replied Hadley.

'If that's the case then this could be a very difficult interview, sir, because I don't think they can all be wrong about her,' said Cooper anxiously.

'Probably not, Sergeant, but whatever she is like, we must be firm and not be browbeaten by her under any circumstances,' replied Hadley with a smile.

'No of course not, sir.'

The maid returned moments later and said 'her Highness will see you now, sir, please follow me.'

They were led upstairs and shown into a large, sunlit, elegantly furnished drawing room and announced. The Princess stood to greet them and Hadley was immediately taken aback by the beauty of the tall, voluptuous woman wearing a red satin dress. She held out her hand and said with a captivating smile, 'good afternoon gentlemen, I am Princess Helena Radomir and this is my cousin, Countess Helga Somovit,' as she waved towards a large, rather plain woman sitting on a plush, gold coloured sofa.

Hadley replied hesitantly, 'good afternoon Your Highness, thank you for seeing us,' as he shook her hand gently before glancing at the woman, nodding to her and murmuring 'Countess.'

'Please be seated, gentlemen,' said the Princess, gesturing them to sit on a large matching sofa opposite the Countess. Hadley could not take his eyes of this lovely Princess when she sat down next to her cousin. Her large brown eyes were mesmerising him and her beautiful face with its flawless complexion and full red lips held him spell bound. Her black hair was lustrous and drawn back before it cascaded down to her shoulders in ringlets with rows of pearls enhancing her graceful neck. She was stunning to behold and Hadley remained speechless for a few moments before he composed himself. He was just about to speak when she smiled at him and asked softly, 'now, how can I help you, Inspector?' which threw him into mild confusion once again. He thought this lovely, gentle creature could not possibly be the strident, forceful woman who had accompanied the Ambassador to Sir Jason's office that morning. Hadley cleared his throat to give him time to clarify his confused mind then said, 'Your Highness, may I ask if you attended a meeting with Sir Jason Thornley at the Foreign Office earlier today?'

'Why yes I did, Inspector... and please thank Sir Jason for his help in asking you to come so quickly to inform me of your progress in the investigation into the cruel murder of dear Igor... he was such a close friend to me you know,' she replied with a disarming smile.

'I'm sure he was, madam, but I've called to...'

'And now having met you, I am certain that you and your young Sergeant here will solve the case quickly and arrest the killer quite soon,' she interrupted as she smiled then looked at Cooper, fluttering her long eyelashes and he blushed.

'As the investigating Officers we will endeavour to do so, madam, but I...'

'You know, Inspector, I am a very good judge of character and I must say that you both look very impressive and are exactly my notion of English Policemen and perfect gentlemen,' she interrupted.

Hadley was not used to such compliments and blushed slightly when he said 'thank you so much… now I have to ask you a few questions about Igor Plovdiv, madam.'

'Of course, Inspector… but may I offer you some tea first?'

'Thank you, madam… that would be most agreeable,' replied Hadley with a smile, glad of a diversion to allow him to marshal his thoughts. The Princess glanced at the Countess who got up and pulled the bell cord by the fireplace. The maid appeared, curtsied and after the Countess spoke to her in Bulgarian, she nodded and disappeared.

'Now while we are waiting, Inspector, please tell us all you know about this terrible tragedy that has upset us so dreadfully,' said the Princess in an imploring tone. Hadley told her all he knew but left out the sordid details of the sexual encounter with Molly just saying that Plovdiv had been stabbed in the back by an unknown assailant as he was leaving the Ten Bells pub.

'Do you have any suspects yet, Inspector?' she asked as the maid brought in the tea and dainties on a large tray, setting it down on a low table for the Countess to pour.

'Yes, madam, we have a list of men who may have committed this crime,' replied Hadley.

'Oh what splendid progress already, may I know who they are, Inspector?'

'I am not at liberty to say at the moment, madam and I'm sure you will understand my position.'

'Yes of course.'

'How do you take your tea, Inspector?' asked the Countess.

'Milk with one sugar please,' replied Hadley, the Countess nodded and poured milk before adding the sugar.

'And for you, Sergeant?'

'The same please, madam.'

'Do help yourselves to the dainties, gentlemen, they are so delicious,' said the Princess.

'Thank you, madam.'

As they were drinking their tea and eating the fondants the Princess asked, 'please tell me, Inspector… at what time was dear Igor murdered?'

'At about nine o'clock, madam.'

'Were there any witnesses?'

'Not really, madam.'

'What does 'not really' mean, Inspector?'

'Well, there was a woman nearby, but she did not actually witness the attack or see the assailant but called for help after Mr Plovdiv fell to the pavement,' replied Hadley, protecting Molly's close involvement.

'What a pity that she did not see the man who did this terrible thing.'

'Quite so.'

'She would have been able to give you a description of him which would have been very helpful, Inspector.'

'Indeed it would, madam, now may I ask you about Igor Plovdiv?'

'Yes of course, Inspector.'

'Do you know if he had any enemies in London?'

'I'm not absolutely sure, Inspector, but of course a career in any Diplomatic service always attracts certain dangers from others who may be hostile to your country,' she replied.

'Can you give me an example, madam?' asked Hadley and she glanced at the Countess who remained impassive whilst sipping her tea.

'Well, I know that dear Igor was suspected of spying by the Rumanians when he was at our Embassy in Bucharest, but I'm quite sure that he was innocent of any such activity,' she replied.

'And do you believe that the Rumanian government is hostile to Bulgaria, madam?'

'Yes I do, Inspector, ever since my cousin Prince Alexander was elected to govern us several years ago,' she replied.

'I see… and do you think that they would harm Igor Plovdiv?'

'That is a possibility, Inspector.'

'And what in your opinion marked him out for such a cruel attack?'

'He was murdered because he was a skilful and popular Diplomat who often exposed their underhand dealings with all our neighbours, the Russians in particular, which led to their ridicule on several occasions,' she replied.

'Then obviously he was a man to be reckoned with in such political circles, madam.'

'Of course and no one, let alone a proud country like Rumania, likes to be shown up to the Russians and the rest of the world as being ridiculous, Inspector,' she replied and Hadley remained silent for a few moments.

'Would you be prepared to name anyone at the Rumanian Embassy who you believe might have been responsible for Plovdiv's murder, madam?' Hadley's question appeared to unsettle the Princess and she glanced at the Countess who remained impassive.

After a few moments she replied 'well... although I will do anything to help you catch the killer, Inspector, I do not wish to falsely accuse anyone, but I believe that their security man is called Bacau and he may be able to help you,' and on hearing that Hadley glanced at Cooper who raised his eyebrows.

'Thank you, madam... and do you know of anybody else who you think may be of interest to us?'

'There is only one other person I know of, Inspector.'

'And who is that, madam?'

'His name is Vadim Osijek, and he is the Secretary at the Hungarian Embassy,' she replied.

'Do you also suspect the Hungarians of some involvement in the murder of Plovdiv, madam?' asked Hadley in a surprised tone.

'It is possible, Inspector, because they are no friends of ours in the Balkans.'

'I see... well thank you, madam, your help has been invaluable to our investigation,' said Hadley with a smile.

'I'm so glad, Inspector and I do hope that you will call again when you have some more news about dear Igor's murder because we wish to know everything,' she said.

'It will be my pleasure, madam.'

'Thank you... and I will write to Sir Jason and your Commissioner to let them know how pleased I am with your close attention,' she said with a smile. Hadley knew instantly that such letters would ensure he was duty bound to visit this beautiful Princess on a regular basis... and the thought did not displease him greatly.

The detectives took their leave, shook hands with the Princess and the Countess before being shown out by the maid.

As the coach made its way back to the Yard, Hadley said 'I think that proved to be a useful line of inquiry, Sergeant.'

'It was, sir, especially as the Princess had such big eyes for you and as a result was very forthcoming!'

'Nonsense, Sergeant, she was only responding to my questioning…'

'Oh yes, I saw the way she looked at you, sir, I bet with half a chance she'd have you to herself between the sheets as quick as greased lightning!' interrupted Cooper with a chuckle.

'Sergeant, that's absolute nonsense and quite unbecoming of you!' Hadley replied before he gazed out of the window, blushing slightly at the thought.

'You wait, sir, just you wait and see what happens!'

On their return to the office they wrote a report for George to type before Hadley went up to see the Chief.

'Well what news, Hadley?' asked Bell as he waved him to sit in the creaking chair.

'It's all here in my report, sir,' he replied before placing the buff folder on the desk.

'Is there anything of particular interest?'

'Yes, several points, sir.'

'Continue.'

'Madam Galati has been sent by her husband to an undisclosed residence in the country to recuperate and is not expected back for a week or so and one of the Diplomats on the suspect list, the Greek named Korinthiakos is also away in the country…'

'Probably with Madam Galati,' interrupted Bell with a grin.

'That's a possibility, sir.'

'Go on.'

'The Hungarian, Rossi Hatvan, has a cast iron alibi, he was with his Ambassador in the afternoon when Brasov was murdered and with his wife at a function at the American Embassy when Plovdiv was killed, sir.'

'None of this is very illuminating Hadley, so is there anything else?'

'Yes, sir, I've been to see Princess Radomir…'

'Good heavens! You shouldn't have done that!' interrupted Bell.

'Why not, sir?'

'She's a Princess who is related to Prince, whatever his name is… and she's far too important a person to be questioned by you, Hadley!'

'Well I must say that she was very amenable and helpful to me, sir.'

'You may think so, but I'm sure she'll complain to Sir Jason or the Commissioner about your intrusive behaviour!'

'She did say she would write to them both to thank us for our close attention, sir.'

'Hadley, you are hopelessly naive when dealing with Royalty or the nobility, and if you're not very careful it could cost you your career,' said Bell firmly which worried Hadley.

'Well I hope not, sir and I would look to you to defend me if the situation arose where my methods or behaviour were called into question.'

'I cannot possibly defend you in such circumstances Hadley, as I have my own position to think of!'

'But surely, sir…'

'There are no 'buts' Hadley, you've brought this on yourself by your ill advised and hasty action,' interrupted Bell.

'This is a difficult and sensitive investigation, sir, and with respect, I am doing my very best to follow up all lines of inquiry.'

'Well it's not good enough, Hadley, you should keep well away from questioning persons of high rank who can give you little information about these murders and consequently add nothing to our sum of knowledge!' said Bell forcefully, Hadley sighed and gently shook his head. There followed a few moments of silence before the Chief asked, 'so what do you propose to do next?'

'I was just about to tell you, sir, that the Princess named two suspects who may be involved in the murder of Plovdiv…'

'And they are?'

'Vlad Bacau, the security head at the Rumanian Embassy and Vadim Osijek the Secretary at the Hungarian Embassy, sir, who if my memory serves me right, you were making inquiries into his background,' replied Hadley.

'Yes I am and Jenkins is preparing a typed report on what we know about this fella… and it appears that he is an unsavoury character,' said Bell.

'Somehow I'm not surprised, sir.'

'Our contact in the Foreign Office says that his behaviour in Budapest was noted by our Ambassador and mentioned in dispatches as being most unbecoming for a Diplomat. It is rumoured that he pursued personal vendettas against the Rumanian and Bulgarian Diplomats,' said Bell.

'That's interesting... when did he arrive in London, sir?'

'Apparently last December... I'll let you have a copy when I take it up to the Commissioner.'

'Thank you, sir.'

'Have you anything else to tell me, Hadley?'

'Yes, sir, I'm going to call at the Russian Embassy again to see if Kamenka is out of his important meeting with the Ambassador to discover if he has an alibi for yesterday afternoon and last night.'

'Good, keep me posted.'

'I will, sir.'

'And see if you can get any sense out of this streetwalker, Molly what's her name.'

'I'll try, sir, but she's already said that the attack was so quick she only caught a glimpse of Plovdiv's assailant,' said Hadley.

Bell sighed and said, 'you can never trust anything these silly women say because they're normally too drunk to know what they are doing or remember anything afterwards.'

'I'm afraid that's sadly true, sir.'

Within half an hour the detectives were on their way to the Russian Embassy in Connaught Square and Hadley remained deep in thought during the journey. They were admitted promptly by the doorman and when Hadley asked to speak to Mikhail Kamenka, the receptionist recognised him, nodded and replied 'please wait here, sir.'

'So he's obviously free now, sir,' whispered Cooper as the man disappeared upstairs.

'It would appear so, Sergeant.'

They waited for several minutes before the receptionist returned and said 'the Ambassador will see you now, gentlemen.'

As they climbed the stairs Cooper whispered, 'I didn't know that Kamenka was the Ambassador, sir.'

'He's not... but perhaps he's still in the meeting with him,' replied Hadley.

They were shown into a large office where a tall, bearded man stood up from his desk to greet them as they were announced.

'I am Nikolei Smolenska, the Ambassador.'

'I think there has been some misunderstanding Your Excellency, we came here to see Mikhail Kamenka, one of your…

'

'There's no misunderstanding, Inspector, please be seated whilst I explain to you,' interrupted Smolenska with a smile.

'Thank you, sir.'

When they were all seated, Smolenska asked firmly, 'now first of all, why do you want to speak to Kamenka?'

'We are conducting inquiries into the murders of two Diplomats, Your Excellency and we wish to eliminate Kamenka from the list of possible suspects…'

'What!' roared Smolenska.

'We wish to…'

'I heard what you said, Inspector and can hardly believe it!' shouted the angry Ambassador.

'Your Excellency, I'm sorry that you are offended, but we have our duty to perform and I would be pleased if you would assist us by calling for Mr Kamenka so we may question him,' said Hadley firmly.

'He's not here, Inspector.'

'Then may I ask where he is, sir?'

'He's been summoned back to Moscow and left this afternoon,' replied Smolenska. Hadley's jaw dropped in surprise before he asked icily 'and when is he due to return to London, sir?'

'I really can't answer that Inspector, but I believe that it may be quite some time as he has important duties to attend to in Moscow,' replied Smolenska.

'I see.'

'But I would be pleased to answer questions on his behalf if that is of any help to you, Inspector.'

'Thank you, sir… can you tell me where Mikhail Kamenka was yesterday afternoon and also late last night?'

'Yes, he was with me all afternoon attending to documents that arrived from Moscow and in the evening, from about eight o'clock, he was at a reception at the American Embassy,

Inspector.'

There followed a few moments of silence before Hadley said 'thank you, Your Excellency, that information eliminates Mr Kamenka from our inquiries.'

'Very good, Inspector, and I am pleased to hear it.'

The detectives left the Embassy and Hadley said, 'Moscow my eye! I don't believe a word of it, Sergeant.'

'Neither do I, sir... he's probably with Madam Galati,' said Cooper before he asked the coach driver to take them to Whitechapel Police station.

When they arrived, Jack Palmer was at his desk and smiled when they entered his office.

'Hello, Jim, you look a bit knackered,' said Palmer with a grin.

'It's been one of those days, Jack,' replied Hadley as he slumped down in a chair.

'Never mind, it could be worse, have some tea... it'll cheer you up,' said Palmer.

'I don't mind if I do, Jack.'

Palmer called out for some tea and then asked Hadley, 'I suppose you've come to see Molly?'

'Yes, I want to know if she can remember anything about this killer... other than he was wearing a Bowler hat,' replied Hadley.

'Well I don't think she can, I've talked to her and she says all she can remember is the man was standing close behind Plovdiv and that he had a large moustache,' said Palmer.

'Well, I'll just have a few words with her in case she can remember something else,' said Hadley with a sigh.

After a reviving cup of tea the detectives went down to the cell where Molly was resting. She smiled when they entered and asked 'have you caught this blimmin' fella yet, guvnor?'

'I'm afraid not, Molly,' replied Hadley.

'Stone the blimmin crows... I'll be in here forever then,' she said.

'No you won't, Molly... we'll catch him don't you worry...besides you're nice and cosy in here for the moment.'

'I am... but I could do with a little drink to keep me spirits up, guvnor.'

'I'm sure, but you'll have to wait awhile for that,' said Hadley.

'Can't you ask Agnes or Florrie to slip me a little gin?'

'No, Molly, I can't for the moment... now please take your time and tell me everything you noticed about the man in the Bowler hat.'

'Guvnor, I keep telling you it was so blimmin quick, my fella suddenly grunted and held on to me tight before he fell down on the step and the bloke in the hat ran off... as Gawd's my witness that's the honest truth,' she said despairingly.

'You told Inspector Palmer that the man had a moustache,' said Hadley.

'Yes, he did.'

'What colour was it?'

'I dunno, guvnor, it was too blimmin dark to see,' she replied.

'Did he have any kind of a beard?'

'No, I don't think so.'

'What about his clothes, did you notice anything at all?'

'No guvnor.'

Hadley remained silent for a few moments then said, 'well thank you Molly, no more questions,' as he realised she could tell him nothing else that would help identify the killer.

Outside the cell Hadley said to Palmer, 'well, all we're looking for now is a man in a Bowler hat with a moustache... so that description narrows it down to about half the men in London.' Palmer smiled and said, 'we'll catch him eventually, Jim.'

'It's the 'eventually' that I'm worried about, Jack.'

'You mean in case he kills again before we get him?'

'Yes, Jack.'

'If you'll take my advice you'll go home and get a good night's rest, Jim,' said Palmer as he gently placed his hand on Hadley's shoulder.

'I think that's a very good idea.'

'Now take your guvnor home, Sergeant,' said Palmer.

'Yes sir,' replied Cooper.

CHAPTER 6

After a worrying and sleepless night, Hadley was not in a good mood when he arrived in the office the next morning. George was already there and had the kettle on for tea as Cooper arrived.

'We've a busy day ahead of us, Sergeant so I want to get cracking as soon as we can.'

'Very good, sir, what do you plan to do first?'

'Pay a visit to the Hungarian Embassy and question their unsavoury Secretary, Vadim Osijek, and see if he's an alibi for Wednesday afternoon and evening, Sergeant,' replied Hadley as George brought in their tea 'then we'll talk to the witnesses to the Brasov murder and question them, hopefully they'll be able to remember something about the incident in the Park.'

'Anything would be a help at this stage, sir.'

'Indeed, then we'll have an early lunch at the Kings Head and talk to the ladies… they may have heard something about our man in the Bowler hat.'

'Quite possibly, sir,' said Cooper.

George re-appeared from his office 'here is the Post Mortem report from Doctor Evans, sir,' he said as he placed the buff folder on Hadley's desk.

'Thank you, George, now let's see what the good Doctor has to say about our victims.' Hadley read through it quickly and said to Cooper 'it confirms that both men were killed instantly by a single stab wound to the heart, made by a stiletto type blade, no more than an inch wide and approximately eight inches long.'

'This does look increasingly like the work of a professional assassin, sir.'

'It does… and it confirms what the Doctor and I believed at the very outset, Sergeant.'

'And that means that if the killer is not the Russian, Kamenka, then he is still in London and may strike again, sir.'

'That's exactly what I'm afraid of, Sergeant.'

Big Ben was striking nine o'clock when the detectives left the Yard in a closed coach and made their way to the Hungarian Embassy. They were admitted to the spacious building in Portman

Square and asked to wait whilst Secretary Osijek was informed they wished to see him. They waited for twenty minutes and Hadley began to get impatient when the receptionist re-appeared and said that the Secretary would see them in half an hour. Meanwhile, they were invited to take a seat and Hadley quietly fumed at the delay, every few minutes he took out his fob watch and tutted, before replacing it in his waistcoat pocket. When the half hour was up Hadley left his seat and made his way over to the reception desk just as a young man appeared from upstairs and informed him that Secretary Osijek was now free to see him. As the detectives were led upstairs Cooper knew that Hadley was not in any mood to be crossed and any confrontation with Osijek would lead to unpleasantness and difficulty. At the end of a long corridor they were shown into a large office and announced to the Secretary, who stood to greet them from behind his ornate desk.

'Good morning, Inspector, I am sorry to have kept you waiting,' said Osijek with a smile.

'Good morning, sir, thank you for finding the time to see us at last,' replied Hadley and Cooper grinned as Osijek waved them to sit. Hadley looked at the tall Hungarian and the first thing that he noticed was the Secretary's large, fulsome moustache that turned up at the ends. He had a swarthy face topped by a mop of black hair, greying at the temples, and dark eyes that seemed to penetrate everything.

'Now how can I help you, Inspector?'

'We are investigating the murders of two Diplomats, sir, and I'd like…'

'Yes, so I've heard,' interrupted Osijek.

'And I'd like to eliminate you from our inquiries, sir.'

'Dear God! You surely don't suspect me of having anything to do with these dreadful crimes do you?' asked Osijek angrily.

'As I said, sir, we only wish to eliminate you from our inquiries, so if you would be kind enough tell us where you were on Wednesday afternoon and evening, it will settle the matter,' replied Hadley calmly.

'This is monstrous, Inspector!'

'I'm sorry that you feel indignant and affronted, sir but I must do my duty and ask you where you were on Wednesday,' said Hadley firmly and there followed a moments silence.

'I shall complain to your Commissioner about your unfounded and offensive accusation, Inspector!'

'You are at liberty to do so, sir, but before you complain, just remember this... I am not accusing you of anything yet, merely asking where you were on Wednesday!' said Hadley angrily and the two men stared at each other for what seemed an age before Osijek replied.

'Well if you must know, Inspector, I took the afternoon off from my duties here and went for a walk in Hyde Park.'

Hadley raised his eyebrows 'what time was that, sir?'

'I'm not quite sure of the time, Inspector, but I arrived back here just after four o'clock.'

'Did you see anything untoward in the Park, sir?'

'No, everything appeared peaceful and very pleasant as usual,' replied Osijek.

'Did you go near the Serpentine Lake, sir?'

'Yes, I walked along it and then over the bridge at the end of the Lake.'

'And you saw nothing?'

'I've already told you, Inspector... other than a few nannies pushing prams and the odd passer by enjoying the afternoon I saw nothing out of the ordinary.'

'I see... now may I ask where you were in the evening, sir?'

'I attended a function at the American Embassy with my wife, we left at about midnight,' replied Osijek.

'Did you leave the Embassy at any time during the evening, sir?'

'Certainly not, I was there all the time with Ambassador Mezotur, Rossi Hatvan and their wives,' replied Osijek.

Hadley waited until Cooper had finished writing his notes and said 'thank you, sir, I have no further questions at the moment.'

'Well I trust that you will not need to question me again, Inspector.'

'It may be that I have to return for another interview as my inquiries broaden out,' said Hadley.

'I hope not as I am a very busy man these days, Inspector... good day.'

The detectives left the Embassy and made their way to Paddington

Green Police station. During the journey Hadley said 'Osijek is now our prime suspect for Brasov's murder and possibly Plovdiv, Sergeant.'

'But if he did murder Brasov in the Park it means that another person killed Plovdiv, sir.'

'Yes of course, Sergeant, but I'm sure that Osijek would have had an accomplice.'

'Perhaps one of his security men, sir?'

'I think that's more than a possibility, Sergeant.'

After arriving at the station they were immediately shown up to Inspector Baxter's office where he greeted them and asked 'any new developments in the investigation, Jim?'

'Well we have a prime suspect for the murder of Brasov but nothing substantial at the moment to prove his guilt,' replied Hadley.

'Who is it then?'

'His name is Vadim Osijek and he's the Secretary at the Hungarian Embassy,' replied Hadley.

'Blimey Jim, that'll be a tough nut to crack!'

'It certainly will and I need all the help I can get so I'm going to question the two witnesses and see what they can remember, Peter.'

'Right, now the nanny is er...' and he opened a notebook on his desk before continuing 'Miss Edith Harkness... she's employed by Mr and Mrs Henry Dudley of 46 Bayswater Road.'

'Thank you... and the gentleman who reported the incident?'

'Ah, he's Major Richard Simmons of 23 Park Lane, Jim,' replied Baxter and Cooper made a note of the details.

'Thanks Peter.'

'Let me know how you get on.'

'I will.'

Hadley decided to call on Miss Harkness first because she had noticed the woman sitting by Brasov and could possibly be of more help in the investigation. Cooper rang the bell at number 46 and after identifying themselves to the butler they were admitted to the house and asked to wait. Within a few minutes they were shown into the drawing room where a tall, distinguished looking man stood to greet them as they were announced.

'Good morning, sir, I am sorry to trouble you but I would like to speak to your nanny, Miss Harkness if I may,' said Hadley with a smile.

'I suppose it's about the murder of this foreign Diplomat in the Park?' asked Dudley brusquely.

'It is indeed, sir.'

'Have you caught the blighter who's responsible for this dreadful incident, Inspector?'

'No sir, our inquiries are ongoing at the moment and are…'

'Well what are you Police people doing about it?' interrupted Dudley.

'We are making good progress in the…'

'I mean to say, the papers are full of it and right minded people are wondering how safe it is to walk in the Park these days,' interrupted Dudley again.

'I'm sure it is perfectly safe sir.'

'You may say that, Inspector but I can tell you that I have forbidden Harkness to take my son there until you catch this murderous blackguard and we see him hanged!'

'I understand, sir, now if I may speak to Miss Harkness then I'm sure that satisfactory moment will arrive sooner rather than later,' said Hadley firmly.

'Very well,' said Dudley with a sigh before he rang for the butler.

Miss Harkness was a plump, pale faced, middle aged woman who looked very anxious when she arrived in the drawing room and was introduced to the detectives. Hadley immediately tried to put her at ease by saying 'thank you for coming forward and helping us with our inquiries, Miss Harkness.'

'Not at all, sir, it was the least I could do, but I have already told the Policeman at Paddington everything I know.'

'I'm aware of that but as I have now taken over the investigation, please tell me exactly what you saw in the Park last Wednesday afternoon,' said Hadley with a smile as Cooper took out his notebook.

'Well, after Master Thomas had finished his lunch I put him in his pram and took him for a walk in the Park as I do every afternoon… weather permitting of course.'

'Of course.'

'And I often meet other nannies who I know and we stop for a chat by the Lake, sir,' said the nanny and Dudley gave her a disapproving look.

'Please continue, Miss Harkness.'

'Well, I'd just finished talking to Polly Browne, she's always there on Wednesdays, and was walking up towards Victoria Gate to come home when I saw a man and woman sitting on a bench. The man looked as if he were asleep because his hat was pulled down over his face and the woman spoke to him… I couldn't hear what she said mind… and then she lifted his hat up and screamed before she dropped it and ran off, sir.'

'Then what happened?'

'I went over to the man because I thought he looked very ill.'

'What did you do next?'

'Nothing, sir, because I didn't know what to do, then a gentleman, who was walking by, came over and asked me what was the matter with the man. I said I didn't know but thought he was ill so the gentleman looked at him and said he was dead… then I saw some blood on the ground,' she faltered and her lip trembled for a moment.

'Please go on.'

'Well I was in a right state after that, so I said we'd better tell the Police and the gentleman said he'd do that and asked me to stay with the dead man.'

'Did you see anybody else close by, Miss Harkness?'

'No sir.'

'What about when you were in conversation with Polly Browne?'

'I did see a gentleman standing by the trees behind the bench and he was looking towards Victoria Gate, as if he was waiting for someone, sir,' she replied and Hadley's eyes gleamed with anticipation.

'Can you describe him to me?'

'No not really… because I didn't take much notice of him at the time but I do remember that he had a moustache that twirled up at the ends and he was wearing a Bowler hat that looked far too big for him, sir.'

'Anything else?'

'No sir.'

'Did you see if the man who was killed and the man waiting by the trees actually met each other?'

'I couldn't really say, sir.'

'And what happened to the man waiting by the trees?'

'I don't know, sir, he disappeared because he wasn't there when the lady came along and sat down next to the dead man,' she replied.

'Did Polly Browne see the man standing by the trees?'

'I don't think so, sir because she never said.'

'Nevertheless I'd like to talk to her, can you give me her address?'

'I don't know it, sir, because she's never told me and I only ever see her in the Park on Wednesdays,' she replied.

'I understand Miss Harkness. Now did you see four men arrive and place the body on a stretcher?'

'Yes I did, and I told them that they should wait for the Police but they took no notice... I think they were foreigners, sir and didn't understand English.' Hadley smiled and said 'thank you for your help Miss Harkness, I have no more questions for you at the moment.'

'You're welcome, sir, I'm sure.'

Leaving the Dudley house in Bayswater Road they went to 23 Park Lane where they were immediately admitted by a butler, shown into a spacious drawing room and announced to Major Richard Simmons.

'How can I help you, Inspector?' asked the Major as he gestured them to sit.

'I have taken over the investigation into the murder of the Rumanian Diplomat in Hyde Park on Wednesday, sir, and I understand from Inspector Baxter that you reported the incident and made a statement.'

'Yes I did, Inspector, would you like me to go over the facts again?'

'If you would please, sir.'

'Right, I was walking along past the Serpentine at about three o'clock when in the distance I saw a man sitting on a bench with his hat over his face then a woman came along, sat beside him and said something to him before she removed his hat, screamed and ran off towards the Victoria Gate. I hurried over to see what was wrong and a nanny pushing a pram had stopped and was looking at the man. When I arrived she said that she thought he was ill so I immediately felt for his pulse but there was none and so I pronounced him dead. Then I noticed a trace of blood on the ground beneath the bench and knew he'd been murdered so I told the nanny to stay there whilst I reported to the Police at Paddington.'

'Did you see anybody else near the dead man, sir?'

'No I didn't I'm afraid… so I think the murderer must have been very quick to have killed this Diplomat and then disappear without trace.'

'Indeed, sir.'

'In my view he was probably a professional assassin, Inspector, the Balkans are full of them you know.'

'So I understand, sir.'

'I served out there in the Crimean war and I know what they are like,' said the Major.

'I'm sure you do, sir.'

'And we've probably got some of them amongst us in London with all the unrest in Eastern Europe.'

'You may be right, sir.'

Hadley thanked the Major for his help before leaving the house in Park Lane and the detectives discussed the investigation as the coach hurried through the traffic to Whitechapel Police station. Hadley came to the conclusion that Brasov's killer must be directly linked to the Embassy security because he knew of Brasov's weekly rendezvous with Madam Galati by the Serpentine.

'I think this afternoon we'll have a very serious talk with Mr Bacau, Sergeant.'

'That will be interesting, sir' said Cooper as the coach arrived outside the Police station. Hadley sent the driver back to the Yard before the detectives entered and went up to see Jack Palmer who smiled when Hadley asked 'how is Molly today, Jack?'

'She's getting a bit impatient now, Jim, and she says she wants to go home,' replied Palmer.

'Well I'm afraid she'll just have to stay put until we can find this killer... it's not safe for her to roam around the streets, Jack.'

'I agree.'

'We're off for an early lunch at the Kings Head and to talk to the ladies, care to join us for a pint?'

'You go on and I'll pop down after I've finished this paperwork, Jim.'

'Right, Jack.'

The sound of the out of tune piano being badly played reached the detectives well before they arrived at the pub. It was packed with noisy, early drinkers and many had spilled out onto the street clutching their beer mugs.

'It'll be blimmin murder in there, Sergeant,' said Hadley before he pushed his way passed them and through the open door towards the bar where Vera and the girls were doing their best to serve everyone at once. Vera caught a glimpse of Hadley and gave a quick nod to him as she pulled a pint before placing it on the wet counter for a sweaty costermonger. Vera served one other customer before she came to the detectives and asked 'the usual, guvnor?'

'Please, Vera.'

'Anything to eat today, gents?'

'Yes, I'll have a ploughman's... what'll you have Sergeant?'

'The same please, sir,' replied Cooper and Vera nodded as she placed the first foaming pint of stout on the counter.

'Want it in the back room, gents?' she asked.

'Please Vera, you can't hear yourself think in here,' said Hadley.

'And don't I blimmin know it!'

'I'm sure.'

'It's the sun what brings 'em out in droves, guvnor, Gawd only knows why they're not all at work,' said Vera as she placed the second pint on the counter.

'When the ladies come in, please tell them I want to have word,' said Hadley and Vera nodded. Cooper paid her and one of the girls unlocked the door to the back room which was cool and quiet compared with the bar. They had just sat down at the table and starting sipping their stout when Agnes and Florrie waltzed in.

'Hello Jim… Sergeant, we saw you walking down the street and thought there's a couple of handsome Bobbies who'll buy us a gin or two on a blimmin hot day,' said Agnes with a smile.

'Hello ladies… and of course you're right as usual. Sergeant, please get the gins while I talk to these lovelies!'

'Blimey Jim, it sounds like you might give in to me at last,' said Agnes as she sat next to him.

'It's too hot today Agnes.'

'Then how about later?'

'Agnes… just behave yourself.'

'Oh Jim, must I?'

'Yes you must… now what's the word down the Lane about the murder of this Diplomat?' asked Hadley.

'Well, I was talking to my friend Nellie Drake about it, just after the Bobbies had come and taken him and Molly away, and Nellie said about the time he was done in she saw some funny fella walking quickly up towards Mitre Square, Jim.'

'Did she describe him?'

'Well, here's the funny thing… she said she noticed him because he walked peculiar like and had a Bowler hat that was too big for him,' Agnes replied as Cooper returned with their gins.

'I'd like to talk to Nellie.'

'You'll have to come back later, Jim, she's gone off to see her old mum in Stepney and won't be back 'til about eight, then she'll be in the Blind Beggar with us,' said Agnes.

'We'll be there,' said Hadley.

'That'll be blimmin good, perhaps we can make a night of it!' said Florrie as the girl brought in their ploughman's lunch. The women were offered a taste but ended up eating half and Hadley complained he was being starved while Cooper just smiled. Jack Palmer arrived shortly afterwards, bought another round of drinks and stayed to talk about the investigation. After hearing about the man in the outsized Bowler with a peculiar walk, Palmer said he would check with all his beat officers to see if they had noticed this strange man while on duty that night.

The detectives left the pub half an hour later and took a Hansom cab back to the Yard and after checking with George that there was nothing requiring their immediate attention set off again in a Police coach to the Rumanian Embassy. Hadley intended to ask Bacau to come back to the Yard voluntarily for questioning but was suspicious when he was told by the receptionist that Vlad Bacau had been sent out by Secretary Galati on Embassy business and would not be back until the next day. Hadley decided to return to his office, write up his report on the day's events and plan his next line of inquiry into the murders.

It was just after four o'clock when Brackley arrived and told Hadley that the Commissioner wished to see him. When Hadley entered the great one's office Bell was already there and looking anxious.

The Commissioner cleared his throat and said 'I've received a letter from Princess Radomir, who, as you know, is related to the ruler of Bulgaria...' and Hadley's heart froze for a moment... 'and she says some very complimentary things about you Hadley and your Sergeant.'

'I'm pleased to hear it, sir.'

'Relieved more likely, Inspector... now tell me, what on earth made you call on this difficult and demanding woman?'

'Well to be truthful, sir, I was following a line of inquiry and found her very charming and polite... and when questioned she gave me some useful information,' replied Hadley with a smile.

'Have you no sense, Hadley?'

'I hope I do have some...'

'You've made a rod for your own back!' interrupted the Commissioner.

'How is that possible, sir?'

'Because you'll be at her beck and call from now on you fool!'

'I told him that, sir,' piped up Bell.

'And you were quite right to do so, Chief Inspector.'

'Thank you, sir,' beamed the Chief and Hadley sighed.

'Now in her letter,' said the Commissioner as he picked it up from his desk 'she says that she wants you to call regularly and inform her of your progress in the investigation to the Plovdiv murder.'

'Very good, sir.'

'There's nothing 'good' about it Hadley, this nonsense will be taking up your valuable time explaining to this silly woman what we are doing… I've never heard anything like it!'

'Neither have I, sir,' added Bell smugly.

'And it's only because she's related to this Bulgarian Prince that we are forced to do this!' exclaimed the Commissioner angrily.

'In that case I'm sorry, sir,' said Hadley.

'She's also written to Sir Jason and he's furious about it all, so God help you Hadley if this all goes wrong and she starts complaining about your lack of progress!'

'Yes, sir,' replied Hadley with a sigh.

When he got back to his office George made him a strong up of tea to calm his nerves while he explained to Cooper what had happened.

'We were told to follow up all lines of inquiry, sir, that's exactly what we did and the Princess was very helpful,' said Cooper angrily.

'I know… but we'll have to be careful with her from now on, Sergeant.'

Working on until Big Ben struck eight o'clock Hadley then said 'let's get up to the Blind Beggar and see what Nellie Drake has to say about our man in the Bowler hat, Sergeant.'

'Right, sir.'

They had just left the office when a messenger hurried up the corridor behind them and called out 'Inspector Hadley, sir… this just came in from the station in Charing Cross Road and the Duty Officer thought you should see it first.' Hadley took the buff envelope, opened it and read the message: *We require the urgent assistance of a senior officer at Covent Garden Opera House where a Hungarian Diplomat has been fatally stabbed. Inspector Blake, Charing Cross Road Station.'*

CHAPTER 7

By the time the detectives arrived at The Opera House there were several Constables guarding the entrance and keeping back a small number of onlookers. Hadley and Cooper swept passed them and into the foyer where Hadley identified himself to a Sergeant.

'This way, sir,' said the Sergeant before he led them downstairs to the gentlemen's cloakroom and through to the toilet where the body of a man lay face down in a pool of blood. There were several officers present and Hadley recognised Inspector Richard Blake, who looked up from the body and said 'I'm glad you're here at last, Jim.'

Hadley nodded at Blake and asked 'so who is he?'

'He's a Hungarian Diplomat called Rossi Hatvan,' replied Blake.

'Oh bloody hell' whispered Cooper and Hadley's face paled.

'You can see here the single stab wound to his back that killed him,' said Blake as he pointed to a small but heavily bloodstained cut in the evening jacket.

'So what do we know, Dick?' asked Hadley with a sigh as Blake stood up.

'Apparently he was with his wife and another Hungarian Diplomat named Vadim Osijek and his wife… they were watching the ballet from their box when Hatvan excused himself after the performance had just started, he came down here to relieve himself and whilst doing so at the urinal, someone stabbed in the back then made their escape un-noticed by anyone.'

'Dear God… it just gets worse and worse' said Hadley.

'Do you think these killings are the work of one man, Jim?'

'I'm certain of it, Dick and this bloody assassin seems to be able to appear and disappear like will o' the wisp… did no one see or hear anything?'

'Apparently not, I've spoken to the cloakroom attendant and he said he left for just a few minutes after the performance had begun, he claims there was no one in here when he left but when he returned he found the body and raised the alarm, Jim.'

'What about the doormen?'

'There were two on duty outside but say they saw nobody leave only people arriving for the performance,' replied Blake.

'Then our killer must be still here,' said Hadley.

'I doubt that, because there are many exits to this place and just along the corridor we found an open fire door which leads out to an alley,' said Blake.

'This killer must be a professional assassin who is able to take advantage of brief unguarded moments to do his deadly work and not get caught in the act,' said Hadley.

'If that's the case then he takes unbelievable risks.'

'He certainly does, Dick.'

'Yes… he must have followed Hatvan into the building then waited for an opportunity to murder him,' said Blake.

'Or be here already.'

'That's also a possibility.'

'But how did he do it and not get caught?'

'I've no idea, Jim.'

Hadley sighed, shook his head and said 'well I suppose we'd better get the body away to the Marylebone for Doctor Evans to examine in the morning.'

'I've sent for an ambulance, Jim.'

'Right, now I'll talk to the cloakroom attendant and then the doormen,' said Hadley.

'I think before you do that you'd better have words with Vadim Osijek and Hatvan's distraught wife, Jim.'

Hadley raised his eyebrows, nodded and said 'yes of course.'

'That's why I sent the telegraph asking for assistance,' said Blake with a smile. Hadley glanced at him and replied 'I don't blame you for not wanting to get involved with a case that has such political ramifications, Dick.'

'Well it could be the ruination a promising Police career if one were to get it wrong,' said Blake with a grin.

'Oh don't I bloody well know!'

Blake led Hadley and Cooper up to the manager's office where Secretary Osijek sat pale faced, looking stunned, whilst his wife tried to comfort a weeping Madam Hatvan.

'I didn't expect to see you again so soon, Inspector,' said Osijek.

'I don't suppose you did, sir.'

'So what are you going to do about this terrible murder?' asked Osijek angrily as Madam Hatvan burst into floods of tears and began to sob. Hadley waited for a few moments for her to compose herself then replied 'Secretary Osijek and Madam Hatvan, I assure you both that we will do everything humanly possible to arrest this man and bring him to justice.'

'Well your record in these murder investigations is not what I would expect from the so called best Police force in the world, Inspector!'

'You're poor opinion of the Metropolitan Police is of no interest to me, sir, all I am concerned with is the rule of law... my duty is to uphold it and arrest those who break it!' replied Hadley firmly.

'Then I suggest from now on you make certain that you expedite matters!'

'I will, sir... so tell me, when you arrived this evening did you notice anybody looking strangely or intently at Mr Hatvan?'

'No I did not but I'm sure that our wives would have noticed if there was such an individual behaving in that manner... and as neither of them made any comment, then I can say with certainty that he does not exist,' replied Osijek.

'Did you go into the gentlemen's cloakroom at any time this evening, sir?'

'Yes, I went in with Rossi to leave our coats when we first arrived, Inspector.'

"Did you notice anybody at the time who may have been loitering, sir?'

"Not really, there were several other gentlemen leaving their coats with the attendant but nobody drew my particular attention.'

Hadley remained silent for a moment before he asked 'did Mr Hatvan have any personal enemies that you know of, sir?'

'Yes, I'm afraid he did, Inspector.'

'Please give me their names, sir.'

'Well there's a Rumanian called Bacau, he's head of security at their Embassy, and he followed Rossi constantly...'

'Do you know why, sir?' interrupted Hadley.

'No I don't, Inspector, but I always suspected that Bacau was a ruthless individual who would stop at nothing to ingratiate himself with the Ambassador...even commit murder,' replied Osijek.

'That's a very serious allegation, sir.'

'I'm aware of that, Inspector.'

'Who else can you name, sir?'

'A Russian called Mikhail Kamenka,' replied Osijek and Hadley glanced at Cooper who raised his eyebrows.

'We know that Mr Kamenka could not have attacked Mr Hatvan because he left London this afternoon to return to Moscow, sir.'

'Well I don't know your source of that information but I can assure you that it is completely wrong, Inspector,' replied Osijek.

'Really, sir?'

'Yes, I saw Kamenka outside in the street when we arrived here this evening.'

Hadley was not unduly surprised on hearing that and asked 'did you see him come into the Opera House, sir?'

'No, but he may have done so later, Inspector.'

'Yes possibly… are there any others who you believe were enemies of Mr Hatvan?'

'Only one that springs to mind, Inspector…he's a Greek called Korinthiakos,' replied Osijek as a Sergeant entered the office and said to Blake 'sorry to disturb you, sir, but the ambulance has arrived to take the body away.'

'Right, we'll be down in a moment, Sergeant,' replied Blake and Madam Hatvan began to sob once again.

Hadley looked at the distressed wives then said to Osijek 'that will be all for now, sir, thank you for your help. May I suggest that you return to your Embassy with the ladies and I will call tomorrow to inform you of our progress in the investigation.'

Osijek nodded and replied with a sigh 'thank you, Inspector.'

The detectives made their way down to the cloakroom where the ambulance men were lifting the body onto the canvas stretcher.

'Let's have a word with the doormen and the cloakroom attendant, Dick,' said Hadley. The three men were brought into the cloakroom and Hadley began the questioning whilst Cooper made notes. The two doormen said that they saw nobody leave the building until the alarm was raised by Charlie Higgs, the cloakroom attendant. A Constable, who happened to be passing by on his beat, was then summoned. However, when Charlie Higgs was questioned, he admitted to slipping out into the alley for a quick smoke when the performance had started, a few minutes later he noticed a man coming out of a fire exit and walking hurriedly away from him down the alley towards St. James's.

'What can you tell me about this man?' asked Hadley with his blue eyes gleaming.

'I couldn't see his face, but he looked a bit peculiar, sir,' replied Higgs.

'In what way?'

'Well, he sort of walked funny… and his hat looked far too big for his blimmin head.'

'When you say he was walking funny… was he limping?'

'Yes, well sort of, sir.'

'Can you be more precise?'

'He just seemed to wobble as he walked, sir,' replied Higgs.

'Did you notice what he was wearing?'

'No not really, sir.'

'Is there anything else you can remember about this person, Mr Higgs?'

'I'm afraid not, sir.'

'Well if you do recall something, please let me know at Scotland Yard,' said Hadley.

'I certainly will, sir… and please don't say anything to the manager about me slipping out for a quick smoke, will you, sir?'

'Your secret is safe with me, Mr Higgs,' replied Hadley with a smile.

Within half an hour Hadley had made a last survey of the murder scene, told Blake that he would now take over the investigation, wished him 'goodnight' and left The Opera House with Cooper. The detectives hurried back to the Yard where Hadley sent a telegraph message to all London Police stations advising them of Hatvan's murder and giving a description of the limping man wearing an oversized Bowler hat and requesting his immediate arrest. Once back in his office he and Cooper began writing a report for the Chief and the Commissioner.

'After we've finished the report, I'll send a quick message to the Chief's home telling him the latest news before he reads it in the newspapers tomorrow, then we'll pop along to the Blind

Beggar and speak to Nellie Drake, Sergeant.'

'Very good, sir… although I was hoping for an early night,' replied Cooper.

'Ah, Sergeant, you never know what awaits us around the next corner.'

'That's very true, sir, but sometimes I just wish that the next corner was a bit further away!' said Cooper and Hadley laughed.

Big Ben was striking ten o'clock by the time they had finished the report and cleared their desks before going downstairs and out to the Embankment, where Cooper hailed a cab.

The Blind Beggar was full of drinkers singing and shouting when the detectives arrived.

'It'll be difficult to talk in there, so we'll have to get Nellie away somewhere quieter, Sergeant.'

'Where do you suggest, sir?'

'I think we'll walk her back to the station, Sergeant, and we can also see how Molly is bearing up without her gin!'

'Good idea, sir.'

They pushed through the crowd at the door and stood in the middle of the noisy bar looking around for the women. Cooper saw them first, sitting at a table in the corner with two men. Hadley led the way to the women and when he said 'hello, ladies' Agnes looked up, smiled then said 'blimey, Jim, we'd given you up for dead!'

'We've been a touch busy this evening, Agnes,' replied Hadley with a smile.

'You're always blimmin busy' said Florrie.

'Indeed we are, now, how's your mum, Nellie?'

'She's fine, thanks guvnor,' replied Nellie with a smile before one of the men asked 'who is this bloke?'

Hadley looked hard at the man and replied 'this bloke's a Bobby Inspector on duty with his Sergeant.'

The man's jaw dropped and he said hesitantly 'Oh sorry, guvnor, I didn't know.'

'I realise that… now ladies, can I persuade you to come for a little walk with me to see Molly?' asked Hadley.

'Why not, Jim,' said Agnes.

'Can I bring her a little tot of gin, guvnor?' asked Florrie.

Hadley grinned and replied 'I'm sure she'll be glad of it, Florrie.'

'What about doing the business with us?' asked the other man in alarm.

'We'll be back later, mate,' replied Agnes.

'We might have gone home by then,' said the first man.

'You'll still be here as usual, Charlie boy, and if you're not, you'll have to wait for another time to do the business with us won't you?' said Agnes as she stood up and led the way out of the pub.

Agnes and Nellie walked either side of Hadley and linked arms with him. Florrie did the same with Cooper as they stepped briskly along the Whitechapel Road towards the Police station.

'This is nice on a warm evening, Jim,' said Agnes with a smile.

'Indeed it is, but I'm afraid we're not on a social outing,' replied Hadley.

'I know and that's a pity... I've told Nellie you wanted to speak to her,' said Agnes.

'Good, we'll talk in the station where it's quiet.'

'I'm not in any trouble am I, guvnor?' asked Nellie anxiously.

'No not at all, Nellie, I just want to talk to you about the man you saw on Wednesday night,' replied Hadley.

'Oh that's alright then,' said Nellie as she squeezed his arm.

When they arrived at the station, Jack Palmer had gone off duty but Sergeant Morris was there and after Hadley told him he wished to question the women, the Sergeant showed them into the interview room. Before Hadley and Cooper joined them, Morris said 'I've seen the telegraph about the murder of the Diplomat at Covent Garden, sir, and I've alerted all the Constables on the shift to look out for this suspect.'

'Thank you, Sergeant.'

'Another terrible tragedy, sir and where will it all end I wonder?'

'Hopefully as soon as we've arrested this man, Sergeant... provided we can find him.'

'I do hope so, sir... now can I get you any tea?'

'Yes please.'

The detectives joined the women, sat down at the table opposite them and Cooper took out his notebook. Hadley cleared his throat and said 'Nellie, please tell me everything you saw on Wednesday night.'

'Well guvnor, I was just going up the Lane when I saw this funny fella walking up towards Mitre Square... and when I heard that the posh fella who was with Molly had been done in, I said to Agnes I said...I bet that funny fella had something to with it and no mistake.'

'What made you think that, Nellie?'

'Because I saw him just after Molly's posh fella was done in, guvnor, and he was in such a blimmin rush,' she replied.

'Describe this funny fella to me.'

'Well, as I said, he walked funny... and that was what I noticed first of all, then I saw his blimmin hat... it was too big for his head.'

'Was he limping?'

'No not really, guvnor, he was just sort of wobbling you might say.'

'As if he was drunk?'

'I don't know... but he didn't look drunk.'

'Can you remember anything else?'

'He kept looking back and hurried up when he heard the Bobbie's whistle' she replied.

'Did you see what he was wearing, Nellie?'

'No not really, I think he just had on a long black coat, guvnor.'

'Did you see him get into a coach or hail a cab in Mitre Square?'

'No... because some fella stopped me just then and asked if I was up for business... so I said I was and we went off down to Fuller Street,' she replied.

'Would you recognise this funny fella again?'

'Oh yes, I saw his face when he turned to look back, guvnor.'

'Tell me what you can remember about him.'

'Well he had a big moustache and his face was quite pale so to speak,' she replied as a Constable arrived with cups of tea on a tray.

'This is nice' said Agnes.

'It's the least we could do at this time of night,' said Hadley with a smile.

When they had finished the tea Hadley asked a few more questions but realised that Nellie had told him everything she knew about the suspect. After thanking her they all went down to see Molly and Florrie slipped her a little tot of gin in a tiny bottle. They left the station and the detectives walked the women to their lodgings in Gypsy Lane and said 'goodnight' to them. Agnes gave Hadley a quick kiss and Florrie did the same to Cooper before the detectives hurried up to Thames Street where Cooper hailed a passing cab.

On the journey back to Camden they discussed the investigation and made plans for the next day.

'Its Saturday tomorrow, Sergeant and I'm afraid we'll be working all through the weekend.'

'And non-stop all next week, sir.'

'Probably… unless we can find this suspect with the big Bowler hat and funny walk.'

'What do you really make of that, sir?'

'I honestly don't know, Sergeant, it's all a mystery to me at the moment... but I'm sure he's our killer.'

'But he doesn't sound like a professional assassin, sir, drawing attention to himself with his funny walk and big hat.'

'As I said, it's a mystery, Sergeant.'

'It certainly is, sir.'

'But everything will be revealed in time,' said Hadley as the cab arrived outside his house.

'Goodnight, sir.'

'Goodnight, Sergeant… I'll see you in the morning at eight as usual.'

'Yes, sir, you will,' replied Cooper with a sigh.

CHAPTER 8

The next morning, to Hadley's surprise, George was in the office and the kettle was on ready for tea.

'Good morning, sir.'

'Morning, George, I didn't expect you in today, it's Saturday.'

'I know, sir, but when I read in this morning's paper what happened last night at Covent Garden, I said to my wife 'the govnor will need me in today for certain'.'

'Yes I do need you, George, and I'm glad you came in,' said Hadley as Cooper arrived and after wishing 'good morning' to them both, expressed his surprise at seeing their clerk.

'Ah, you can rely on me when duty calls, sir... I will always be there,' said George and Cooper nodded.

'Yes we know, George... and thank you,' said Hadley with a smile before the clerk went off to make the tea while the detectives checked their reports ready for him to type.

Hadley expected that the Chief Inspector would arrive in his office at any moment and want a full report on Hatvan's murder. He did not have to wait for long. Big Ben was striking the half hour at eight thirty and coupled with the clacking sound of George's typewriter it allowed the Chief Inspector to enter the office unnoticed for a brief moment, Hadley was suddenly aware of someone, glanced up from the paperwork on his desk and said 'ah... good morning, sir.'

'Morning Hadley... Sergeant.'

'Morning, sir.'

'Come up to my office now... both of you,' said Bell firmly before he turned and strode out. The detectives followed on in silence up the stairs and only after Bell was seated at his desk did he wave them to sit on the creaking chairs.

'Hadley, when I received your message about this Hungarian's murder at Covent Garden last night, I was more concerned than I have ever been in my whole career with the Metropolitan Police,' said Bell as he fixed the Inspector with a piercing look.

'I'm sorry to hear that sir, but I thought you should know about it immediately.'

'Of course and you acted quite correctly, Hadley, but do you fully appreciate the ramifications of this terrible act in Covent Garden of all places?'

'Well, sir…'

'It is the centre and very heart of British cultural civilisation where London's high society and foreign dignitaries, go to be entertained.' interrupted Bell angrily.

'I'm sure they do…'

'And they do not expect to be murdered in the gentlemen's cloakroom!'

'No, of course not, sir.'

'And in the middle of a performance of Swan Lake of all things…my God, what sort of killer are we dealing with?'

'I'm sure he's a foreign assassin, sir.'

'And what are you doing about arresting this bloody foreigner?'

'Last night I advised all London stations of Hatvan's murder and gave a description of the suspect for his immediate arrest, sir,' replied Hadley.

'And?'

'I intend to follow up various leads this morning, sir, and talk to Secretary Osijek for his full account of what happened at The Opera House,' replied Hadley.

'That may have to wait, Hadley, because when I advised the Commissioner last night he said he would arrange a meeting at midday to discuss this spiral of tragic events with Sir George at the Home Office and we are expected to attend with detailed written reports,' said Bell.

'Very good, sir… my clerk is already typing out my initial report.'

'I'm pleased to hear it… now the Press are having a field day with these Diplomat murders… The Times editorial this morning claims that we are still baffled and have no idea who the killer is!'

'Well I'm afraid that's the truth at the moment, sir.'

'Hadley, you don't have to side so readily with these sneering troublemakers in Fleet Street who regularly deride us!'

'I don't, sir!'

'May I remind you that this situation is becoming politically very serious for our country with such turmoil and uncertainty raging in the Balkans?'

'And why is that, sir?'

'It's obvious, Hadley, we cannot hope to exert our proper and civilising influence in Eastern Europe when their Diplomats are being slaughtered at random and unhindered in London by one of their own .'

'I suppose not, sir.'

'And if we don't bring this murderous mayhem to a halt then who knows what will be the outcome for Britain?'

'I'm really not quite sure, sir.'

'Then I'll tell you…our worldwide reputation for the rule of law in our safe, civilised society will be severely tarnished, Hadley.'

'Yes, sir.'

'Her Majesty and the Government would be distraught beyond all measure if that were to happen.'

'I'm sure, sir.'

'We must apprehend this killer before he strikes again!'

'Of course, sir.'

'So what else do you propose to do?'

'I plan to search all the lodgings within a mile around Mitre Square in Whitechapel, sir.'

'Was he seen in the vicinity?'

'Yes, sir, he was observed hurrying up Gypsy Lane towards the Square at the time Plovdiv was stabbed in Church Alley.'

'I see, well get on and ask Palmer to do that immediately.'

'I know he's very pressed at the moment, sir, so I wondered if we could send officers from here to search the lodgings.'

'It's out of the question, Hadley, because as you know, we're suffering severe financial constraints from the Government and our manpower is limited,' replied Bell.

'Very well, sir,' said Hadley with a sigh.

'Before you return to your office, tell me in detail what happened last night at Covent Garden,' said Bell.

Hadley gave his account of the events and when he had finished the Chief said 'this sounds preposterous, a man with some form of walking disability and wearing a Bowler hat that's too big for him… what sort of description is that?

'I'm afraid it's all we have at the moment, sir.'

'And more to the point, Hadley, what kind of political assassin goes round in such a fashion which is bound to get him noticed?'

'It's a complete mystery to me, sir, but he has been seen by independent witnesses near the crime scene on each occasion,' replied Hadley.

'Dear God, what are we dealing with I wonder?'

'I really don't know, sir.'

Bell sat back in his chair, gazed at the ceiling and remained silent for a few moments before he asked 'now what information have you about this Galati woman and all her foreign paramours?'

'None, sir… and I'll have to wait until she returns to London before I can question her.'

'Nonsense Hadley, this is the most serious investigation that we have ever undertaken and we must follow every line of inquiry so find out where this woman is and question her rigorously!'

'Yes, sir, but I fear her husband will complain when I insist that he gives me her whereabouts.'

'Then let him complain, Hadley, you heard what the Commissioner said about diplomatic immunity and all that nonsense!'

'Very well, sir.'

'These blasted foreigners must learn that we will not be diverted from our lawful duties when murder has been committed on our streets,' said Bell firmly.

'Of course not, sir.'

'Now do you intend to find and question this Russian, what's his name, who was supposed to have gone back to Moscow but was seen outside the Opera House?'

'His name is Kamenka, sir, and I will be making inquiries at the Embassy.'

'Well don't let anyone there fob you off with lame excuses and demand to see the Ambassador if necessary.'

'I will, sir.'

'And get after the Greek and question him closely.'

'Yes, sir.'

'I've never trusted the Greeks you know.'

'No, sir.'

'And if you must go gallivanting off this morning Hadley, make sure that I have your detailed report before you go, so I can add my comments to it before the midday meeting with Sir George and the Commissioner.'

'I will ensure that you have it within the hour, sir.'

'Good… and whatever you do… don't be late for the meeting, Hadley!'

'No of course not, sir.'

The detectives returned to their office and Hadley told George to hurry with the report.

'I'm doing my best, sir,' the clerk replied above the clacking noise of the typewriter.

'That's all I ask, George,' said Hadley before he started to plan the morning with Cooper. It was decided to call at the Russian Embassy to see if Kamenka was there and after that, if time allowed, see Secretary Galati and request the whereabouts of his wife.

'I'm sure that will be a difficult conversation, sir,' said Cooper.

'I must admit I'm not looking forward to it, but we must do our duty without fear or favour, Sergeant.'

'Yes of course, sir.'

'And we need to find Mr Vlad Bacau, because he's got some questions to answer!'

Hadley sent a telegraph to Jack Palmer requesting he begin searching the lodgings around Mitre Square for the suspect and by the time he had returned from the telegraph office, George had finished typing the report. Hadley read and signed it before the clerk took it up to the Chief's office. If the day went according to plan then Hadley would call on Secretary Osijek later to question him about the events at Covent Garden, before going on to the Marylebone to see Doctor Evans and then down to Whitechapel.

Big Ben was striking ten o'clock when the detectives set off in a Police coach to the Russian Embassy. The receptionist informed the detectives that Mikhail Kamenka was not there and had left for Moscow yesterday. Hadley demanded in a firm tone to see the Ambassador and the anxious receptionist asked him to wait before he hurried upstairs. He returned minutes later and said 'Ambassador Smolenska will see you now, sir, so please follow me.'

They were shown into the office where the Ambassador stood to meet them and waved them to sit.

'Good morning, Your Excellency, thank you for seeing us so promptly.'

'Good morning gentlemen… how can I help you today?'

'You told us that Mr Kamenka had been recalled to Moscow and left London yesterday afternoon, sir.'

'That is correct, Inspector.'

'We have a reliable witness who claims that he saw Mr Kamenka outside the Covent Garden Opera House last night, sir.'

'Then whoever saw him must be mistaken, Inspector.'

'I don't think so, sir.'

'Are you calling me a liar?' roared Smolenska

'The gentleman who claims he saw Mr Kamenka is a Diplomat who knows him well, sir, and…'

'I don't care who he is, Inspector, I know for a fact that Kamenka was urgently recalled to Moscow and left in the afternoon!'

'But you cannot be certain that after he left the Embassy he did not remain in London until much later, sir,' said Hadley which seemed to take Smolenska by surprise.

'Well, no, I suppose not, he may have caught a later train to Dover.'

'That is one possible explanation, sir.'

'But that doesn't mean he was at Covent Garden when this latest atrocity took place, Inspector!'

'Sir, our witness claims that he was seen outside...'

'I am not interested…'

'And you can't be sure that he is not still here in London… unless you know otherwise, sir,' interrupted Hadley.

'Are you suggesting that for some reason I am deliberately misleading you about Kamenka's whereabouts, Inspector?'

'Sir, with respect, it is my duty to follow up every possibility in such a high level investigation and further more I am instructed by the Commissioner to leave no stone unturned…'

'I find your assertions most offensive so I will be making a serious formal complaint about you to your Home Secretary!'

'You are free to do so, sir, and I will inform him of your

intentions when I attend a meeting with him later today,' replied Hadley which made Smolenska turn pale.

'Well, er, I…'

'Do you know if Mr Kamenka knew Mr Rossi Hatvan, the Hungarian Diplomat who was murdered last night?' interrupted Hadley.

Smolenska composed himself and replied 'yes, Inspector, I'm sure he did, they must have met at various functions and I believe they shared a mutual friendship with the Rumanian Secretary, Mr Galati and his charming wife.'

'Did Mr Kamenka ever mention anything of a hostile or jealous nature regarding Mr Hatvan's friendship with the Galati's, sir?'

'No, never, Inspector, and as far as I knew they were all good friends,' replied Smolenska and Hadley remained silent for a few moments.

'Finally, sir, is it your firm belief that Mr Kamenka left the Embassy yesterday afternoon to immediately return to Moscow?'

'It is, Inspector.'

'And you know of no reason why he should stay in London until the evening, sir?'

'No, Inspector, I don't.'

'Thank you, sir, that will be all for the moment.'

The detectives left the Russian Embassy and made their way hurriedly to the Rumanian Embassy, where they were promptly admitted and the receptionist went to inform Secretary Galati that they wished to see him. When they were shown into the Secretary's office he did not seem pleased to see them and said firmly 'I suppose you have come to question me about this latest tragic murder, Inspector.'

'No, sir, but if you have any information regarding the events at The Opera House last night then I'd be glad to hear it.'

'So it's right what the papers are saying this morning, you're baffled and have no idea who the killer is.'

'Don't believe everything you read in the Press, sir, they have their agendas and we have ours and at the moment I can assure you that we have several suspects for the murder,' replied Hadley with a smile.

'Really… so why do you wish to see me, Inspector?'

'I've come to ask you where Madam Galati is staying at the moment, sir.'

'Why?'

'I wish to ask your wife a few questions regarding her friendship with Sergei Brasov and Rossi Hatvan, sir,' replied Hadley and Galati looked distinctly uncomfortable.

'I fail to see why you need to waste time speaking to my poor wife about the unfortunate victims of some crazed lunatic killer roaming freely around London, Inspector.'

'It is a line of inquiry that I am ordered to follow, sir.'

'You'd do better to concentrate on finding and arresting this killer.'

'We are, sir, I assure you.'

'Let me tell you, Inspector, my wife is distressed beyond all reason over the death of Brasov, made doubly worse by finding his body in Hyde Park!'

'I'm sure that is so, sir, but nevertheless I need to speak to her… so where is she?'

Galati hesitated for a while before Hadley prompted him by saying 'well, sir?'

'I'm not sure that I should tell you, Inspector.'

'Sir, please consider your position very carefully…in this country, obstructing Police Officers in their inquiries is a very serious matter that usually leads to imprisonment,' said Hadley calmly, Galati shrugged his shoulders, raised his eyebrows and replied 'she is staying with friends at Pangbourne, near Reading.'

'May I have the full address, sir?'

Galati wrote the details on a slip of paper and handed it to Hadley.

'Thank you, sir. Now I also need to speak to Mr Bacau… is he here?'

'No, Inspector, he's away on Embassy business at the moment.'

'And where has he gone to on this business, sir?'

'I'm not at liberty to say, Inspector, but he will be back soon,' replied Galati.

'Good, then I will call again, sir.'

'As you wish, but I must warn you to be very careful with your inquiries from now on, Inspector.'

'And why is that, sir?'

'I have many powerful friends who are watching you and your dismal failed attempts to deal with these tragic events...'

'And so have I, sir... good morning,' interrupted Hadley before he and Cooper strode from the office, leaving Galati open mouthed.

Outside the Embassy, Hadley glanced at his pocket watch and ordered the driver to return to the Yard as quickly as possible. They arrived just before noon and Hadley hurried up to Bell's office.

'You're late, Hadley!'

'I'm sorry, sir, but...'

'Never mind now, let's get to the Home Office quickly... Sir George and the Commissioner will not be best pleased if we keep them waiting!'

When they arrived at Sir George's palatial office, Bell apologised for being a few minutes late. The Commissioner's side whiskers bristled as the Home Secretary gave a nod and waved them to sit. Bell placed the buff folder containing the report on the edge of the desk before he sat down.

Sir George cleared his throat and said 'before I read your report, Chief Inspector, tell me where we are at the moment with the investigation into Hatvan's murder.'

'Very good, sir,' replied Bell and then he gave a full account of what was known and the action taken by Hadley after the murder.

'That all seems positive, Chief Inspector,' said Sir George and Bell smiled.

'Thank you, sir.'

'Now Commissioner, I suggest that you place armed Officers outside all the Balkan Embassy's until the suspect is apprehended,' said Sir George.

'I think it very unlikely that he would attempt any further killings within the confines of the Embassy's, sir,' said the Commissioner.

'I'm sure that is so, but my decision is a political one, designed to calm troubled nerves within the diplomatic community and it is sanctioned by the Prime Minister,' said Sir George.

'Then of course I will arrange that protection immediately, sir,' replied the great one.

'Very good, now I also want extra manpower deployed for a thorough search around Whitechapel for this suspect,' said Sir George and Hadley was pleased that he and Palmer would have assistance in looking for this limping, Bowler hatted man... a veritable needle in a haystack.

'Yes, sir,' said the Commissioner with a sigh.

'And alert all London stations to be extra vigilant for this dangerous man and arrest anyone who vaguely fits the description, Commissioner.'

'I will, sir.'

'And I think that the Officers who are conducting the investigation should be armed at all times, Commissioner.'

'Very well, sir.'

'This man is obviously extremely dangerous and I do not want him to slip away when he is found and challenged... in other words, gentlemen,' and Sir George paused, glanced at Hadley and Bell, before continuing 'do not hesitate to shoot him down if necessary.'

'We will not hesitate, sir,' said Bell and Hadley nodded.

'Good... so thank you, gentlemen... and if you will now carry on with your important duties while the Commissioner and I discuss your report and other matters,' said Sir George with a smile.

'Of course, sir... Commissioner,' said Bell before he stood up.

'Oh... and Inspector Hadley,' said Sir George.

'Yes, sir?'

'Sir Jason Thornley has asked that when you have a moment to spare, would you please call on Princess Radomir and give her some vague information as to where we are in apprehending Igor Plovdiv's killer?' asked Sir George. On hearing that the Commissioner's side whiskers bristled as his face coloured up, Bell's jaw dropped and Hadley replied brightly 'yes of course, sir.'

'You must understand that it's all become very political,' said Sir George with a sigh.

'I do understand, sir,' replied Hadley with a smile.

As the detectives hurried along Whitehall towards the Yard, Bell was seething with anger and said 'never mind about politics and wasting valuable time calling on that silly woman, Hadley, get yourself armed and after this bloody, murdering foreigner!'

CHAPTER 9

Back in his office Hadley asked George to get some sandwiches from the canteen and make a pot of tea whilst he briefed Cooper on what had transpired at the meeting. After Hadley had finished the briefing he said 'and from now on we're to be armed at all times, Sergeant.'

'I'm not surprised, sir.'

'It's desperate that we catch this blighter before he strikes again and Sir George has given us a direct order to shoot him down if he attempts to escape when confronted.'

'Then I won't hesitate this time, sir.'

'No don't, Sergeant … because I want you to finish this investigation completely unhurt for a change!'

'So do I, sir... and so does my wife.'

'Of course, now after lunch we'll call on Osijek and see what else he can tell us about last night and then we'll see the Doctor before going on to Whitechapel.'

After a hurried lunch, the detectives went down to the armoury and booked out two .45 calibre revolvers and 12 rounds of ammunition before setting off in a Police coach to the Hungarian Embassy.

On being admitted to Secretary Osijek's office and announced, he waved them to sit. He was pale and looked anxious when Hadley asked him to recount the tragic events at Covent Garden. When Osijek finished speaking, Hadley asked various questions which seemed to confuse the Secretary and he gave conflicting answers, which aroused some suspicion in Hadley's mind. The interview was not very satisfactory and Osijek contributed little to what was already known, so, realising there was nothing more to be gained, Hadley thanked him for his help and the detectives left the Embassy.

As the coach hurried onto the Marylebone Hospital, Hadley said 'there's something not quite right about Osijek's account of last night's events, Sergeant.'

'Can you say what for instance, sir?'

'I don't know, I can't quite put my finger on it but I'm damned sure he knows more than he's telling us!'

'Ah, Balkan intrigue, will we ever get to the bottom of it, sir?'

'I do hope so, Sergeant,' replied Hadley as the coach turned into the Marylebone.

When they entered the mortuary office, Doctor Evans looked up from his paper-strewn desk and said 'you two are beginning to become a nuisance!'

'Why's that, Doctor?' asked Hadley with a grin.

'It's Saturday in case you haven't noticed… and I was due to play golf with Bob Andrews, he's the Chairman of the Hospital Trust, you know,' replied Evans.

'No, I didn't know.'

'Well I was just about to set off from home when a messenger called with a note from your Chief Inspector asking me to examine this Diplomat who was murdered last night and write an interim report for the Commissioner!'

'Ah, you can't say we don't keep you busy with our murdered clients, Doctor,' said Hadley with a smile.

'I know, but on a Saturday?'

Hadley ignored the remark and asked 'have you had a chance to look at him yet?'

'Only a quick cursory one I'm afraid, Jim… Smythe laid the body out last night when it first arrived and it appears that he was killed by a single stab wound to the back, which is similar to the other two Diplomats,' replied the Doctor

'May we see?'

'Of course,' replied Evans before he stood up and led them out into the cold, white tiled mortuary.

The Doctor uncovered the body of Rossi Hatvan and with the help of Smythe, the dour mortuary assistant, turned it on to one side so that the detectives could see the neat stab wound to the back.

'It looks like the same stiletto dagger was used, Jim… you can plainly see that the entry wound is not more than an inch wide,' said Evans.

'Well it all ties up nicely with the suspect who was seen at all three murders, Doctor.'

'So our professional assassin was observed then?' asked Evans as he and Smythe lowered the body to the slab.

'Yes he was.'

'And what does he look like, Jim?'

'Well it is a little strange to say… but according to the witnesses, he walks with a limp and wears a Bowler hat that appears to be too big for him,' replied Hadley.

'Good heavens… surely that would draw attention to him and a professional killer would not countenance that under any circumstances, Jim.'

'I agree with you, Doctor, and I must admit it's a mystery to me.'

'It is to me as well, Jim,' said Evans. They remained silent for a few moments before Hadley said 'we'd better leave you to it, Doctor, and I would be grateful if your report was with the Chief as soon as possible.'

'Of course, Jim, I will send my initial conclusions over to him within a couple of hours.'

'Thank you, Doctor.'

On the journey across London, Hadley said nothing, remaining deep in thought and only glanced at his fob watch as the coach arrived at Whitechapel Police station. It was just after four o'clock and he said to Cooper 'I could do with a nice cup of tea, Sergeant.'

'So could I, sir, it's quite hot today.'

'True, and there's nothing so cooling as a hot cuppa!'

'I'm sure we can twist Inspector Palmer's arm, sir.'

'Provided he's not out searching for our suspect,' said Hadley with a grin before he stepped down from the coach.

Palmer looked up from his desk as they entered his office and said 'I've got as many men as I can spare searching all the lodgings for this suspect, Jim, and before you ask for me to do any more…'

'Jack, let me stop you right there… the Home Secretary has just ordered the Commissioner to send as many men as necessary to assist you,' interrupted Hadley with a smile.

'Well thank God for that!'

'And they should be arriving at any moment.'

'I'm relieved to hear it, Jim.'

'So while we're waiting perhaps we could have a pot of tea, Jack?'

'That's a very good idea... so why not?'

After Palmer had ordered tea, they discussed the case so far and Hadley briefed him on what had transpired since they last met.

'My God, it all gets darker by the minute, Jim.'

'It does... and I think we're clutching at straws at the moment and unless we get a major breakthrough then I fear there's little chance of catching this killer,' said Hadley gloomily.

'You think he may skip the country when he's finished his deadly work?'

'I'm sure of it, Jack, and he may have already gone if the last victim on his list was Hatvan' replied Hadley as the tea arrived. They had just started to sip the golden reviver when a Constable entered with a buff envelope.

'This just arrived for you, sir.'

'Thank you.' Palmer opened it and read the telegraph message out aloud.

'Inspector Palmer. Inspector Walters with Sergeants Wells and Gibson will be leaving Scotland Yard shortly with forty Constables to assist you in a search for the Diplomat murder suspect in the area around Mitre Square. They will remain with you until 10.00pm and if the suspect is not apprehended they will resume the search from 9.00am tomorrow and continue until 9.00pm. Commissioner of Metropolitan Police.'

'There... what did I tell you, Jack?'

'That's the first time the Commissioner has ever sent me a message, Jim.'

'At last he knows you exist,' said Hadley with a grin.

'Will wonders never cease!' exclaimed Palmer.

'Apparently not, Jack,' replied Hadley.

The detectives planned to search a much greater area now that reinforcements were on their way. Palmer ran his finger over the street map of Whitechapel and said 'as you know, Jim, it's a rabbit warren around these alleyways leading up to Mitre Square.'

'Oh, indeed I do.'

'And our suspect could be hidden away in any number of doss

houses or lodgings.'

'I'm afraid it's like looking for the proverbial needle,' said Hadley with a sigh.

'Yes it is… and I've only been able to allocate Sergeant Morris and four Constables for the search so I'm very glad that we're receiving help from the Yard.'

'And we need all the help we can get if we're to catch this murderous foreigner,' said Hadley before he paused for a moment and added 'I think I'll have a word with the ladies, Jack, and get them to put the word out to the other streetwalkers that I'm offering a reward for any information that leads to his arrest… that should get things moving.'

After planning the new extended search area for the Yard Officers with Palmer, Hadley and Cooper left the station and made their way down to the Kings Head to find Agnes and Florrie. The ladies were standing outside the noisy pub talking to a woman called Dot when the detectives approached them.

'Hello, ladies,' said Hadley with a smile.

'Oh, Jim… and Sergeant Bobby, what a nice surprise on a sunny afternoon!' replied Agnes.

'Are you going to treat us to a gin, guvnor?' asked Florrie.

'Only if you're good!'

'Oh, I'm very good don't you know!' replied Florrie as she gave him a wink.

'So I've heard,' said Hadley with a grin.

'But I think you need to find out for yourself, guvnor,' said Florrie with a coy smile.

'Now, now, Florrie, let's get you ladies a couple of gins before things start getting out of hand,' said Hadley.

'Well, Agnes deary, looks like you and Florrie will be doing the business with these gents, so I'll catch you later in the Ten Bells,' said the woman with a smile.

'No, Dot, there's no business with these fella's because we can't get them to lift our skirts no matter how hard we try,' said Agnes.

'Quite right too,' said Hadley with a grin and Cooper nodded.

'Blimey, Agnes… you must be slipping in your old age girlie,' said Dot with a sly grin before she waltzed away up the road towards the Ten Bells pub.

'Old age my foot! She's got a blimmin cheek!' said Agnes as she put her hands on her hips and glared after the woman.

'Take no notice of her Agnes, she's well passed it now and I know she only does it for a shilling so she can get any poor drunk old bugger who nobody else wants,' said Florrie.

'Ladies... I think it's time for a drink,' said Hadley.

'Too blimmin right, Jim,' said Agnes before she turned and led the way into the busy pub.

Vera and her girls were doing their best to serve the early evening drinkers and when she caught sight of Hadley, she nodded. They waited at the end of the bar until Vera finished serving a sweaty costermonger and came to Hadley.

'The usual, guvnor?'

'Please Vera... and gins for the ladies,' replied Hadley. Vera nodded before she began pulling the first pint of stout and when she placed it on the wet counter, Hadley asked 'can we go into the back room, Vera?'

'Of course, guvnor, I'll get one of the girls to open up for you.'

'Thanks.'

As soon as they were settled in the cool, quiet back room with the door closed, Hadley said 'now ladies, I need your help as well as all the other girls you know in the area.'

'What's in it for us, Jim?' asked Agnes.

'I'm going to offer a reward of ten Guineas...'

'Ten Guineas, Jim!' interrupted Agnes.

'Yes...'

'Blimey, that would keep us off the blimmin streets for a couple of months or more!' said Florrie.

'I'm sure it would.'

'So what do we have to do, Jim?'

'Help us quickly find this man with the limp and big Bowler hat.'

'Well we don't know where he is, Jim,' said Agnes.

'And neither do we, but I'm sure he's probably staying somewhere in Whitechapel, Agnes, and if you or any of the girls find out where... then the ten Guineas are yours,' said Hadley.

'Well for ten Guineas I'd blimmin go looking for him all night long in just me hat and knickers!' exclaimed Florrie.

'You don't wear any knickers,' said Agnes with a grin and Cooper blushed.

'Just me hat then,' added Florrie with a giggle.

'And I would arrest you if you went out like that, Florrie,' said Hadley.

'Oh I know guvnor... but I think I'd quite like that!'

'Now now, Florrie,' said Hadley with a smile.

'And can you imagine me waltzing up Whitechapel Road with you to the Police station in just me hat?' she giggled.

'We can... and it's an 'orrible sight!' said Agnes as Cooper raised his eyebrows and blushed while Hadley chuckled.

'So what's a girl got to do to earn these ten guineas?' Florrie asked.

'I've just told you, find this man before we do... there's a number of Constables on their way from the Yard who will be searching all the lodgings and doss houses for a mile or more around Mitre Square... so if you want the money you'd better drink up and get cracking ladies,' said Hadley.

'Blimey, Jim, it's all rush with you these days!' said Agnes.

'We're in difficult times, Agnes and the devil drives,' said Hadley.

Within ten minutes they had left the pub and whilst the women made their way to Gypsy Lane to tell all the girls and then start calling at the doss houses in Hanbury Street, the detectives hurried back to Whitechapel Police station where the Yard Officers had just arrived in four Police wagons.

Whilst the Constables waited in the Watch Room, Palmer briefed Hadley, Cooper, Inspector Walters, Sergeants Wells and Gibson in his office. They studied the street map carefully and were each assigned areas which were clearly defined. It was decided that the Constables would be split up into parties of ten. Palmer would lead the first, searching around Mitre Square whilst Walters would lead another ten with Sergeant Wells, Hadley the third with Cooper and Sergeant Gibson would follow on with his men to their designated area. The armed senior Officers went down to the Watch Room and Palmer briefed the Constables before they all boarded the Police wagons and set off to search for the suspect.

As Hadley led his party around the area's doss houses and lodgings it brought back memories of his early days as a Constable. It depressed him to see the poor living in such squalid conditions and nothing seemed to have improved with the passing of time. There were many Russian Jewish immigrants now living in the East End cheek by jowl with others from Europe, which made for a dangerous and difficult situation as they tried to live together in such an overcrowded area. Successive Governments had done little to ease the situation and were much more concerned with looking after their wealthy, influential friends. The popular author Charles Dickens, with his accurate storytelling of the poor in his wonderful books, had begun to awaken society's conscience to their plight and at last questions were being asked but it came too late for many who had died needlessly.

Having searched the area thoroughly without finding even a trace of the limping man, Hadley led his party back to their wagon and proceeded to Whitechapel Police station. It was just after ten o'clock when the tired officers climbed down from the wagon and went inside for some tea and sandwiches. The other three parties arrived shortly afterwards and joined them in the Watch Office. None of the others had discovered anything that could give a possible lead to the whereabouts of this man and it seemed that he had just disappeared into thin air.

In Palmer's office, the detective's planned for the continuing search in the morning. It was decided to extend out as far as Bishopsgate in the west, Cable Street to the south, Cambridge Heath to the east and Hackney Road to the north.

'If he's anywhere within this boundary we'll find him for sure,' said Palmer.

'I hope so, Jack, but I'm afraid that Cooper and I will not be with you first thing,' said Hadley.

'Why's that, Jim?'

'We're following up another line of inquiry down at Pangbourne,' replied Hadley and Cooper looked surprised.

'Ah, so while we do all the work you'll be gallivanting off to the country,' said Palmer with a grin.

'It's on the strict orders of the Chief Inspector, Jack'.

'That's alright then,' he said.

'But we'll join you as soon as we get back.'

'Maybe we'll have caught him by then.'

'Oh, may it please God to make it so… then we can all take a breather,' said Hadley with a sigh.

'Amen to that, Jim.'

After wishing their colleagues 'goodnight', Hadley and Cooper left the station and waited for passing Hansom cabs to take them home. In the warm night air they stood in the Whitechapel Road and Hadley said 'meet me at Paddington Station at eight tomorrow, Sergeant, and we'll catch the first train down to Reading.'

'Very good, sir' replied Cooper with a sigh.

'And when we get back from seeing Madam Galati, we'll pay a quick visit to the Princess to keep her well informed… and hopefully stop any complaints that she may make regarding our slow progress in the Plovdiv case.'

'This blimmin investigation is now getting a bit too complicated, sir,'

'Indeed it is, Sergeant,' said Hadley with a sigh as he waved at a passing cab.

It was just before eleven thirty when Hadley arrived home to find Alice still up and waiting for him in the parlour.

'Oh Jim, my poor tired husband… have you eaten anything?'

'Not really, Alice, just sandwiches and plenty of tea I'm afraid.'

'Then let me get you something…'

'No, it's alright dearest, I think I'll just go to bed,' he interrupted.

'Listen to me, Jim… you will soon be very ill if you don't stop…'

'Alice, we've just had a holiday!' he interrupted.

'And much good it's done you! Just look at yourself will you?'

'I'm alright…'

'You can't see yourself James Hadley… I promise you that…'

'I'm going up to bed!' he interrupted.

'You're the most stubborn man I've ever met!'
'Goodnight Alice dear,' he said as he strode out of the parlour.

CHAPTER 10

Cooper was already waiting at Paddington ticket office when Hadley arrived at station just before eight o'clock. After buying day return tickets they boarded the 8.15 express to Bristol and had a compartment to themselves.

'We should be in Reading within an hour or so, Sergeant,' said Hadley as he glanced at his fob watch.

'Right, sir.'

'And the trip out to Pangbourne should take about another hour, so all being well, we should be with Madam Galati by ten thirty at the latest.'

'I wonder if her Greek friend is with her, sir.'

'We'll find out all in good time, Sergeant, and if he is there we'll be able to kill two birds with one stone.'

'Well according to Bacau, he's the last one on the list of suspects we can question, sir, because Hatvan is dead, Kamenka is supposed to be in Moscow, so it only leaves this fella Korinthiakos who may have murdered Brasov in Hyde Park,' said Cooper.

'And not forgetting our friend Osijek, who went for a walk alone at the time Brasov was killed, Sergeant,'

'Oh… yes, sir… but what motive would Osijek have for killing Brasov?'

'I don't know yet, Sergeant.'

'It's all a mystery, sir.'

'It certainly is, but it will be interesting to see if Mr Korinthiakos is at Pangbourne and walks with a limp, has a large moustache and a Bowler hat that's too big,' replied Hadley.

'It will indeed, sir and if he fits the description are you going to arrest him?'

'If he hasn't got a watertight alibi for the times of the murders, Sergeant, then I'll have him in custody without a moment's hesitation.'

They discussed the case during the journey and when the express pulled into Reading station at 9.20, the detectives hurried from the platform and out into the warm sunshine. Cooper hired a waiting trap to take them out to Pangbourne and gave the driver the address. The chestnut mare clip clopped along at a good pace through the town and out on the Oxford Road towards Pangbourne. Hadley glanced at his fob watch occasionally as he was anxious to get back to London as soon as possible. He believed that the killer was still there and this trip to speak to Madam Galati was probably a waste of his time but a necessary exercise to placate Bell and the Commissioner. However, if the Greek was with her, then the journey out to Pangbourne would not have been in vain.

Within the hour the trap had reached the village of Pangbourne, made its way up the hill overlooking the gently flowing Thames and turned into a drive leading up to an elegant Georgian House.

'This is it, sir,' said the driver as he stopped the trap by the portico.

'Thank you... will you please wait for us?' asked Hadley before he stepped down.

'Yes, sir.'

'We shouldn't be too long.'

'Very good, sir.'

'What a beautiful view, Sergeant,' said Hadley as he surveyed the gently rolling green hills that surrounded the valley.

'It certainly is, sir.'

They stood for a few moments before climbing the steps to the front door where Cooper rang the bell. The door was eventually opened by a butler who looked them up and down before asking 'yes, can I help you?'

'Is this the home of Sir Rodney Phelps?' asked Hadley.

'It is, sir.'

'We're Police Officers from Scotland Yard and wish to speak to Sir Rodney,' said Hadley.

'Please come in, sir' said the butler as he stood back and allowed them to enter the spacious hallway.

'Please wait while I'll let Sir Rodney know that you're here, sir.'

'Thank you.'

The butler soon returned and said 'Sir Rodney will see you now, so please follow me.'

They were led into a study where a tall, grey haired, elderly man stood up from his desk.

'Good morning, sir, I'm Inspector Hadley and this is Sergeant Cooper, we're from Scotland Yard.'

'Good morning, gentlemen, you've come a long way first thing on a Sunday, so it must be important,' said Sir Rodney in a suspicious tone.

'It is, sir.'

'So how can I help you?'

'I believe that you have Madam Galati staying with you at present, sir.'

'Indeed, she is one of my guests, Inspector.'

'May I speak to her, sir?'

'As I'm sure this is in connection with the tragic murder of Sergei Brasov, then I have to tell you, Inspector, that Madam Galati is still in a state of great distress and I'm not certain that she should be disturbed,' replied Sir Rodney firmly.

'I understand your concerns, sir, but I am here on direct orders from the Metropolitan Commissioner to interview Madam Galati.'

Sir Rodney frowned and replied 'that may be so, but the poor lady is still in a very fragile state and any untoward questioning may throw her headlong into some form of mental relapse… from which she may never recover.'

'I'm truly sorry to hear this, but nevertheless I must insist on speaking to her, sir.'

Sir Rodney sighed and said 'then on your own head be it, Inspector, but if you say anything that harms Madam Galati's emotional state, then I will complain vigorously to your Commissioner as well as others in high authority.'

'You are at liberty to do so, sir.'

'And I'll have you know that I am not without influence, Inspector.'

'I'm sure of that, sir.'

'Until I retired, I was Her Majesty's Ambassador in Rumania for many years and know Secretary Galati and his wife very well…'

'I'm sure that you have all the right connections, sir, but as we're a little pressed for time this morning, I'd be obliged if you would send for Madam Galati,' interrupted Hadley.

'I'm not sure I approve of your tone, Inspector.'

'Well I'm sorry about that, sir but I have my duty to perform.'

'Yes, I suppose so.'

'I must also ask if, amongst your other guests, you have a Greek Diplomat named Mr Korinthiakos staying here?' asked Hadley and Sir Rodney was taken aback.

'Why yes, yes, he's here… but how did you know?'

'Ah, we have our sources, sir, when conducting such high profile murder cases,' replied Hadley triumphantly while Cooper tried to hide his grin.

'Well, er…'

'So would you be good enough to tell Mr Korinthiakos that we also wish to speak to him, sir?'

'Well, yes, Inspector,' replied Sir Rodney hesitantly.

'But before you do, sir, can you confirm when he arrived here?'

'Yes, it was yesterday afternoon… about three o'clock if I remember correctly.'

'Thank you, sir.'

'I'll go and ask Madam Galati if she will see you now, Inspector.'

'Thank you, sir.'

'And I'll let Cristos know that you wish to speak to him.'

'If you would, sir.'

After Sir Rodney had left the study Hadley said 'well this is a turn up for the book, Sergeant.'

'Indeed, sir, and the Greek only arrived yesterday, which puts him on the list of prime suspect for the murders.'

'Quite so, Sergeant and I wonder if he has a large moustache and walks with a limp!'

'We'll soon find out, sir.'

'And if he fits the description and has no alibi… then it's back to London with him on the first available train.'

The detectives waited for quite awhile before Sir Rodney entered the study with Madam Galati, and a short, dark haired man who was holding her arm. Hadley assumed it was Korinthiakos. Sir Rodney made the introductions and Hadley was impressed by the beauty of the pale woman, but less so by her Greek companion who appeared to walk with a slight limp. However, his moustache was clipped and quite neat, which in Hadley's opinion did not rule him out as a suspect. Hadley had wanted to speak to them individually but realised that it was foolish to insist on that at the moment with Madam Galati in such an anxious state. The Greek was obviously a comfort to her and would be a calming influence if she became too distraught.

After they all sat down and Cooper took out his notebook, Hadley said gently 'I realise that you are still very distressed by the tragic loss of Sergei Brasov, madam, but I must ask you a few questions about that dreadful afternoon.'

'If you must, Inspector,' she replied in a whisper.

'First of all please tell me what happened, madam and leave nothing out.'

She nodded, took a moment to compose herself and said slowly 'I had been shopping at Harrods as usual and was making my way back to the Embassy through Hyde Park when I noticed Sergei sitting on a bench overlooking the Lake.' She paused and dabbed at her eyes with a handkerchief before continuing 'I sat beside him and said 'hello' but he didn't reply... then I saw blood on the ground and screamed before I ran back to the Embassy as fast as I could and told my husband what I had seen.' She began to sob and the Greek put his arm around her to comfort her.

'I think that's enough now, Inspector,' said Sir Rodney firmly.

Hadley ignored the remark and asked 'at the time, did you see anyone standing close by?'

She shook her head and whispered 'no.'

'Or walking quickly away?'

'No,' she whispered again before dabbing her eyes once more.

'Did you happen to see anybody in the Park that you knew or recognised before you found Mr Brasov?'

'Now that's enough, Inspector!' said Sir Rodney firmly.

'Please keep quiet for the moment, sir,' said Hadley calmly.

'You're damned impertinent, sir!' exclaimed Sir Rodney.

Hadley ignored the remark and asked 'well did you, madam?'

'No, Inspector, I didn't.'

There followed a few moments of silence before Hadley said 'thank you, madam, I'm sorry that I had to ask such questions at a time when you are so distressed.'

Madam Galati just nodded and wept into her handkerchief.

Sir Rodney glared at Hadley and said 'I'm appalled by your behaviour, Inspector, and I will be making a serious complaint about you to the Commissioner!'

'As you wish, sir… Now, Mr Korinthiakos.'

'Yes, Inspector?'

'Would you please tell me where you were last Wednesday afternoon and evening?'

'This is intolerable!' exclaimed Sir Rodney.

'Sir, your frequent interruptions are interfering with my investigations and if you persist then I will arrest you for obstruction! Do I make myself perfectly clear?' said Hadley and Sir Rodney's jaw dropped as his face coloured with anger. There was a stunned silence before Hadley asked Korinthiakos 'so, please tell me where you were on Wednesday, sir.'

'I was invited to lunch at the Dreyfus Club in Curzon Street by friends and then in the evening I attended a function at the American Embassy in Grosvenor Square, Inspector,' he replied.

'Did you leave the American Embassy at any time during the evening, sir?'

'No, Inspector, I stayed until about eleven o'clock and left with our Ambassador.'

'And what time did you leave the Dreyfus Club after your lunch, sir?'

'I'm not absolutely sure… but it must have been well after three o'clock'

'Did you hire a cab or walk back to your Embassy, sir?'

'I walked, Inspector.'

'Did you go into Hyde Park, sir?'

'No, I had no reason to.'

'And where were you last Friday night, sir?'

'I went out with the same friends for the evening, Inspector.'

'Where to, sir?'

'Well if you must know… they took me to a music hall in Shaftesbury Avenue, Inspector.'

'And who are these friends, sir?'

'You want their names?'

'Please.'

'Well there's Sir William Pettigrew, Mr Charles Wright and Mr Rupert Wentworth, I had lunch with them at the Club and they invited me out for the evening on Friday… you can ask them if you wish, Inspector.'

'I intend to, sir.'

'Sir William and Mr Wright are members of the Dreyfus Club so I'm sure the secretary will confirm that we had lunch together on Wednesday,' said Korinthiakos.

'Thank you, sir, and finally… do you know of anybody who would wish to kill Mr Brasov and the other Diplomats?'

'I've no idea who would want to do such a terrible thing, Inspector.'

'Thank you once again for your help, sir,' said Hadley with a smile.

'I'm glad to have been of assistance, Inspector.'

'It is appreciated, sir, may I know when you intend to return to London?'

'I plan to leave Pangbourne this afternoon as I have duties to attend to at the Embassy in the morning,' he replied.

'And will Madam Galati be leaving with you, sir?'

'Possibly… but I'm sure we will make that decision after lunch, Inspector.'

'Thank you, sir… we will leave you now… goodbye Madam Galati, Mr Korinthiakos, Sir Rodney,' said Hadley with a smile before he stood up and strode from the study.

As the Greek's alibi clearly ruled him out as a suspect for the murders, Hadley had no option but to leave Sir Rodney and his guests. The butler showed the detectives out of the house and Hadley paused for a moment by the trap to look at his fob watch. It was just eleven o'clock and after he climbed aboard he asked the driver to hurry back to Reading station where they caught the 12.15 to Paddington.

Arriving back in London they stopped at the kiosk on the station concourse for some tea and sandwiches before taking a cab to the Dreyfus Club in Curzon Street. Hadley asked the receptionist, Smethurst, who recognised the detectives from their previous visits, if the secretary would see them. Smethurst hurried away and within minutes they were shown into Mr Bolting's office and announced.

'Good afternoon, Inspector, it seems like only yesterday when you called before,' said Bolting with a smile.

'Indeed, sir, but time does have the habit of flying by you know,' replied Hadley.

'So how can I help you?'

'Would you kindly look at your lunch bookings for last Wednesday and confirm if Sir William Pettigrew, Mr Wright and Mr Wentworth dined here with a Greek gentleman named Mr Korinthiakos?'

'Yes of course, Inspector,' replied Bolting before he rang a bell and the receptionist appeared.

'Smethurst, please bring me the lunch appointments book.'

'Yes, sir,' he replied before disappearing.

'While we're waiting, sir, can you tell me about Sir William and Mr Wright?'

'In what connection, Inspector?'

'Well… their backgrounds and what business they are involved in… that sort of thing, sir.'

'Sir William has been a member of this Club for many years and is well respected… I believe his Merchant Bank is involved with overseas investments in Europe, Inspector.'

'Do know what those investments are, sir?'

'I understand that he is currently involved in financing rail links in the Balkans.'

'And Mr Wright, sir?'

'Ah, he's a relatively new member, sponsored by Sir William, and has something to do with steel production… railway tracks, steam locomotives, that sort of thing, Inspector.'

'Thank you, sir, that's very helpful information,' said Hadley as Smethurst returned with the book.

Bolting opened it and confirmed that Sir William, Mr Wright and their two guests had booked lunch for one o'clock last Wednesday and judging by the bill, had enjoyed a substantial meal.

'Is there anything else, Inspector?'

'Yes, my I have Sir William's London address?'

'Of course,' said Bolting before he opened a drawer in his desk, took out a large leather bound ledger opened it, traced down the list of club members and replied 'he lives at 26 Connaught Square, Inspector.'

'Thank you once again, sir.'

Hadley decided to leave until later the interview with Sir William confirming the evening at the music hall. It was after two o'clock when the Hansom carrying the detectives arrived at Princess Radomir's house in Berkeley Square.

'I don't plan to be too long with the Princess, Sergeant' said Hadley as Cooper rang the bell.

'Right, sir.'

'We've more important business to attend to in Whitechapel,' said Hadley as the maid opened the door.

CHAPTER 11

The Princess smiled and stood to greet them holding, out her hand as she purred 'Inspector Hadley and Sergeant Cooper, what an unexpected pleasure to see you today.'

'Good afternoon Your Highness and thank you for seeing us.'

'I'm delighted… please be seated and we'll have some tea.'

'Thank you, madam.'

The Princess rang a small hand bell as the detectives sat down opposite then she said with a smile 'I am all alone today as the Countess has gone to visit friends.'

'Well I must say that it's a very nice day for visiting, madam,' said Hadley, Cooper grinned at the small talk while the Princess nodded as the maid arrived and tea was ordered. Hadley was mesmerised again by the Princess who looked radiant in a white lace dress, contrasting with her dark, beautiful complexion and full red lips.

'So, have you some news for me, Inspector?' she asked and Hadley had to gather his composure before replying 'I have indeed madam, we now have a fairly accurate description of the murderer.'

'That's very encouraging.'

'It appears that he is a man of medium build who has a disability which causes him to limp and witnesses report that he has a large moustache.'

'I see…' she paused for a moment then continued 'but surely that is not much to go on, Inspector?' she asked with raised eyebrows and Cooper wanted to laugh as he wondered if Hadley would mention the oversize Bowler hat.

'Well it's a positive start, madam and we are now conducting a full search of an area around Whitechapel were the suspect was seen after the murder of Mr Plovdiv,' replied Hadley as the maid arrived with the tea and placed the silver tray on a low table by the Princess.

'So are you anticipating an early arrest, Inspector?'

'We are confident that the net is closing on the killer, madam.'

'I do hope so… I believe its milk and sugar for you Inspector?' she said as she poured the tea from a silver teapot into porcelain cups.

'Yes, thank you madam.'

'And the same for you, Sergeant?'

'Please, madam.'

'There, it's so nice to enjoy a relaxing cup of tea… don't you agree, Inspector?' she asked as she poured the milk and added the sugar.

'I do, madam.'

'Good… now I've sent a letter to my cousin, Prince Alexander, telling him how wonderful you are and that the murderer of dear Igor will be arrested quite soon and then hanged.' Hadley was taken aback by her abruptness and replied hesitantly 'we'll certainly do our best, madam.' The Princess gave him a long hard look and said in a firm tone 'well I hope your best is good enough to find this man quickly, Inspector.' Hadley's mind raced with the warnings given to him about the Princess by the Chief and the Commissioner.

'Of course, madam' he replied and Cooper raised his eyebrows before sipping his tea.

'From now on I'm sure that Prince Alexander will be taking a close personal interest in your success in bringing this killer to justice,' she said with a curious smile.

'I'm sure he will, madam.'

'And you don't want to disappoint the Prince do you, Inspector?'

'Absolutely not, madam,' replied Hadley realising that he was now straying into deep political danger.

'Good, and as I am planning to return to Sofiya at the end of the week I will expect to tell the Prince that you have arrested this man,' she said with a smile and Hadley gulped.

'I'm afraid I cannot promise…'

'Nonsense, Inspector, I'm quite certain that you will have this dreadful killer behind bars before I leave London next Saturday,' she interrupted.

'Yes, well, as I say, we'll do our best…'

'Would you like some more tea?' she interrupted again and Hadley just nodded as he realised that he was now a hopeless pawn in a political game that could have far reaching consequences for him. He suddenly felt very exposed and quite alone in the company of this beautiful woman, who appeared to have contrasting sides to her character. One moment she was charming and light hearted... the next, demanding and forceful. Hadley felt decidedly uncomfortable with the situation in which he now found himself.

'So, can you think of anyone else who may be implicated in Igor Plovdiv's murder, madam?' he asked casually as she poured more tea into his cup.

The Princess looked hard at him before she replied sharply 'Inspector, I've told you everything I know and besides, you say that you have a description of this man who killed dear Igor and are searching for him somewhere in London.'

'Yes, yes, madam, we are, but...'

'But what, Inspector?' she interrupted.

Hadley was hesitant before replying 'you may have remembered someone or something that will assist us in making sure that we have the right suspect when we bring him to justice, madam.'

She looked into his eyes and asked firmly 'Inspector... have you ever sent an innocent man to the gallows?'

Hadley gulped and replied 'I am sure I haven't, madam.'

'Then I am relieved... and my judgement of your good, honest character is quite correct,' she said with a smile.

'Thank you, madam, you're too kind.'

'And I'm sure you'll find the right person... now when do you expect to arrest this murderer and hang him?'

'I really can't give an accurate date...'

'Why not?'

'Madam...'

'Surely you have enough Policemen to search all of London to find him quickly,' she interrupted in an angry tone.

'The Commissioner has alerted all London Police stations with an immediate search and arrest order for the suspect, madam and...'

'I should think that's the very least he could do, Inspector, after all, the murder of a Diplomat is a very serious crime and will be seen that way throughout Europe!' she interrupted and Hadley felt extremely uncertain by the behaviour of this difficult and demanding woman.

'I assure you…'

'If you fail to catch his dreadful man in the next few days then all of Europe will think less of the British,' she interrupted again and Hadley's heart sank. He knew that he was now up to his neck in a political quagmire and escape would not be easy. He decided to leave as he was not ready for any more difficult conversation with the Princess when he could be assisting in the search for the killer. He took a deep breath and said firmly 'I trust that you, madam, the Prince and our friends across Europe will not be disappointed with our endeavours. So with your permission, we will leave you now because we're duty bound to visit all the Police stations in the East End of London to follow up the Commissioner's order… please excuse us and thank you for the tea.'

'You are welcome, Inspector, but make sure you keep me well informed of your progress.'

'I most certainly will, madam… good day.'

'Good day, Inspector… Sergeant.'

Once outside the house, Hadley breathed deeply and composed himself as Cooper hailed a passing cab. On the journey back to the Yard, Hadley said 'that woman is difficult and dangerous, Sergeant.'

'That she is, sir.'

'And I was very foolish to have contacted her in the first place.'

'But you were following up a legitimate line of inquiry, sir.'

'Indeed I was… but I should have thought about the consequences more carefully, Sergeant.'

'Well if I may say so, sir, that's hindsight.'

'True… both the Chief and the Commissioner advised me against seeing her again but I had no option after the Home Secretary's request to keep her informed.'

'So you can't be blamed for what may happen if she complains, sir.'

'Oh yes I can, Sergeant.'

'Why, sir?'

'Because she is a person of high rank, Sergeant and it appears that if we trespass into their social world we do so at our own peril,' replied Hadley.

'Surely we must follow our lines of inquiry where ever they lead us, sir.'

'In the main that is true, Sergeant, but sometimes we must make an exception, and the Princess is such an exception; I should have known better,' said Hadley as the cab stopped outside the Yard.

After checking with the telegraph office and finding that no messages had arrived for him, Hadley returned to his office to read Cooper's notes while the Sergeant organised a Police coach for the rest of the day's activities.

Within half an hour the detectives were on their way to Whitechapel Police station. Hadley remained silent during the journey and Cooper knew not to disturb him with any questions. When they arrived in Palmer's office, he was discussing extending the search area with Inspector Walters.

'Ah, Jim, you're with us at last,' said Palmer with a smile.

'I am... so have you any good news?'

'None at all I'm afraid ... this bloke seems to have just disappeared into thin air,' replied Palmer.

'And we've searched every nook and cranny in every blimmin doss house and lodgings for miles around,' added Walters.

'That we have,' said Palmer

'So what now?' asked Hadley.

'We're extending the search area up to Dalston in the north, Southwark to the south, Holborn to the west and to Bow in the east,' replied Palmer.

'And we'll do our best to get most of it covered before we go off duty at nine tonight,' said Walters.

'I'm sure.'

'By then we'll have been at it for twelve hours, Jim,' said Palmer.

'What about tomorrow?' asked Hadley.

Walters raised his eyebrows and replied 'I don't know about tomorrow, Jim, because the Commissioner ordered the search to end tonight when we went off duty.' Hadley shook his head and whispered 'this nightmare will go on and on if I don't have the manpower to find him.'

'Then I think you'd better ask the Commissioner for more men tomorrow, Jim,' said Palmer. Hadley sighed and replied 'that I will, Jack,'

'Our lads are taking a short break and having something to eat before we start again, so in the meantime tell us how you got on at Pangbourne,' said Palmer.

Hadley gave them a brief account of what had transpired and when he finished Palmer said 'not much to go on then with the Galati woman, Jim and a waste of your time if you ask me, other than the Greek's alibi for Wednesday that is.'

'Yes it was, but I will check with Sir William if Korinthiakos did go to the Music Hall on Friday night with him,' said Hadley.

'And if he didn't, will you arrest the Greek?' asked Palmer.

'Possibly.'

'Rather you than me, Jim, arresting a Diplomat will not be easy,' said Palmer with a grin.

'That I'm sure of, Jack.'

Half an hour later, Hadley and Cooper were aboard a Police wagon taking the Constables to the designated search area around Holborn. House to house inquiries were fruitless and when they returned to Whitechapel Police station at six o'clock, Hadley was feeling depressed. Whilst the Constables were having a tea break, Hadley told Palmer that he would not continue the search with the officers.

'I think it's important that I speak to Sir William this evening about the Greek's alibi for Friday night, Jack.'

'Of course, Jim, besides there's not much more you can do and I'll send my Sergeant with the Constables for the last stint around Holborn,' said Palmer.

'Thanks, Jack.'

It was almost seven o'clock when the Police coach pulled up outside 26 Connaught Square and the detectives stepped down. Cooper rang the bell and the door of the imposing residence was opened by the butler.

'Good evening, gentlemen, may I help you?'

'Good evening, I'm Inspector Hadley and this Sergeant Cooper, we're from Scotland Yard and we'd like to speak to Sir

William Pettigrew, please.'

'May I ask in what connection, sir?'

'A murder inquiry,' replied Hadley in a firm tone and the butler blanched.

'I will inform the master immediately, sir, please come in and wait if you would.'

'Thank you.'

The detectives waited for a few minutes before the butler returned and asked them to follow him. They were led upstairs and into a large drawing room where Sir William was standing with his back to the fireplace while his wife was seated close by. The butler announced them and Sir William looked quizzically at Hadley then said 'I'm informed that the purpose of your visit is to speak to me about a murder, Inspector.'

'That is quite correct, sir.'

'You'd better tell me what this all about, Inspector before I make a complaint to the Commissioner about being disturbed on a Sunday evening in such a distressing manner!'

'Of course, sir, and I'm sorry to disturb you but we have a pressing inquiry to conduct,' said Hadley.

'I presume I'm part of your inquiry, Inspector?' asked Sir William but before Hadley could reply Lady Pettigrew said in alarm 'surely you're not accusing my husband of murder are you?'

'No madam…'

'Well that's a relief,' she interrupted and waved her fan vigorously closer to her face.

'I have come to ask you, sir, if you can confirm that a Greek Diplomat named Mr Korinthiakos, was with you and two other gentlemen last Friday night?' On being asked Sir William looked decidedly uncomfortable before he stuttered 'yes, yes, Inspector he was.'

'What time did you meet him, sir?'

'We all met at my club… about seven o'clock if I remember correctly.'

'And where did you go afterwards, sir?' asked Hadley and Sir William looked concerned.

'Does it matter, Inspector? I mean I can confirm that he was with me all evening.'

'Just for the record, sir, it is important as I am on direct orders from the Commissioner to leave no stone unturned regarding the murders of the three Diplomats, which I am sure you've read about in the press.'

Lady Pettigrew drew in her breath and her husband now looked decidedly uncomfortable.

'Yes, yes, the papers are full of dreadful news regarding these terrible murders… but surely Mr Korinthiakos is not a suspect?' asked Sir William.

'Please answer my question, sir, it is important.'

'Well we… er, er, went to another place for some entertainment, Inspector.'

'Where exactly, sir?'

'Well if you must know…'

'I must, sir.'

'We went to a Music Hall in Shaftesbury Avenue,' said Sir William and his wife let out a shriek before her jaw dropped and she asked angrily 'you went to a Music Hall?'

'Yes, my dear, but it was only to let Cristos see what they were like,' replied Sir William sheepishly.

'Well I am very disappointed in you, William and we'll speak about this later.'

'Yes of course, my dear,' replied Sir William and Cooper tried to hide his grin

'Did he leave the Music Hall at any time during the evening without you, sir?' asked Hadley.

'No Inspector, he was with me all the time until we returned to my club,' replied Sir William.

'And what time was that, sir?'

'About eleven o'clock, Inspector.'

'Thank you, sir, you've been very helpful.'

The detectives left the hapless Sir William to his wife's angry disapproval of his visit to the Music Hall which, in her opinion, was a hot bed of drunkenness and lewd behaviour by common working class people and not a proper place for a Knight of the Realm.

Hadley ordered the driver to take them to Bishopsgate Police station then back to Whitechapel.

'What's of interest to us at Bishopsgate, sir?' asked Cooper as the coach rattled over the cobblestones

'I want to have a quick word with Inspector Blakemore about the efforts to find the suspect before we go back to Whitechapel, Sergeant.'

'Do you think he's not pulling his weight, sir?'

'I'm sure he is, but I'm just a little concerned to know that everything that can be done is being done by all London stations to find this assassin and Blakemore will tell me because he has his ear closer to the ground than most,' replied Hadley.

'Well I must admit our man in the Bowler hat certainly appears to be very elusive, sir.'

'That he does, Sergeant... and it is a constant worry to me.'

When they arrived at the reception at Bishopsgate Police station the Desk Sergeant smiled and recognising Hadley said 'we've got him, sir!'

'What are you telling me?' asked Hadley in surprised anticipation.

'The murder suspect with a limp, sir... we arrested him not more than half hour ago, walking along Broad Street... as bold as brass he was...'

'Oh well done, Sergeant, very well done!' interrupted Hadley excitedly.

'Inspector Blakemore and Sergeant Newman have got him in the interview room and are questioning him now, sir.'

'I'm very relieved to hear it.'

'He's a nasty foreign bugger mind, he pulled a knife on our lads when they stopped him and they had to give him a few hefty whacks to persuade him to come quietly, sir.'

'Bloody good show!' said Hadley before he and Cooper hurried down the corridor to the interview room, knowing they were about to come face to face with the assassin who had caused such mayhem in the foreign Diplomatic corps.

CHAPTER 12

Inspector Harry Blakemore was leaving the interview room as the detectives arrived at the door. Blakemore looked surprised and said with a grin 'well blow me down, Jim, you're here already!'

'It's only by chance, Harry,' replied Hadley with a smile.

'Well I'm glad to see you... I've telegraphed all stations with the news that we've got him, so I knew you'd be here soon.'

'That I am, now tell me everything,' said Hadley.

'I will after I telegraph the Yard and ask them to find an interpreter,' replied Blakemore.

'So what's his nationality?'

'From what I can gather, Jim, I think he's a Russian.'

'That's interesting.'

'Why?'

'I thought he'd be someone from the Balkans,' replied Hadley.

'Well he may be because there's plenty of them about at the moment.'

'Very true, Harry.'

'These Europeans have been flooding in for months now and only God knows where they all are because we can't keep track of them,' said Blakemore.

'I'm sure we'll never know, Harry, but you go and call for an interpreter while we see our man.'

'Right... Sergeant Newman and two Constables are with him because he's a violent bugger.'

'So we understand.'

When the detectives entered the interview room, Sergeant Newman stood up and the two Constables came to attention.

'Good evening, gentlemen, please be at ease,' said Hadley as he gave a nod to them then looked hard at the man sitting at the table. He was about forty years old, appeared disconsolate and dishevelled, only glancing at Hadley as he sat down opposite. He had a full moustache but had several days of stubble on his pale face, his long black hair was lank and his clothes looked dirty and were threadbare in places. Hadley surmised he had been hiding somewhere and sleeping rough. He was not how he imagined the assassin would be.

'I'm Inspector Hadley from Scotland Yard.' The man just raised his eyebrows, nodded with disinterest and looked down at his clasped hands resting on the table.

'Are you a Russian?'

'Da, Ruskie, Ruskie,' he nodded as he looked up.

'Good, we'll have someone here soon who will translate for us.' The Russian did not understand Hadley and just repeated 'Ruskie,' before staring down at his hands again.

Within minutes Blakemore returned and said 'I'm sure they'll find an interpreter at the Home Office tonight, so hopefully we'll get some sense out of him.'

'I've been waiting for this moment, Harry.'

'I'm sure, Jim.'

'So give me all the details.'

'About an hour ago, two of my Constables noticed him limping along in Broad Street and as he fitted the description of the suspect, they stopped and questioned him. He obviously did not understand what they said and pulled a knife, so they dealt with him accordingly, cuffed him and brought him in. He was searched and all we found was a pocket book written in Cyrillic and a few coins, which didn't amount to much money. I immediately telegraphed all stations with the news if his arrest and started to question him, but he obviously didn't understand English, then you arrived, Jim.'

'Was he wearing a Bowler hat?'

'Yes he was and it was too big for him.'

'What type of knife did he have?'

'It's a thin stiletto engraved with a Cyrillic pattern I've not seen before, so I presume its Russian,' replied Blakemore.

'Sounds as if it is, Harry… may I see it?'

'Of course, Jim.'

'Then we'll send it over to Doctor Evans at the Marylebone for him to examine and see if it's the murder weapon,' said Hadley.

'I'll do that first thing in the morning.'

'Thanks, now after we've had the interview with our friend and the interpreter, we'll take him back to the Yard tonight, so we can begin the detailed questioning in the morning.'

'Right you are.'

'And thanks to you and your bright lads, Harry, it's hopefully the end of this bloody affair and I will be able to sleep at night,' said Hadley with a sigh.

Whilst waiting for the arrival of the interpreter the two Inspectors left the Sergeants' with the Russian in the interview room and made their way to Blakemore's office where Hadley examined the stiletto. On the blade of the grey, pitted steel knife was engraved a double headed eagle which gave the impression that it was a Russian army issue. Hadley looked at it carefully before placing it back on the desk. He then confided in his friend the concerns he had about the whole investigation and the political involvement of Diplomats that could possibly have ruined his career.

'It's been a nightmare, Harry and made worse by all of them, from the Commissioner to Princess Radomir, putting their oar in and demanding action and the immediate arrest of this lunatic, so I am truly grateful to your lads for picking him up.'

'You must feel as if a great weight has been lifted, Jim,' said Blakemore with a smile.

'Yes, it's a blessed relief and I can't wait to tell them all that we've got him at last.'

An hour later the interpreter arrived with a Sergeant from the Yard and they were shown into Blakemore's office and introduced themselves before the Inspector explained the situation to the serious looking, elderly man named Gustav Orenko.

'We believe our prisoner is a Russian and he faces very serious charges of murder, so our questioning will be intense,' said Blakemore.

'I understand, Inspector,' replied Orenko.

'And we will need you tomorrow morning at Scotland Yard, when he faces more questioning,' said Hadley.

'I will be available to you, sir,' replied Orenko.

'Good, now let's go and see what he has to say for himself,' said Hadley.

Once the officers were seated at the table with Orenko, Hadley began the questioning whilst Cooper took notes.

'What is your name?' Orenko translated and the reply was 'Boris Ivanovich Karpov.'

'Where do you live?'

'At various Doss houses in Whitechapel when I have the money to pay.'

'How long have you been in London?'

'About two weeks.'

'Have you any family here?'

'No.'

'Do you know anybody here?'

'No.'

'Where were you last Wednesday afternoon?' asked Hadley, Orenko translated and Karpov looked uneasy and hesitated before replying 'I looked for work.'

'Where?'

'At some places.'

'Where exactly?'

'At warehouses in the docks.'

'Did you get any work?'

'No.'

'Where were you on Wednesday evening?'

'At a pub in Whitechapel.'

'Name the pub.'

'The Ten Bells.'

'What time did you arrive at the pub?'

'About seven o'clock.'

'Were you there all evening?'

'Yes.'

'When did you leave?'

'It was after eleven o'clock.'

'Did anybody see you who could confirm that?'

'No.'

'Where were you last Friday night?' asked Hadley and Karpov looked concerned when Orenko translated the question.

'At the Ten Bells pub again.'

'All evening?'

'Yes, until about eleven.'

'Did you go to the Opera House at Covent Garden?'

'No... why should I want to go there? I have no money for food let alone opera.'

Hadley waited for a few moments before asking 'when the

Constables stopped you this evening why did you attempt to attack them with a knife?'

'I was scared and thought that they would arrest me.'

'You were right to be scared if you've done something wrong… like commit murder!'

'No, I've done nothing wrong! In Russia the Police arrest you for no reason and you can end up in prison for years without a trial.'

'Where did you live in Russia?'

'In a small village called Laticia, it's near Moscow.'

'Why did you come to England?'

'For work and a better life.'

'Anything else?'

'No.'

'Not to kill Diplomats?'

'No, of course not.'

Hadley waited for a few minutes, collecting his thoughts and said 'Boris Karpov, you've no alibi for Wednesday afternoon or evening or Friday evening when three foreign Diplomats were murdered by stab wounds made by a knife similar to yours, so I'm arresting you on suspicion of murdering Sergei Brasov, Igor Plovdiv and Rossi Hatvan. Anything you say will be taken down and used in evidence against you.'

When Orenko finished translating, Karpov cried out 'Niet! Niet! Niet!,' before slamming his clenched fists on the table then clasping his head and shaking it vigorously.

'No! No! No!' translated Orenko un-necessarily.

'You will now accompany me to Scotland Yard where you will be held in custody for further questioning before formal charges are made against you.'

After Orenko translated, Karpov just shook his head and began to sob which took Hadley by surprise and he wondered for a fleeting moment if Karpov really was the assassin.

Half an hour later the Russian was on his way to the Yard in a prisoner wagon with Sergeant Newman and two Constables. After Hadley had said 'goodnight' to Blakemore and Orenko, he and Cooper followed on in the Police coach.

'Well at last the investigation is over, sir.'

'I hope so, Sergeant.'

'Have you any doubts, sir?'

'Just a nagging little one.'

'Oh?'

'Yes… the man is not what I expected and when he sobbed, I thought for a moment that he was genuinely innocent and possibly tragic coincidences may have put him in jeopardy,' replied Hadley.

'But sir, he fitted the description and was carrying a stiletto, so surely we've got the right man.'

'Perhaps… but let's see what our witnesses say and of course Doctor Evans, his opinion on the murder weapon will settle it,' replied Hadley as the coach rattled passed Blackfriars and made its way along the Embankment to the Yard.

Karpov was booked into Custody by the Duty Sergeant and taken to a cell for the night whilst the detectives went up to their office.

'I'll send a good news message to the Commissioner with the copy to the Chief and that should give them a restful night before all the palaver in the morning, Sergeant.'

'Good idea, sir, because they are not at their best on Monday mornings so anything positive to help ease them into the week I'm sure would be welcomed,' said Cooper and Hadley chuckled 'quite so, Sergeant.'

After writing a short informative note to the Commissioner with a copy to Bell advising them of the arrest of Karpov, Hadley took the envelopes down to the Duty Sergeant for despatch to the officer's homes by Police messenger.

On returning to his office he said 'well, I think we've done our duty for today, Sergeant, so let's go home now and sleep peacefully.'

'A good idea, sir… I must admit I've had enough.'

Alice was pleased to see her husband and felt relieved when she saw him smile as he took his coat off.

'It's all over my dear…Harry Blakemore's lads at Bishopsgate caught our man this evening.'

'Oh, Jim, that's a relief.'

'It most certainly is,' said Hadley as he went into the parlour.

'Have you eaten anything?'

'Only tea and sandwiches for lunch at Paddington station, dear.'

'Right, I've got some game pie with a salad of tomatoes, spring onions and cucumber for you.'

'Sounds delicious… and I'll have a glass of stout to settle me before I eat.'

'I'll get it now for you, Jim.'

'You're an angel.'

'Oh, I know I am,' she said as she went out to the kitchen.

Hadley sat and reflected on the days' events but the sight of Karpov sobbing troubled him once again. The words of the Princess came back to him, 'have you ever sent an innocent man to the gallows?' He shuddered inwardly and only the arrival of Alice with his stout chased away the terrible thought from his mind. He tried to relax and after the meal he sat talking to Alice about his concerns.

'I know you'll do the right thing, Jim… and if there is any doubt about this man's guilt then I'm sure you'll not let him hang.'

Hadley smiled and replied 'no I won't my dear.'

'Let's go up, dearest, because you do look tired,' said Alice gently and he nodded.

CHAPTER 13

The next morning Hadley arrived in his office as Big Ben was striking eight o'clock and was surprised to find the Chief Inspector talking to Cooper and George.

'Morning, Hadley,' beamed the Chief.

'Morning, sir.'

'So how are you feeling now that it's all over and we've got the blackguard?' asked Bell with a smile.

'Well, relieved obviously…'

'I know the feeling, when the messenger arrived last night with the good news I said to my wife 'now I can relax, have a drink and sleep like a baby,'' interrupted Bell and the thought of him as a baby made Hadley grin.

'That's good to hear, sir.'

'I've been down and seen the wretch first thing and I must admit he's not what I expected.'

'Me neither, sir… and I'm...'

'But never mind, he fits the description and he attacked our Constables with a knife, so that's good enough for me, Hadley.'

'Yes, sir, but I do wonder…'

'And if you can a get a confession out of him today then there will only need to be a quick court appearance before we take this foreign bugger over to Pentonville and hang him.'

'Yes, sir, but I must…'

'Now I've told Mr Brackley that we will be up to see the Commissioner at eight thirty to fully brief him so he can release a press statement,' interrupted Bell.

'Very good, sir.'

'I'll leave you now and make sure you're with me before eight thirty with an initial report, Hadley.'

'Yes, sir.'

Bell nodded at him then swept out of the office and in the moment of silence that followed, George asked, 'tea, sir?'

Over tea, the detectives put the finishing touches to their notes for George to type and whilst he was busy with the urgent report, Hadley planned the rest of the day.

'When I'm with the Commissioner, find Jack Curtis and get him to prepare his studio to take photos of Karpov, Sergeant.'

'Very good, sir.'

'After questioning him further, we'll take the photos to all the witnesses then call at the Marylebone to see what Doctor Evans has to say about the knife.'

'Right, sir.'

'That should keep us pretty busy until lunchtime!'

'And will it be an early one at the Kings Head, sir?'

'Very probably, Sergeant,' replied Hadley with a grin.

When the Chief Inspector and Hadley entered the Commissioner's office at exactly eight thirty, the great one looked up from his paperwork and beamed as he waved them to sit.

'Here is Hadley's initial report on the arrest, sir,' said Bell as he placed the buff folder on the edge of the Commissioner's desk.

'Thank you, Chief Inspector, well I must say Hadley, I was delighted and very relieved when I received your note last night.'

'I'm glad, sir.'

'And you must be relieved.'

'I am, sir, but...'

'Good... Blakemore and his lads will be commended for their actions in arresting this bloody assassin.'

'Yes, they deserve it, sir.'

'Now, down to practicalities, what chance is there of getting this Russian to confess?'

'I really don't know until I question him further, sir,' replied Hadley.

'Well if he does confess, it'll mean a quick court appearance before we hang him,' said the Commissioner.

'That's what I said to Hadley this morning, sir,' said Bell with a smile.

'You were quite right, Chief Inspector.'

'Thank you, sir.'

'So Hadley, if you can extract a confession, then it will save time and above all, costs, as we are so financially restricted by Government cut backs at the moment,' said the Commissioner.

'I'll do my best, sir, but I must tell you from the outset that I do have some doubts about Karpov's guilt...'

'What?' interrupted the great one as Bell's jaw dropped in alarm before he asked in a loud whisper 'what are you saying, Hadley?'

Hadley took a deep breath and replied 'frankly, the man looks like a down and out and he doesn't have the appearance of an assassin who could kill in such a professional manner, so I do believe that there may be some doubt about his guilt and possibly we have the wrong man, sir.'

'I can hardly believe what you're telling me, Inspector,' thundered the Commissioner whilst Bell shook his head in disbelief.

'I'm sorry, sir, but it's what I believe at the moment.'

'So what will alleviate your fears, Hadley?'

'I plan to photograph Karpov and show his photos to the witnesses and if they identify him, along with what Doctor Evans says about the knife, that will be the proof I need to continue with this suspect for the time being, sir.'

'Dammit man, that will all be quite un-necessary if this Russian confesses to killing these Diplomats,' said the Commissioner firmly.

'Quite so, sir,' added Bell.

'I agree, sir, but he may not,' said Hadley.

'Oh dear God, what complications plague us these days,' muttered the Commissioner.

'Well I think we should proceed as if he is guilty, sir,' said Bell firmly.

'I tend to agree, Chief Inspector but we must be sure he is before we hang him,' replied the great one whilst shaking his head.

'I suppose so… but what are you going to say to the press, sir?' asked Bell.

'Only that we have the prime suspect in custody and our inquiries are ongoing, Chief Inspector.'

'That's a very wise statement if I may say so, sir.'

'Well it should hold the Fleet Street wolves at bay for a day or two with their un-necessary comments about our failings, whilst Hadley confirms the guilt of this Russian,' said the Commissioner.

'And it will calm all the foreign Diplomats, sir,' added Bell.

'Yes of course.'

'Should we remove the armed officers from outside the Embassy's, sir?' asked Bell.

'Yes, I think we can safely withdraw them now, Chief Inspector.'

'Very good, sir.'

'And despite Hadley's reservations, I believe we're almost at the end of this difficult investigation and Sir George will be relieved when I inform him of the welcome news,' said the Commissioner.

'I agree, sir... so it's all down to you now, Hadley,' said Bell.

'Yes, sir.'

'Then go to it, Inspector and keep me well briefed,' said the great one.

'I will, sir.'

Mr Orenko was waiting in Hadley's office when he returned.

'Ah, good morning, sir... you're just the person I need right now,' said Hadley.

'Good morning, Inspector... I thought I might be.'

'Sergeant... have you alerted Jack Curtis?'

'Yes, sir, he says he's all ready in his studio whenever you are,' replied Cooper.

'Good... and have you retrieved the Bowler hat?'

'Yes, sir, it's with the Desk Sergeant in Custody.'

'Right, gentlemen, let's go down and get things started!'

On the way down to Custody, Hadley explained to Orenko that he wanted to photograph Karpov then question him further. They waited in Custody whilst the Russian was brought from his cell by two Constables and Cooper collected the hat. Afterwards they all made their way along to Jack Curtis's studio. Orenko told the Russian that he was to be photographed and then questioned. Karpov became quite animated on being told and just kept saying 'niet!, niet!, niet!'

'Good morning, sir... I'm all ready for you,' said Jack with a smile when Hadley led the way into his studio.

'Thanks, Jack... now I want you to photograph this man full face and then from either side.'

'Very good sir.'

'Then I want you to do the same again, but this time with his Bowler hat on,' said Hadley.

'Right, sir.'

Karpov was told to sit on a stool in front of a white background board whilst Curtis busied himself fitting plates into the box wood camera on its tripod. They watched in silence as Curtis photographed the Russian full face then side face. When told to put on the Bowler hat, Karpov refused, Hadley became suspicious and asked Orenko to discover what the Russian's objection was to the request. After an animated discussion, Orenko said 'it seems he doesn't want to be seen in the hat, he says it makes him look ridiculous.'

'Well I can't help that, so just tell him he has to wear it,' said Hadley firmly. Orenko told the Russian and when Cooper handed it to him he put it on with great reluctance. Hadley grinned because the hat did make him look foolish as it came down almost to his nose and only his ears kept it up. He looked like a circus clown. Curtis photographed him as requested and when it was all over, Karpov was led away to the interview room.

'Please get these prints done as fast as you can, Jack,' said Hadley.

'Yes, sir, you'll have them by midday,' replied Curtis.

'Good man.'

Hadley questioned the Russian for almost two hours but nothing substantial relating to the killings came from the interview. Karpov had arrived in London penniless and tried to get work but failed as he spoke no English. Several streetwalkers took pity on him and gave him some money for a drink and occasionally four pence for a night in a doss house in Hanbury Street. The night's he did not have four pence for the doss house he slept in the outfall sewer in Mellish Street, where he had fallen over and damaged his left knee, causing him to limp. He claimed that an old costermonger had given him the Bowler hat out of pity one rainy day and, although it was too big, it kept him warm at night in the sewer. When asked about the stiletto, he said had given it to him years ago by his father who had been a soldier in the Crimean war and had fought at Sebastopol. He said the knife was very precious to him as it was the only memento of his late father.

After Hadley had finished the questioning he felt even more uncertain of Karpov's guilt and it troubled him. The Russian claimed he was innocent of the murders and was returned to his cell shouting 'niet!, niet!, niet!' whilst Hadley thanked Orenko before he left the Yard and returned to the Home Office. The detectives made their way up to their office as Big Ben struck eleven o'clock.

George made a pot of tea whilst they wrote out their report on Karpov's interview. Whilst they sipped their tea and George typed as fast as he could, Hadley said 'once we have the photo's from Jack Curtis we'll get off to see all the witnesses, Sergeant.'

'Very good, sir... and when will we call at the Marylebone?'

'I think that will have to wait until after lunch now... it'll give the Doctor a good chance to examine the stiletto.'

When George finished typing the report, Hadley read it through, signed it and the clerk placed it in a buff folder before taking it up to the Chief's office.

'Any minute now Jack Curtis should arrive,' said Hadley and no sooner had he finished the sentence when the cheerful photographer entered with the sepia tints.

'Here you are, sir, as promised,' said Curtis as he placed the folder on Hadley's desk.

'Thank you, Jack.'

The photographs were clear and Hadley was pleased with the results and after thanking Curtis again, he left the office with a smile.

'Right, Sergeant, let's get going!'

'Yes, sir,' replied Cooper as George arrived back and said 'there's a letter that's come for you in the midday post, sir, and it's marked private.' The clerk placed the envelope on Hadley's desk and he waited for the Inspector to open it.

'I wonder who it's from, sir,' said George wistfully and Hadley glanced at him but did not reply. He opened the letter, read it and chuckled.

'Would you believe it's from the Princess?'

'What does she say, sir?' asked Cooper.

'We're invited to have lunch with her and the Countess on Wednesday... she says she has something important to tell us,

Sergeant.'

'Well I'll be blowed, sir!'

'We're to be there at one o'clock… so we'd best be clean and tidy for that appointment!'

'Indeed, sir, and we'll be able to tell her that we've got the murderer in custody, sir.'

'Yes… and hopefully we've got the right man, Sergeant.'

Half an hour later the detectives were in a Police coach on their way to see Miss Edith Harkness at the address of her employer in the Bayswater Road.

After being admitted by the butler they were shown into the drawing room and announced to Mr Dudley.

'I hope you have news of this murderer, Inspector, because I have forbidden Harkness to take my son into Hyde Park until I know the culprit is in Police custody,' said Dudley.

'Have no fear, sir, I'm pleased to tell you that we have arrested a suspect and I have called to show Miss Harkness photographs of the man to see if she recognises him,' replied Hadley.

'Ah… some good news at last, Inspector.'

'Yes indeed, sir.'

Miss Harkness was summoned from the nursery and shown all the photographs. She looked carefully at each one and then said to Hadley 'I can't be sure if it's the man I saw standing by the trees, sir.'

'What?' asked Dudley in an impatient tone.

'I'm sorry, sir, I really can't be sure,' she replied anxiously.

'Do you realise the importance of this, Harkness?' asked Dudley, she nodded and looked tearful. Hadley said calmly 'Miss Harkness, I do understand your uncertainty, in my experience people seldom clearly remember someone they've seen who is an unremarkable stranger to them.'

'Thank you, sir,' she whispered.

The detectives left the house and made their way to The Opera House at Covent Garden.

On the journey Hadley said 'well that was a little disappointing but perhaps we'll have better luck with Charlie Higgs.'

'I wouldn't be too sure about that, sir, because if I remember rightly, he only saw the man from the back as he made his way down the alley.'

'So he did, Sergeant,' said Hadley with a sigh.

When shown the photographs, Charlie Higgs confirmed Hadley's fears and could not positively identify the suspect.

The next stop was Whitechapel Police station where Palmer greeted the detectives in his office with a beaming smile and said 'well thanks to Blakemore's lads we've got him, Jim, and you must be as relieved as we are.'

'Yes, Jack, but I am slightly worried about this Russian.'

'Why is that, Jim?'

'I'm not absolutely sure he's the killer,' replied Hadley.

'I see… well you'd better tell me your reservations,' said Palmer.

'I will… but first, is Molly still here?'

'She is, Jim, I decided to ask her to stay until you arrived and confirmed it was safe for her to leave.'

'Good, I'd like her to see these photo's of the Russian,' said Hadley as he handed the folder to Palmer, who quickly glanced through them.

'He does look a bit of a rum character in his hat,' said Palmer with a grin.

'I agree, Jack and that concerns me.'

'Why, Jim?'

'Well, he just doesn't look like a professional assassin hired to kill Diplomats,' replied Hadley.

'Perhaps that's his strength, Jim… he may be much cleverer than you give him credit for.'

'Possibly… now let's go and see if Molly recognises him.'

Molly was all smiles when the detectives entered her open cell.

'The Bobbies tell me you've got him, guvnor,' she said.

'Indeed we have, Molly,' replied Hadley.

'Well thank Gawd for that… so I can go home now can't I?'

'Yes of course, Molly, but first I want you to look at these photo's and tell me if you recognise him.'

Molly looked carefully at each sepia tint and said 'he's a funny looking fella and no mistake.'

'But do you recognise him?' asked Hadley.

She hesitated the replied 'no, not really guvnor, as I said before, it was all so blimmin quick and he was gone in a flash.'

Hadley sighed and said 'well thank you, Molly… you're free to go when you wish.'

'Thanks guvnor… and I'm blimmin glad you've got him.'

'We are as well, Molly.'

After saying 'goodbye' to her, the detectives returned to Palmer's office where Hadley told him about his reservations regarding Karpov's guilt and Palmer knew the dilemma Hadley faced and sympathised.

'So if Nellie Drake can't identify him from the photo's then I think your doubts are well justified, Jim.'

'And if Doctor Evans tells me that the knife is not the one used to kill the victims then I will have to conclude that Karpov is not our man,' said Hadley.

'I'm sure that is so, Jim.'

The detectives left the station and made their way down to the Kings Head to start the search for Nellie. As luck would have it, they found her sitting at a table in a corner of the busy pub talking to Agnes and Florrie. Hadley strode over to them whilst Cooper went up to the bar and ordered drinks from a sweaty Vera.

'Hello, ladies.'

'Hello,' they chorused with smiles and Agnes added 'Jim, we're so glad to see you… we've heard he was caught in Broad Street… so tell us, is it true?'

'Indeed it is, Agnes.'

'Well, that's a blimmin relief I must say,' said Florrie.

'Too right, now are you buying us all a drink to celebrate?' asked Agnes.

'Cooper is ordering them for you as we speak.'

'That's blimmin good to hear on a hot day!' said Agnes.

'Now Nellie, I want you to look at these photo's of the man we have in custody and tell me if he is the man you saw last Wednesday night near Mitre Square,' said Hadley as he gave her the folder. She took out the photo's and said with a shriek 'that's him alright! I'd know that blimmin 'orrible face anywhere!'

'Oh, Nellie Drake… I could kiss you!'

'Then what's stopping you, guvnor?' she asked with a broad smile.

'I'm sure it would make Agnes jealous if I did… but the nice thought is there!' replied Hadley with a grin as Cooper arrived with their drinks on a tray.

After toasting their good health, Cooper went back to the bar and ordered a Ploughman's lunch for them all whilst Hadley outlined the events leading to Karpov's arrest. When they had finished eating, the detectives said 'goodbye' to the women and hurried back to the Police station to inform Palmer of Nellie's positive identification of Karpov.

'All we have to do now is find out what the Doctor says about the stiletto and if it is the weapon, then I'm very relieved,' said Hadley and Palmer nodded.

'You'll know that you're not sending an innocent man to the gallows, Jim.'

'Indeed not, Jack… so Sergeant, let's get over to the Marylebone!'

CHAPTER 14

On the journey to the Marylebone Hospital the detectives said little and Hadley was becoming more impatient the closer the coach got to its destination. He was very anxious to hear what the Doctor had to say about the knife and if he confirmed that it was the weapon used Hadley could put aside all his doubts regarding Karpov's guilt. Coupled with Nellie Drake's positive identification of the Russian, the stiletto would seal his fate if it proved to be the murder weapon.

The detectives alighted from the coach and hurried through to the mortuary where they found Doctor Evans in the dissecting room with Smythe, examining the naked body of Brasov. The stiletto lay amongst surgical instruments on the marble slab close to the corpse.

'Afternoon, Doctor... Mr Smythe.'

They looked up, Evans smiled and replied 'afternoon, Jim... Sergeant, you've arrived just in time.'

'Excellent... so do tell us, Doctor.'

'Well, I've examined all three victims now and can confirm that the stiletto sent by Inspector Blakemore this morning is identical to the weapon used to murder each of them,' said Evans.

'Thank heavens for that,' said Hadley with relief and Cooper nodded.

'The blade width and penetration to each victim is exactly the same, so without any doubt this knife or... as I must say to be correct... an identical one was used, Jim.'

'Well I'm very relieved, Doctor because I did have some doubt about the suspect's guilt.'

'Well I'm pleased that I've been able to put your mind at rest, Jim.'

'Yes, thank you, Doctor.'

'I'll write up my report and you'll have it by the end of the day,' said Evans.

'I'm obliged, now can I take the knife back to the Yard?'

'I see no reason why not, Jim,' replied Evans and he handed the stiletto to him.

'Thank you once again, Doctor.'

The journey back to the Yard was very relaxed and Hadley's relief was palpable.

'On this occasion I think I ran before my horse to market with my doubts of Karpov's guilt, Sergeant.'

'And with good cause I might say, sir.'

'Possibly… but as it's all over now, we only have to do the paperwork for the trial.'

'Well I think it's good to have doubts when a man's life is at stake, sir.'

'Indeed, none of us would want to send an innocent man to the gallows.'

'Do you think Karpov will confess when he's told about the knife?'

'I really don't know, Sergeant, because he steadfastly refutes any suggestion of his guilt.'

'I suppose only time will tell, sir.'

'Of course, now when we get back to the Yard, please arrange for Karpov to be brought up from his cell, then find Mr Orenko and ask him to join us in the interview room while I let the Chief know the Doctor's verdict.'

'Very good, sir.'

Chief Inspector Bell looked up from his desk when Hadley entered the office holding the stiletto.

'Well Hadley, you look like the cat who's been at the cream.'

'Yes, sir… and with good reason.'

'So I take it that the Doctor confirms that the knife is the murder weapon?'

'He does, sir.'

'Thank heavens for that, now we can hang this foreigner without any qualms!'

'Only after his trial sir.'

'Hadley, you're nit picking again… the trial is now a mere formality and will be a very quick hearing if this Russian confesses!'

'Of course, sir.'

'So, I hope after you've confronted him with the news about his knife he'll capitulate and we'll get a signed confession.'

128

'Possibly, sir.'

'While you're getting his confession, I'll let the Commissioner know so he can put out a press statement to that effect.'

'I think that might be a little premature if I may so, sir.'

'Nonsense Hadley, the public must be informed immediately of our success, which will comfort the powers that be along with the worried Diplomats whilst giving all those drunken Fleet Street mongrels who daily report our so called 'shortcomings' a good poke in the eye!'

'As you wish, sir,' said Hadley with a sigh.

'I do wish... now let me have a good look at this murder weapon.'

Ten minutes later, Hadley strode into the interview room where Karpov sat looking very dejected whilst Cooper made some notes. Mr Orenko arrived a few moments later and apologised for keeping them waiting. Through the interpreter Hadley informed the Russian of the Doctor's findings and showed him the knife. The man reacted immediately, saying 'niet! niet! niet!' over and over again as he slammed his fists on the table. When asked to confess, Karpov replied 'no never, not ever will I confess to murders that I did not commit!'

Hadley then formally charged him and the Russian was taken back to his cell, still shouting his innocence, to wait his appearance in front of a Bow Street magistrate the next day.

Before the detectives left the interview room, Orenko said in a calm voice 'Inspector, it's not my place to say anything, I'm just the interpreter, but I know the Russian temperament and I must tell you in all conscience, that I think Karpov is innocent of these murders.'

Hadley was concerned once again and asked 'what makes you say that, sir?'

'Well, he's a simple, un-educated man and his speech makes me think that he's a little slow mentally... and his very appearance is not what I would expect from a trained and well paid political assassin.'

'I must admit I shared your doubts at first, sir, but I have an eye witness who identified him near the scene of the murder in Whitechapel and you know the Doctor confirmed his knife was the weapon used to kill all three Diplomats,' replied Hadley.

Orenko sighed and said 'I understand Inspector, but I must tell you that the knife he carried is one of many that were issued to soldiers in the Crimean war, even my uncle has one although he was never a soldier. I am sure there must be many in London brought in by Russian immigrants and I ask you to consider this question... how reliable is the witness who identified him that night?'

'I believe my witness when she said she saw him hurrying away from the crime scene and caught sight of his face as he turned when he heard the Police whistle sounding the alarm,' replied Hadley

'Well, in that case I can say no more, Inspector, I've voiced my doubts to you and everything must now take its inevitable legal course, but I say again... I believe Karpov is innocent... good day.'

As Orenko left the room Hadley glanced quizzically at Cooper who raised his eyebrows and said 'what he thinks is his opinion, sir... but you have no option, other than to proceed with the evidence before you.'

Hadley nodded and said 'you're quite right, Sergeant, let's go and have a pot of tea, write our reports then I'll inform the Chief that Karpov has not confessed.'

'He won't be happy about that, sir.'

'Indeed he won't.'

Big Ben was striking five o'clock when Hadley entered the Chief's office with his typed report.

'Well Hadley?'

'He did not confess, sir and still claims he is totally innocent...'

'By God, Hadley, he's a liar as well as a murderer!' interrupted Bell.

'He probably is, sir.'

'Probably? You mean he certainly is... the black guard should be hanged twice!'

'Mr Orenko gave me his opinion that...'

'I'm not interested in his opinion, Hadley... the man's a foreign interpreter employed by the Home Office, not a Police

Officer!'

'Quite so, sir.'

'This Russian's refusal to admit his guilt will not save him from the hangman, it'll just mean we have to bear the cost of a tawdry trial, which will enable the legal worms to get even richer, before we cart this bloody foreigner across to Pentonville and hang him!' shouted Bell with passion. Hadley remained silent and just nodded.

'The Commissioner shall hear of this before he goes home tonight, Hadley.'

'Yes, sir.'

'So stay in your office until I say you can go, just in case the Commissioner needs you to clarify any details.'

'Very well, sir.'

An hour later Hadley sent Cooper and George home just before the Chief arrived in the office and said 'I've advised the Commissioner of all the facts and the Russian's denial of the murders, but he is quite content.'

'That's a relief, sir.'

'He believes, as I do, that we have enough evidence against this troublesome foreigner to secure his conviction, Hadley.'

'Yes, sir.'

'But tell me one thing... this witness, who saw him in the Lane, is she a woman of good repute?'

'I'm afraid to say she's a streetwalker, sir.'

'Oh dear God, you know how unreliable these women are and once the defence lawyer's find out what she is, they'll destroy her and her evidence in court!'

'I believe she is an honest person...'

'You can't know that for certain Hadley... in my opinion they're normally too drunk on gin, or whatever else they drink nowadays, to even know, let alone, state the truth!'

'That's harsh and very unfair, sir.'

'It may be to you... but you know full well what the legal worms will make of her and without doubt it'll cast a shadow of uncertainty over her testimony.'

'Well in her defence I must say she knows she will be on oath to tell the truth and that means as much to her as someone of 'good repute',' replied Hadley firmly.

Bell sighed and, after a moment's pause, said 'you may be right, Hadley.'

'I know I am, sir.'

'Very good… you may go home now.'

'Thank you, sir.'

Hadley was deeply troubled by the events of the day and Orenko's opinion of Karpov's innocence kept coming back to his thoughts during the journey home. Alice was delighted to see him early for once and she told him what she had prepared for dinner but he only half listened as he made his way into the parlour. After the meal, Hadley told Alice of his concerns regarding the Russian's guilt.

'Don't worry so, Jim, I'm sure that you will discover a vital clue or perhaps something will happen that'll prove his guilt one way or another, just you wait and see,' she said with a smile as she placed a comforting hand on his.

Hadley sighed and said 'I don't know what I'd do without you, dearest.'

'Neither do I, Jim, now let's go up to bed.'

When Hadley arrived in his office the next morning Mr Orenko was already there talking to Cooper.

'Morning, gentlemen.'

'Good morning, sir.'

'Morning, Inspector,' said Orenko as George arrived with a pot of tea on a tray.

'If I remember correctly… Karpov is due in front of the Bow Street magistrates at ten o'clock,' said Hadley as he sat at his desk.

'Yes, sir, he is.'

'I've already been to see him this morning and told him what will happen in court,' said Orenko.

'Good… and how is he today?'

'Not very well I'm afraid to say.'

'Is he ill then?'

'Not that I can see… but he's very distressed about his situation and keeps saying he is completely innocent,' replied Orenko.

'I'm not surprised he's distressed.'

'He is begging me to do something to save him from the death sentence but I've explained that the law must take its course and I can do nothing,' said Orenko sadly.

'Indeed it must... so I suggest we have our tea and then make a move to Bow Street with the prisoner,' said Hadley.

The detectives led the way in a Police coach with Orenko whilst the prison wagon carrying Karpov and two others followed on through the busy traffic. Hadley went over the paperwork for the Russian's court appearance whilst Cooper chatted to Orenko. Half an hour later, the convoy turned into the yard behind the magistrate's court and Hadley stepped down from the coach with the others. While Cooper and Orenko made their way towards the back entrance to the court, Hadley stood watching the three handcuffed prisoners as two Constables helped them down from the wagon. Karpov was the last to appear and when he was standing on the cobbled yard he looked about and seeing Hadley he shouted 'Niet!' before he head butted the nearest Constable in the chest and swung his clenched fists wildly at the other, catching him full on the side of his face. Both Officers gasped then fell like trees to the ground as Karpov sprinted towards the open gate and out into the busy street. Hadley had only time to shout 'after him, Sergeant!' before he ran across the yard to the gate as Police whistles blew.

Cooper was alongside Hadley as they turned into the street and they could see the Russian as he weaved through the crowd and occasionally into the road, much to the annoyance of cab drivers as their horses shied away from the running fugitive. Cooper was now gaining on Karpov as Hadley began to trail his fit young Sergeant.

'For God's sake... don't let him get away!' gasped Hadley and Cooper shouted back 'I won't, sir!'

As they ran, the sound of Police whistles and shouts were heard from behind them followed by a clanging Police bell with cries of 'Police! Clear the way! Police! Clear the way!' A Police coach was being driven at speed along the street after the Russian. As Cooper narrowed the distance between them, Karpov glanced back at him and then darted across the busy thoroughfare causing a

Hansom cab to swerve and collide with a packed omnibus. Hadley heard the screams of the frightened women passengers on the open top deck, the shouts of the cab driver and the neighing of the horse as he endeavoured to keep up with Cooper. The Police coach, which had now overtaken Hadley, pulled up by the accident and blocked the road. It was carrying four Constables who quickly jumped out and continued the chase on foot. Hadley could see Cooper in the distance closing on the Russian who was literally running for his life. Within moments Cooper was close enough to grab the Russian's shoulder, he spun the man around and knocked him to the ground as the Constables arrived on the scene. Hadley breathed a sigh of relief as he slowed to a fast walk and gasped for breath. By the time he reached the Officers, they had pulled Karpov to his feet and were marching him back towards the Police coach.

'Well done, lads,' said Hadley between gasps, they nodded and murmured 'sir.'

'I thought for a moment that he'd get away, sir,' said Cooper.

'I knew you'd catch him, Sergeant.'

'Thank you, sir, but I must admit it was touch and go,' said Cooper with a grin as a Sergeant and two more Constables arrived to deal with the accident.

The detectives hurried back to the magistrate's court and arrived in the yard to see Karpov being manhandled out of the coach and escorted into the building. They followed the prisoner in and took their seats inside the court alongside Orenko, who looked visibly shocked. Hadley explained what had taken place in the street and assured him that the Russian would soon face the magistrates. Orenko just nodded and remained silent.

Karpov was the last prisoner to be brought up to the dock and Orenko crossed the court to stand beside him to interpret the proceedings. The elderly leading magistrate, Mr Crossley Milton, flanked by two others, who looked similarly grave and aloof, gazed at the Russian before he asked Karpov his name. After it was given to the court by Orenko, Mr Crossley Milton told Hadley to proceed.

The Inspector gave a succinct account of the arrest of Karpov and the murder charges against him. Other than occasional muttered cries of 'good heavens' from the public gallery, which was almost entirely made up of Press reporters, the court remained silent as the hideous murders were recounted in detail by Hadley. When he had finished speaking and resumed his seat, Mr Crossley Milton whispered to each of his dour colleagues before he addressed the prisoner. Karpov was informed that he would be remanded in custody until a date could be fixed for him to face trial at the Old Bailey accused of murdering the three Diplomats. When Orenko had finished translating, the Russian shouted 'niet niet! niet!' before he was bundled down from the dock by two burly Constables. Hadley glanced at Cooper before casually turning to face the public gallery, where to his astonishment, he noticed a pale faced man with a large moustache, wearing an oversized Bowler hat, get up and limp out of the court room.

'Sergeant... follow me outside as quick as you like!'

CHAPTER 15

The detectives hurried out from the court into the busy street and glanced around for the limping man but saw no one who fitted the description. Hadley's attention was immediately drawn to a closed coach standing nearby which suddenly pulled away from the kerb before being driven at a fast trot towards Aldgate.

'I bet our man is in that coach, Sergeant!'

'I'll hail a cab and we'll follow it, sir,' said Cooper as he stepped into the road and flagged down an oncoming Hansom. They clambered aboard after Hadley pointed at the fast disappearing coach and said 'driver, follow that coach as quick as you can!'

'Right you are, sir,' he replied before he shouted and whipped the chestnut mare which startled the animal into a fast trot. The driver weaved through the slow moving traffic whilst the detectives tried to keep the coach in sight but it was proving difficult because of the sheer volume of cabs, coaches, omnibuses and drays heading towards the City.

'Dear God, I hope I've not made a terrible mistake and charged the wrong man with murder, Sergeant.'

'I'm sure you haven't, sir.'

'I hope you're right.'

The Hansom was slowly overhauling the mystery coach when suddenly a loose horse ran out into the busy road from a side street causing the traffic to come to an abrupt halt. The detectives watched the coach disappear in amongst several omnibuses and cabs whilst they waited for the errant horse to be caught and led away by its owner, who nodded his thankful appreciation to the drivers of the stationary vehicles.

'Damn! I think we may have lost it, Sergeant.'

'What now, sir?'

'We'll carry on for a little and see if we can catch it up,' replied Hadley as the driver whipped up the mare and they proceeded at a fast trot. By the time they reached Aldgate the trail had gone cold amongst the myriad of traffic and the driver called down 'I'm sorry, sir, but I think I've lost it.'

'No matter... thanks for your efforts, now please take us back to the Kings Head in Whitechapel,' said Hadley.

'Right you are, sir.'

'I could do with a drink after this morning's events, Sergeant.'

'So could I, sir.'

The pub was as busy as usual when they arrived and they had to push through the drinkers to get to the bar. Vera saw them and nodded as she placed pints of stout on the wet counter for her customers.

'Let's have a quiet lunch in the back room and discuss what has happened today, Sergeant.'

'That's a very good idea, sir.'

'What will you have to eat?'

'A ploughman's, sir, it's too warm for anything hot,' replied Cooper as Vera appeared before them.

'The usual, gents?'

'Please, Vera.'

She nodded and began to pull the foaming stout and asked 'anything to eat today?'

'Yes, two ploughman's in the back room if you please, Vera.'

'Right you are, guvnor, I'll get one of the girls to open it up,' she said with a nod as she placed the pints of stout on the counter and Cooper paid her. They sipped the cool stout whilst remaining silent and deep in thought, waiting for the girl to open the door.

In a short while, they were seated in the room with the door closed enjoying the lavish portions of cheese with onions, ripe tomatoes, pickles and fresh bread rolls. When they had finished eating Hadley said 'I think we need some time to think about all the suspects and re-evaluate their alibis, Sergeant.'

'Right, sir... so I take it that despite all the evidence against him, you are not absolutely convinced Karpov is the killer?'

'I am dreadfully un-certain, especially so after seeing that man in court this morning' replied Hadley as the door opened and Agnes walked in followed by Florrie.

'Agnes...'

'Oh, Jim... I'm glad we've found you... Molly's disappeared!'

'What?'

'She's just blimmin disappeared, Jim!'

'And we've looked everywhere for her,' added Florrie wide

eyed with concern.

'Dear God,' whispered Hadley as he feared the worst.

'Have you seen her at all today?' asked Cooper.

'No we haven't,' replied Agnes.

'We saw her in the Blind Beggar last night, but when we called at her lodgings this morning she wasn't there and no one down the Lane has seen her,' said Florrie.

'Did you see her with anyone last night?' asked Hadley.

'No, Jim, she just had a glass or two with us before she went off,' replied Agnes.

'We thought she'd gone back to her lodgings as she was a bit worse for wear as you might say,' said Florrie.

'Well now, I'm very concerned about her so we'll go up and see Jack Palmer and get a missing persons notice out to all stations,' said Hadley.

They hurried to the Police station where the women were asked to wait in an interview room whilst the detectives went up to Palmer's office.

'Hello, Jim, I thought you were in court so I didn't expect to see you today.'

'No I'm sure you didn't, Jack, but Agnes has just told me that Molly Barnet is missing.'

'Oh, bloody hell.'

'She was seen last night in the Blind Beggar but has now disappeared and I'm very concerned for her, Jack.'

'Why are you so troubled, Jim?'

'Because I think that the killer may still be at large, Jack.'

'But you've got this Russian in custody and had him up before the magistrate.'

'Quite right… but I think he may be the wrong man.'

'Whatever makes you say that, Jim?'

'Two things, Jack… firstly, he persists in claiming he's totally innocent and, secondly, in court this morning I saw a man who exactly fitted the description of the suspect,' replied Hadley.

'Well you obviously didn't arrest him.'

'No… because he left the court before I could catch him and made off in a coach, which we followed but lost it in the traffic near Aldgate.'

'This is all most unfortunate, Jim.'

'So it is, Jack.'

'Do you want to put out a missing persons notice for Molly?'

'Indeed I do.'

'Right.'

'Agnes and Florrie were the last to see Molly and they'll be able to give us a good description of what she was wearing.'

'Are they here?'

'Yes... they're waiting in the interview room.'

The detectives questioned the women carefully regarding the time that Molly left the Blind Beggar and a description of what she was wearing. After the women had given all the details, they thanked the Officers as they left and made their way back to the Kings Head for a drink or two to calm their nerves. A detailed missing persons notice was telegraphed to all London stations whilst Palmer briefed Sergeant Morris and the Constables who were about to go out on their beats in the local area.

'I think that's all we can do for the moment, Jim,' said Palmer.

'Yes... thanks, Jack.'

'So what do you plan to do about the suspect you saw in court?'

'Start all over again and go through every part of the investigation in the hope that I've overlooked something that will lead me to the right suspect,' replied Hadley with a sigh.

'Do you really believe that the killer was in court?'

'Jack, I have to eliminate him from the investigation if I am to be sure that the right man will face trial,' replied Hadley.

'That's a monumental task, Jim and I don't envy you,' said Palmer with concern.

The detectives arrived back at the Yard as Big Ben struck two o'clock and hurried to their office where Hadley asked George to make some tea.

'Right you are, sir.'

'And we've a great deal of work to do this afternoon, George... so I don't want to be disturbed,' said Hadley as he sat behind his desk and Cooper drew up a chair.

'Very good, sir,' replied the clerk before he left to make the tea.

'Now, Sergeant, we must go right through the investigation to see what we may have missed and when we've finished, a prime suspect may emerge who we've previously overlooked.'

'Yes, sir.'

'Then we'll arrest and question him relentlessly until we get the truth.'

'Are you going to tell the Chief before or after the arrest, sir?'

'A good point… and I think before would be the best option,' replied Hadley.

They worked tirelessly until just after six o'clock when two suspects emerged as the likely killers. Hadley decided that either Vadim Osijek or Vlad Bacau, probably assisted by their security men, carried out the murders and with that information he went up to inform Bell.

The Chief Inspector looked up from his paperwork as Hadley entered and asked 'how did you get on in court today?'

'Karpov was remanded in custody as expected sir, until a trial date can be fixed.'

'Excellent… now I've told the Commissioner and he's released a further press statement giving more details and confirming we've got the killer under lock and key.'

Hadley hesitated before he said 'but I'm afraid to say that I think we may have the wrong man, sir.'

'Good God Hadley! You're not starting all that nonsense again are you?' demanded Bell angrily.

'I have good reason to believe…'

'Listen to me, Inspector, we've got the killer, who's been positively identified by an eye witness near the crime scene and he was carrying the knife that killed all three Diplomats!' interrupted Bell.

'I appreciate that, sir, but…'

'There are no 'buts', Hadley, we've got him and that's final!'

'But there are doubts…'

'Nonsense! I mean, for God's sake… what more proof of his guilt do you want?' interrupted Bell angrily.

'Sir, if Karpov goes to trial we may end up hanging an innocent

140

man!'

'But we both know he isn't innocent, Hadley!'

'I'm really not sure, sir… because Molly Barnet is now missing and I saw a man in court this morning who fitted the description of the prime suspect and he escaped in a closed coach before I could apprehend him.'

'And so what, Hadley? The silly woman could be anywhere and there must be many men in London who fit this ridiculous description of a limping man with a large hat,' said Bell firmly.

'Precisely so, sir… you're absolutely right!'

Bell remained silent, clasped his hands behind his head, lent back in his chair and gazed at the ceiling. Hadley waited patiently for the Chief to resume his upright position. When he had done so, he said 'I think you'd better sit down and tell me about your doubts, Inspector.'

Hadley sat in the creaking chair and gave an account of all his misgivings after a full review of the evidence and informed Bell that he believed Osijek or Bacau were now behind the murders of all three Diplomats. When he finished speaking, Bell muttered 'bloody foreigners.'

'So I propose to bring them in for intense questioning, sir.'

'Very well then… but who do you think is this limping man?'

'He's probably one of their security men or a paid assassin,' replied Hadley.

'I think it unlikely that he's a professional assassin, he's more of a stupid security man.'

'You may be right, sir.'

Bell sighed and said 'I'll hold off letting the Commissioner know about all this until you're satisfied one of them may be behind the killings or possibly they both have blood on their hands,' said Bell.

'That is a strong probability, sir.'

'Well if they are both guilty it'll cause huge political ructions, Hadley.'

'I realise that, sir.'

'Then go to it, Hadley, you've got plenty of time before Karpov comes to trial.'

'Thank you, sir and I must tell you that Princess Radomir has written to say that she has some vital information that may assist our investigation.'

'Has she now,' said Bell in a suspicious tone.

'So I propose to call upon her tomorrow, sir,' said Hadley, thinking it would be better if the Chief did not know of her invitation to lunch.

'Oh, be careful... be very careful, Hadley,' said Bell as he shook his head slowly.

'I will be, sir.'

Hadley returned to his office and made plans with Cooper for the following day. It was decided that they would arrest Osijek and Bacau after they had lunch with the Princess, which would enable them to question the suspects armed with the Princess's new information. Hadley now expected a positive breakthrough narrowing the investigation down to the true suspects.

The detectives left the Yard and Cooper hailed a cab to take them to Whitechapel. They were anxious to see if there had been any sighting of Molly by Palmer's men but knew that the women would be more likely to have news of her whereabouts.

As they entered Palmer's office he looked up and shook his head.

'No news yet I'm afraid, Jim.'

'It's as I feared, Jack, this killer has got to her and it worries me deeply after we told her she was safe,' said Hadley with a sigh.

'I know... I think we've failed her, Jim.'

'It could cost the poor girl her life if we don't find her soon.'

'I'm fully aware of that, Jim.'

'We'll go and see what the ladies have to say and let you know if anything comes up, Jack.'

The Kings Head was full and noisy by the time the detectives reached it. They pushed their way through to the bar where Vera and the girls were doing their best as usual. After ordering their drinks Hadley looked around for Agnes and Florrie and spotted them sitting in the corner by the piano.

'Ah, there they are, Sergeant, get a couple of sixpenny gins will you?'

'Yes, sir.'

Hadley pushed his way across to the women who looked up when he said 'hello, ladies.'

'Oh Jim, were still so worried about Molly... have you heard anything yet?' asked Agnes.

'No, I'm afraid not,' Hadley replied as he sat down.

'Well what could have blimmin happened to her I wonder,' said Florrie.

'Don't think about it, Florrie... but it could be bad, couldn't it Jim?' said Agnes.

'Let's not be too pessimistic until we know more,' said Hadley brightly hiding his own fears for Molly's safety.

'We should have gone home with her last night when she was in such a state,' said Agnes as Cooper arrived with their gins.

'Oh thanks, Bobby blue eyes, you've just cheered us up,' said Florrie with a smile.

'And we need cheering up and no mistake,' said Agnes.

'Glad to be of service, ladies,' replied Cooper with a grin.

'So, Agnes, what's the word down the Lane?' asked Hadley.

'There's no word, Jim, nobody we've asked has seen her,' replied Agnes as Florrie looked up, let out a scream and said 'oh my Gawd... she's only blimmin well here!'

They all turned to see Molly pushing her way through the drinkers towards them.

'Molly!' exclaimed Agnes.

'Where have you been, girlie?' asked Florrie wide eyed when a smiling Molly reached them.

'I've had a bit of a blimmin adventure and no mistake,' replied Molly.

'All the Bobbies are out looking for you, girlie,' said Agnes.

'Why?'

'Because we didn't know where you were!' said Agnes.

'Please tell us all about it, Molly' said a very relieved Hadley as she sat down at the table.

'Can I have quick snifter of your drink, Agnes?'

'Need fortifying do you?' asked Agnes as she pushed the glass across to Molly.

'I blimmin do.'

'Take your time, Molly,' said Hadley calmly as she downed the gin.

They waited in silent anticipation for her to speak.

'Well, after I left you in the Blind Beggar, a bit worse for wear as you might say…'

'Oh we know alright!' interrupted Agnes.

'I was walking along the Whitechapel Road when a coach pulled up beside me and who d'you think was hanging out the blimmin window?'

'No idea, but I'm sure you'll tell us,' said Agnes.

'It was only my mate Lucy… Lucy Talbot!'

'Blimey! what was she doing in a coach?' asked Florrie.

'She was only with a posh gent who had just picked her up for business and Lucy said he wanted another good girl to come along for his friend,' replied Molly.

'So you went off in the coach and then what?' asked Agnes.

'Uncle Billy, that's what he likes to be called, took us to his lodgings out in Hackney where his friend, Uncle Bob, was waiting for us.'

'Go on,' said Agnes in a disapproving tone.

'Well, they gave us drinks and we got undressed… but they told us to keep our corsets on, then they spanked us, not hard mind, before they started…'

'Yes… yes, thank you Molly… I think that's enough detail for the moment,' said Hadley.

'You can tell us later,' said Florrie as she nodded and smiled.

'So where have been until now?' asked Hadley.

'We stayed all night with the old gents, lovely they were, and this morning they gave us a Guinea each for our troubles…'

'A Guinea each!' exclaimed Agnes.

'Yes, they said they were blimmin well satisfied and completely knackered!'

'Sounds like it,' said Florrie.

'Then we went round to Lucy's sister, Gertie, who lives in Hackney with her kids and we stayed there for the day before we caught a 'bus back here,' Molly replied.

'Well I'm very glad you're safe, Molly but there's been a development so I must take you into protective custody once again,' said Hadley.

'Whatever for, guvnor?' asked Molly in surprise.

'I believe that the man we've arrested may not be responsible for the murders,' replied Hadley.

'Oh stone the blimmin crows! Am I going to be stuck up at the station again?'

'I'm afraid so, Molly… but I'm sure it won't be for long,' replied Hadley reassuringly.

'I blimmin hope not!'

The detectives escorted Molly back to the station and booked her in to custody before going up to see Palmer. He was pleased that she had been found and immediately ordered a telegraph to be sent out to all Police stations with the news.

'That must be a weight of your mind, Jim,' said Palmer.

'Indeed it is, Jack.'

'So all you've got to do now is find this limping man.'

'Yes, and I hope tomorrow I may have some more positive information from the Princess that will lead me to him… and now Molly has turned up safe and sound, I can sleep tonight with one less thing to worry about,' said Hadley with a smile.

CHAPTER 16

The next morning the detectives spent their time preparing documents for the Crown Prosecution Service for the impending trial of Karpov. Hadley felt distinctly uneasy as he filled in the details but he knew it had to be done. Other than reviving cups of tea served occasionally by George, they were not distracted from their tiresome work. When Big Ben struck midday, Hadley glanced at his fob watch to check its accuracy and said 'we'll make a move soon, Sergeant.'

'Yes of course, sir, we wouldn't want to keep the Princess waiting.'

'Quite so, and let's hope she has something of value to tell us over lunch.'

'Yes, sir… I wonder what we'll be eating.'

'Probably some awful Bulgarian dish with lots of flavouring to hide the taste of the meat,' replied Hadley with a grin.

They hailed a cab to take them to Berkeley Square and arrived outside the Princess's house at quarter to one. After Cooper rang the door bell, they were admitted by the maid and escorted upstairs to the elegant drawing room where the Princess stood to greet them.

'Good afternoon, gentlemen, I'm so glad that you found the time to join me for lunch,' she said in a purring tone.

'Good afternoon, your Highness, and thank you for inviting us.'

'It's my pleasure.'

'I assure you the pleasure is all ours, madam,' replied Hadley as he was struck once again by her beauty and decorum. She was dressed in a shimmering light blue satin gown with dark blue roses embroidered on the bodice. She wore a dark blue choker studded with a large diamond and pendulum earrings that sparkled in the sunlight as it streamed in from the open window. Her appearance was breathtaking and Hadley wondered about her private life. Why wasn't this beautiful woman married to some rich, handsome, Prince?

'Please sit down, gentlemen, lunch will be served shortly,' she said with a smile.

'Thank you, madam,' said Hadley as he and Cooper sat on the large sofa.

'I'm afraid the Countess will not be joining us for lunch today as she is unwell at the moment and confined to her bed.'

'I'm very sorry to hear that madam, I trust it's nothing too serious.'

'No, she has developed a summer cold, Inspector.'

'Ah, I believe that is a common complaint this time of year,' said Hadley and Cooper wanted to laugh at the silly statement. He realised that Hadley was quite overawed by this lovely woman and had lost his equilibrium.

'Well I just hope that it doesn't develop into something more serious, Inspector,' said the Princess in a worried tone.

'I'm sure it won't, madam.'

'Thank you for your concern, Inspector, now may I offer you something to drink?'

'Please, madam.'

'I can recommend my own favourite Bulgarian wine if you would care to try it.'

'That would be most agreeable, madam,' replied Hadley with a smile, Cooper nodded and murmured 'yes, please.'

The Princess rang her hand bell and the maid appeared immediately. After speaking to her rapidly in Bulgarian the maid curtsied and left, returning minutes later with a carafe full of a dark red wine and three cut glass wine glasses on a silver tray. The wine was poured and the detectives were offered a glass each after the Princess took hers from the tray.

'Gentlemen, here's to your very good health.'

'And here's to you, madam … and also the speedy return to health of the Countess.'

'Thank you, Inspector.'

Hadley took a good sip of the wine which he found to be very smooth and palatable.

'This is very pleasant, madam.'

'It's my favourite and I have it specially brought over from Sofiya,' she said with a smile.

'It obviously travels well, madam,' said Hadley before he took a large mouthful.

'Yes it does... now would you do me a great favour, Inspector?'

'Why of course, madam, you only have to ask.'

'Would you please call me Helena?' she asked with a bewitching smile that left Hadley gasping for words. He eventually stammered out in a whisper 'yes, madam... I mean Helena, if that's what you wish.'

'I do wish it... and may I call you James?'

'Why yes of course, I am deeply honoured.'

'That's very good... I think we are now firm friends... don't you agree, James?'

'I do indeed, Helena.'

'I like to have friends whom I can trust no matter what,' she said with a smile as the maid returned and spoke to her.

'Ah, lunch is served, shall we go through?'

Hadley nodded and replied 'by all means, Helena.'

The Princess stood up and made for the door held open by the maid. Hadley glanced at Cooper who winked at him, grinned and whispered 'you'll soon be between the sheets, sir.' Hadley blushed and shook his head before they followed the Princess through to the dining room.

The table was set out beautifully with a centre piece of fresh flowers in a silver bowl. Cut glass goblets and tall wine glasses were positioned by the gleaming silver cutlery and china side plates adorned with blue and gold rims accompanied each place setting. The Princess sat at the head of the table and the detectives sat either side of her.

'I hope you both enjoy the meal I've chosen, James.'

'Oh, I'm sure we will,' replied Hadley whilst having some misgivings as Cooper grinned at him across the table. The maid brought in soup plates and a tureen of cold soup. As it was being served the Princess said 'this is Tarator, it's a soup made from cucumber and yoghurt with herbs and spices... it's very tasty.'

'It looks it,' said Hadley with a smile as he gazed down apprehensively at the green, creamy soup before he picked up his spoon. To his surprise, the Tarator was more palatable than he expected and he finished the soup with relish.

Hadley was anxious to know what information the Princess had that would assist his investigations and he was about to ask when she said with a smile 'now, James, I'm sure you'll enjoy the chicken Yahniya which has been specially prepared in your honour.'

'Thank you, Helena, I'm sure I will,' he replied as the maid brought in a carafe of rose Rakia wine and poured generous amounts into their glasses. When she had completed the task she spoke rapidly to the Princess who replied before the maid nodded, curtsied and left the dining room.

'It seems that the Countess has refused to eat anything, which is unusual and I'm very concerned about her, James.'

'I'm sorry to hear that, Helena but I'm sure she will recover quickly.'

'We can only pray she does,' replied the Princess as the maid appeared with a large tureen filled with chicken and vegetables. Generous portions of the Yahniya was served to them before the Princess raised her glass of Rakia and proposed a toast to the speedy recovery of the Countess.

The food was delicious and the detectives thoroughly enjoyed the spicy chicken with the myriad of beautifully cooked vegetables. After another glass of the Rakia they felt relaxed and Hadley decided that his questioning of the Princess could now wait until after lunch. The dessert was another of the Princess's favourites and consisted of baked pumpkin with walnuts and honey. They finished the meal with Kashkaval cheese and dry biscuits washed down with more Rakia.

'That was absolutely delicious, Helena,' said Hadley as he put down his empty wine glass.

'It was indeed,' said Cooper with a nod.

'I'm glad you both enjoyed it,' she replied with a smile then added 'I think we'll have coffee in the drawing room.'

After the maid had brought in the coffee and served it to them, Hadley decided that it was now time to ask the Princess about her information.

'Helena, I was delighted to receive your kind invitation to lunch and I'm intrigued to know what information you have that would help in our investigations.'

She waited for a moment to compose herself then said in a serious tone 'James, what I am about to tell you is...' she hesitated, 'is so confidential that if ever you disclosed it to anyone else it would be the ruination of me forever.'

'You have my solemn word that anything you say now will never be repeated to anyone and I know that Sergeant Cooper will be as honour bound as I am to keep that promise,' replied Hadley.

'Indeed I will, Princess, you have my word,' said Cooper with a nod.

She smiled and said 'thank you gentlemen, I know I can trust you both implicitly.'

'So... please tell us, Helena.'

'It may surprise you to know that I have many loyal informants who are employed by most of the European Embassies and I receive so much valuable information that I am frequently overwhelmed by it.'

'Are you now,' said Hadley, slightly bemused by the thought of her network of spies.

'And I wish to help you with your investigations into the murders by naming the killers responsible for these tragic and unnecessary deaths of three wonderful men who only lived to give service to their respective countries.'

'Then I am truly grateful to you and your informants,' said Hadley.

The Princess nodded before she said 'I am reliably informed that the murder of Sergei Brasov in Hyde Park was committed personally by the Hungarian Vadim Osijek.'

'That confirms my suspicions about him, Helena, because he was in Hyde Park at the time and has no alibi.'

'You must arrest him and get him to confess, James.'

'I intend to as soon as we leave you, Helena.'

'Good... now dear Igor Plovdiv and Rossi Hatvan were both killed by Vlad Bacau and his wicked security henchmen,' she said with passion.

'Do you know why, Helena?'

'I believe it was mistakenly in revenge for the murder of Brasov, which that awful Rumanian Secretary, Galati, blamed on them both,' she replied.

'So Galati never suspected Osijek?'

'It appears not, James.'

'What motive did Osijek have for killing Brasov?' asked Hadley.

'I'm sure it was in a fit of jealousy over Galati's wife, she's a disgraceful harlot who sleeps with any man and was having a torrid affair with Brasov after rejecting Osijek,' she replied.

'I see,' mused Hadley.

'You have to understand our Balkan mentality, James, we are not calm like you English... we smoulder with consuming passions that sometimes rise up and cause us to commit terrible acts of violence,' Helena said with her eyes blazing.

'I now realise that, Helena,' said Hadley and he was becoming slightly afraid of this powerful woman.

'And so you must arrest Bacau and his men, they are all implicated in the murders, James.'

'I fully intend to, Helena.'

'Thank you so much, James... I knew I could rely on you and I am glad that I have told you what my informants have discovered,' she said with a smile.

'So am I, Helena, because without doubt you have saved an innocent man from the gallows,' said Hadley.

'I am pleased to hear that, James.'

'Of course... I will have to interview your informants and get them to make statements, Helena.'

'I will arrange everything as soon as you say, James,' she replied as the maid entered and spoke to the Princess in an anxious tone. She replied quickly, the maid nodded and disappeared.

'I'm afraid the Countess has now developed a raging fever and I must send for our Doctor,' said Helena.

'Oh dear, I am so sorry to hear that,' said Hadley as the maid returned with a coachman in livery. The Princess spoke to him, he nodded and left hurriedly.

'I've sent Uri for the Doctor, so you must please excuse me, James, while I go up and see my cousin.'

'Of course, Helena, and please give the Countess our best wishes for her speedy recovery,' said Hadley as he and Cooper stood.

'I will... and thank you,' she replied.

'We will be in touch, Helena, before you leave London on Saturday.'

'Of course, James,' she replied before they shook hands with her and quickly left the house.

Cooper hailed a cab and during the journey back to the Yard they discussed the information given to them by the Princess. Big Ben struck three o'clock as the Hansom stopped on the Embankment and Hadley strode into the building whilst Cooper paid the fare. Once they were in the office, Hadley made out arrest warrants for Osijek and Bacau then hurried up to Bell's office for his authorisation signature.

The Chief looked up as Hadley entered and asked 'any interesting developments today, Hadley?'

'Yes, sir, I've been to see Princess Radomir and she has named Osijek and Bacau as the murderers and says she can provide informant's who will make statements to that effect and testify in court,' replied Hadley, gilding the lily.

'Has she by God!'

'Indeed she has, sir.'

'Well this is a turn up for the book.'

'I believe it is the turning point in the case and I have brought the arrest warrants for your signature, sir.'

'Now hold your horses, Inspector, we need a little more than a strident woman's say so before we rush off and arrest Diplomats willy-nilly,' said Bell.

'But sir…'

'Hadley, we must proceed with caution so I suggest we speak to the Commissioner before we get ourselves into a pickle over this.'

'As you wish, sir,' said Hadley with a sigh.

They were just about to leave the office when a messenger arrived and said 'Chief Inspector, this just arrived for you from West End Central station.'

Bell tore open the buff envelope, read the message and whispered 'good God.'

'What is it, sir?'

'Here, read it yourself, Hadley,' replied Bell as he handed the note over. Hadley paled as he read: *To the Duty Inspector at Scotland Yard. Sir, I have just been alerted to an incident regarding the fatal attack on a woman at Harrods Department Store. The manager has identified the woman as Madam Galati, the wife of a Diplomat at the Rumanian Embassy. Please send senior officers to assist me at the crime scene as soon as possible. Inspector Briggs, West End Central.'*

'My God,' whispered Hadley.

'Get over there right away Hadley and take charge of everything while I inform the Commissioner!'

'Right, sir.'

'I'll follow on as soon as I'm free,' said Bell as Hadley made for the door.

'Very good, sir.'

CHAPTER 17

Hadley raced down the stairs to his office and startled Cooper when he rushed through the door and said 'Madam Galati has just been murdered in Harrods!'

'Blimey, sir!' exclaimed Cooper as he stood up from his desk

'Find Jack Curtis quick as you can and tell him to follow us to the scene, the Chief will be there as soon as he's informed the Commissioner!'

'Right, sir.'

'So let's go to it, Sergeant!'

Within minutes the detectives were in a Police coach racing through the busy traffic towards Kensington High Street. Hadley remained silent and deep in thought as the coach swayed along, passing slower coaches and cabs. His mind was filled with doubts and complicated thoughts regarding the murder of Madam Galati. This investigation was a spider's web of Balkan intrigue and unfathomable motives. The Princess was right when she remarked that they were bound by smouldering passion which could erupt at any moment into violence. He hoped that there were witnesses to this latest killing who would ensure the immediate arrest of the culprit. He now knew with certainty that Karpov was not the killer this time and he felt quite relieved.

The coach pulled up at the main entrance to the prodigious store and the detectives rushed into the building to find three Constables stationed in the large vestibule talking to anxious looking customers. Hadley identified himself to them and one Constable said 'please follow me, sir.' They hurried up the stairs to the first floor and along to the Millinery department where there was a group of people surrounding the body of a woman laying on the floor. Hadley knew Inspector Sidney Briggs, who was kneeling beside the body with Sergeant Rush standing close by while a Constable held back several onlookers; customers and staff, some of whom were crying.

Briggs looked up and said 'I'm glad you're here, Inspector Hadley.'

'So am I… and Chief Inspector Bell will be on his way after he's informed the Commissioner of this incident,' said Hadley.

'Well I'm pleased that my telegraph has gone right up the chain of command,' said Briggs with a smile.

'It has… now what do we know so far, Inspector?'

Briggs stood up and said 'according to the sales assistant, the victim was trying on several hats and when she asked the assistant for one on display over there,' Briggs pointed to a hatless mannequin nearby, then continued 'the girl obliged her and when she turned round with the hat, the lady was on the floor. The assistant rushed over to her thinking she'd fainted in the heat but when she saw the blood, she screamed out and all hell was let loose.'

'Did the girl see the attacker?' asked Hadley.

'No I don't think so, but I've not spoken to her yet to get a full account of exactly what happened,' replied Briggs.

'I'll speak to her in a minute, now where's the manager?'

'I'm here, sir,' said a tall, well-dressed man in a frock coat.

'And you are?'

'I'm Mr Robinson, the floor manager, sir.'

'Can you confirm who this lady is, Mr Robinson?' asked Hadley pointing down at the body.

'Yes indeed, sir, I reported to the Police that she is Madam Galati, a regular and highly esteemed customer of Harrods,' he replied.

'Was she shopping alone?'

'I believe so, sir, Madam always shopped alone on a Wednesday but on Saturday's she was usually accompanied by another lady who I think is her maid,' Robinson replied.

'Very interesting… now, I will need to speak to you and the…' Hadley began when he was interrupted by the arrival of another well-dressed gentleman wearing a frock coat who said angrily 'Robinson, get all these people away from here and close the department at once!'

'Yes, Mr Goldfinch, right away.'

'Nobody leaves this crime scene until I say so,' said Hadley firmly.

'You have no right…'

'Oh I have every right, sir, and I presume you are the manager in overall charge?' interrupted Hadley as Robinson stood looking uncertain of whom he should obey.

'I am indeed… and who are you?'

'I'm Inspector Hadley from Scotland Yard and this is Sergeant Cooper.'

'Well I'm glad that someone's turned up at last to help Inspector Briggs,' said Goldfinch.

'I can inform you that Chief Inspector Bell will be arriving shortly after he has briefed the Commissioner about this incident,' said Hadley.

'Incident? You call it an incident! My God, an important lady customer has been murdered here…in Harrods… in the Millinery department… and you call it an incident… as if it were something akin to a costermonger having some of his fruit stolen from his street barrow!'

'Sir, with respect…'

'It is your duty, sir… to protect the law abiding public from such outrages as we have witnessed this afternoon in Millinery!' interrupted Goldfinch angrily.

'Indeed it is, sir, now…'

'Please arrange to remove the body of this unfortunate customer immediately, Inspector,' interrupted Goldfinch.

'I'm afraid I can't do that, sir, because this is now a crime scene and under my jurisdiction until Chief Inspector Bell arrives to take…'

'I'm not interested in any of your tiresome Police procedures, Inspector, I'm Mr Oswald Goldfinch, the manager of Harrods and what I say in this establishment must be obeyed without question!'

'Sir, I suggest you return to your office and I will come and see you when we have finished here,' said Hadley firmly.

'How dare you address me in such a cavalier and off hand manner!'

'Oh I dare, sir, and if you don't do as I ask then I'll have you arrested for Police obstruction!'

'My God, I believe you would!'

'Be in no doubt whatsoever, sir!' replied Hadley with a smile.

'Very well then, Inspector, but you've not heard the last of this I promise you… Mr Robinson.'

'Yes, sir?'

'Report to my office as soon as you have closed the department and found other duties for all the assistants downstairs in the food hall... that is, after Inspector Hadley has finished with them!'

'Very good, sir,' replied Robinson as Jack Curtis arrived with his photographic paraphernalia.

'And what the devil is all this?' asked Goldfinch as he stared wide eyed at the equipment.

'We will be taking photographs of the crime scene, sir,' replied Hadley.

'Dear God! You are depraved voyeurs of the very worst kind!' said Goldfinch before he hurried away.

'Mr Robinson... who was serving Madam Galati when she was attacked?' asked Hadley

'Er, it was Miss Tucker, Inspector.'

'Where is she now?'

'She's been taken to the staff room in a very distressed state.'

'Right, I'll need to speak to her in a minute so please come back when you have completed your instructions and take me to her before you go to the manager's office.'

'Very good, Inspector,' said Robinson with a nod before he walked away.

'Now Jack, photograph the scene from all angles and get me close ups of the body,' said Hadley.

'Right you are, sir,' replied Curtis before he set up his tripod and lifted the camera into position.

Hadley knelt down beside the body of Madam Galati and looked at the single stab wound to the middle of her back. Her head was turned to one side and he glanced at her open, lifeless eyes. In her left hand she was still clutching a large hat while her right arm was trapped beneath her lifeless body as she had fallen. Hadley shook his head in sorrow, stood up and said to Cooper 'I'm sure it's our limping man who's responsible for this, Sergeant.'

'Yes, sir... and of course we know it isn't Karpov.'

'No, but what concerns me is that apparently no one saw him here... he's like will o' the wisp... he just strikes a fatal blow and melts away,' said Hadley.

'Perhaps Miss Tucker can give us some helpful information, sir,' said Cooper.

'We can only hope so, Sergeant... Inspector Briggs.'

'Yes, Inspector?'

'When you arrived on the scene tell me what you saw.'

'Mr Robinson met me at the entrance to the department and I only noticed the victim on the floor with several customers and shop assistants standing around the body,' replied Briggs.

'Did no one else attract your attention?'

'No... we'd received the urgent message from Mr Goldfinch stating that a customer identified as Madam Galati had been attacked and fatally wounded so I telegraphed the Yard and hurried over here as quickly as I could, the assailant obviously had made his escape by the time we arrived,' replied Briggs.

'Well now it all rests with what Miss Tucker can tell us,' said Hadley as Chief Inspector Bell arrived, nodded at the officers, looked down at the body and asked 'are you certain that this is Madam Galati?'

'Yes, sir, Cooper and I recognise her and the floor manager, Mr Robinson, also confirms that it is Madam Galati,' replied Hadley.

'Dear God Almighty,' whispered Bell.

'I'm just about to question the sales assistant who was serving her when she was attacked, sir,' said Hadley.

'Did she witness the attack?'

'Apparently not, sir because...'

'Why the devil didn't she see what happened?' interrupted Bell.

'She was removing a hat from that mannequin for Madam Galati, sir,' replied Hadley pointing at the nearby figure then continuing 'and when she turned round the victim was on the floor, at first the girl thought she'd fainted in the heat but soon realised she'd been stabbed.'

'Did she see the assailant?'

'I don't know until I speak to her, sir.'

'Where is she now, Hadley?'

'In the staff room, sir.'

'Right, let's talk to her and see if we can some sense out of the girl,' said Bell.

'Very good, sir.'

'And when we've finished here, the Commissioner has ordered us to inform Secretary Galati of his wife's murder before Sir

George contacts the Embassy officially,' said Bell with a sigh.

'That will not be an easy meeting, sir,' said Hadley.

'No it won't,' said Bell testily as Curtis started photographing the body aided by his flash gun that lit up the scene.

The detectives watched Curtis at work for a few minutes before Robinson arrived back and said to Hadley 'would you like to speak to Miss Tucker now, Inspector?'

'Please, Mr Robinson.'

'Then follow me if you would, sir,' said Robinson before he strode away.

'Inspector Briggs, stay here with your Officers and take statements from everyone who was here at the time of the murder,' said Bell.

'Very good, sir.'

Miss Tucker sat quiet, pale faced and tearful at a table surrounded by several assistants in the staff room. She clutched a handkerchief to her eyes every so often and sipped at a glass of water. When the detectives arrived with Robinson, she appeared anxious until Hadley spoke to her calmly.

'Miss Tucker, I'm Inspector Hadley, this is Chief Inspector Bell and Sergeant Cooper, we're from Scotland Yard.'

'Yes, sir,' she whispered.

'Now, we'd like you to take your time and tell us exactly what happened when you were serving Madam Galati this afternoon,' said Hadley with a smile as he sat down opposite the frightened young woman. He waited patiently for her to gather her thoughts and compose herself.

'Well, sir, I'd come back from my lunch break and was told by Mr Robinson to tidy up the new stock of summer hats and display some of them on mannequins,' she said anxiously then paused as she glanced at Robinson.

'Please go on Miss Tucker,' said Hadley gently.

'I had just finished when I saw Madam Galati arrive in the department and I hoped she come to my counter.'

'Why was that?'

'She's such a nice lady and was always very kind to us, she never was cross, unlike some customers I could mention,' she replied glancing again at Robinson.

'Was she alone this afternoon, Miss Tucker?'

'Oh yes, sir, she always came alone on Wednesdays but sometimes she had another lady with her on Saturdays,' she replied.

'Please continue.'

'Well, after she looked at some other hats she came to my counter and I said 'good afternoon, madam, can I help you?' and she said 'yes, I'd like to try on that hat... the one on the mannequin over there' and she pointed to it.'

'Then what happened?'

'I went over to get the hat and I heard a noise behind me and when I turned round she was on the floor...'

'What sort of noise did you hear?' interrupted Hadley.

'It was a gasp and then it must have been the sound of her falling down, sir,' she replied before she began to cry.

Hadley waited for her to compose herself but the Chief was impatient and he asked 'did you see who attacked Madam Galati?'

Miss Tucker shook her head, burst into tears once again and Bell tut-tutted as Hadley gave him a disapproving glance.

'I think it best I leave you to interview Miss Tucker, Hadley while I go and find out if any of the other witnesses saw the attacker,' said Bell.

'Very good, sir,' replied Hadley, glad to be left alone to question the distressed young woman.

After a few moments Hadley asked 'Miss Tucker, I'd like you to think very carefully and tell me if you saw any gentlemen nearby when Madam Galati came into the department.'

She nodded and replied 'there were several gentlemen with their ladies but there was one on his own.'

'Tell me about him.'

'I noticed him when I first saw Madam Galati coming into the department and he looked at her then turned away.'

'Then what happened?'

'Well, she came over to my counter and I didn't take any notice of him after that,' she replied.

'Can you remember what he looked like?'

'Not really, sir.'

'Was he wearing a hat?'

'Yes, he had a Bowler hat which was a bit too big for him,' she replied and Hadley glanced at Cooper who gave a slight nod.

'Did you notice anything else about him?'

'He had a large moustache... that's all I can remember, sir.'

'Did you see him leave the department?'

'No, sir, I didn't.'

'Have you ever seen this man before in the shop?'

'I don't think so, sir.'

Hadley realised that she was not going to add any more significant information about the attack and so he said 'you've been very helpful Miss Tucker, we will leave you now but I may wish to ask you a few more questions at a later time when you are feeling better.'

'Yes, sir, thank you.'

The detectives left the staff room and made their way back to the crime scene. Jack Curtis had just finished taking photographs and was dismantling his paraphernalia while the Chief was talking to Briggs. He stopped mid sentence to ask 'did she come up with anything useful, Hadley?'

'Miss Tucker says she noticed a man wearing a large Bowler hat when Madam Galati arrived, sir.'

'Did she now?'

'Yes .. apparently he was looking at the victim and then turned away but unfortunately Miss Tucker lost track of him after she was distracted by Madam Galati arriving at her counter.'

'That's understandable I suppose,' said Bell, then added 'none of the witnesses here saw anything unusual.'

'That's a pity, sir.'

'It is... now if we've finished here I suggest we get the body away to Doctor Evans at the Marylebone whilst we advise Secretary Galati of his wife's untimely death, Hadley.'

'Very good, sir.'

'Inspector Briggs, will you arrange everything?'

'Yes of course, sir, leave it to me.'

'Thank you... and tell Mr Goldfinch that we've left and I will be in touch with him in due course,' said Bell with a nod before he strode off followed by the detectives.

As the Police coach made its way towards the Rumanian Embassy,

Bell said to Hadley 'after we have advised Galati of the sad, unwelcome news, we are, on the Commissioner's instructions, to arrest Vlad Bacau and then Vadim Osijek on suspicion of murder.'

'I presume this latest killing has prompted the arrests that I originally called for, sir.'

'Yes, after careful thought I put it to the Commissioner that we should proceed with your request, bearing in mind the political ramifications, Hadley.'

'I'm pleased to hear it, sir.'

'I have the warrants and the Commissioner will advise the Home Secretary so he may prepare for any unwelcome back lash from the foreigners,' said Bell as the coach pulled up outside the Rumanian Embassy.

'Very good, sir.'

'As I believe that these desperate killers may try to resist arrest I must ask if both of you are still armed?'

'We are, sir,' replied Hadley and Cooper murmured 'yes, sir.'

'Good… and don't hesitate to shoot them if they resist,' said Bell before he climbed out of the coach.

CHAPTER 18

Cooper rang the bell and the door of the Embassy was eventually opened and they were admitted by the swarthy doorman. The Chief told the receptionist that he wanted to see Secretary Galati urgently.

'I believe he is in a meeting with our Ambassador, sir, and cannot be disturbed,' replied the receptionist.

'Then please interrupt their meeting as I must speak to Secretary Galati immediately on a private matter,' said Bell firmly.

'I'm afraid I can't do that, sir.'

'Inspector Hadley... arrest this man for Police obstruction then follow me to the Ambassador's office wherever it is!' said Bell.

'Very good, sir... '

'No, no, sir... I assure you that will not be necessary because I will accompany you to the Ambassador's office right now!' wailed the frightened receptionist.

'Very well then... Inspector Hadley...'

'Yes, sir?'

'Disregard my order to arrest this man,' said Bell.

'Very good, sir,' replied Hadley with a grin as the receptionist left his desk and hurried up the stairs. The detectives followed on and at the end of the long corridor the receptionist asked them to wait for a moment. He knocked gently at the door which was eventually opened by Vlad Bacau, who glanced at the detectives in turn before stepping out into the hallway, closing the door behind him and asking 'what are you doing here, gentlemen?'

'We've come to speak to Secretary Galati on a private matter,' replied Bell.

'I'm afraid he cannot be disturbed at the moment as he is in an important meeting with our Ambassador,' replied Bacau.

'We must insist on seeing him immediately!' said Bell firmly.

'Insist all you want but I tell you he cannot be disturbed!'

'I'm afraid you don't understand my good man...'

'I must remind you, sir that you are in a foreign Embassy and have no right of entry under agreed diplomatic law!' interrupted Bacau firmly.

'We are here on the direct orders of the Commissioner, so allow us to see Secretary Galati immediately or you will be arrested for obstruction!' said Bell angrily. Bacau looked surprised, waited for a moment, nodded and said 'very well,' then opened the door for the detectives to enter the room.

Galati stood up immediately looking angry whilst Ambassador Sulina remained seated at his desk.

'What is the meaning of this intrusion?' asked Sulina firmly.

'I am Chief Inspector Bell from Scotland Yard with officers whom you know already your Excellency and we've come to speak to Secretary Galati on a private matter.'

'This is outrageous!' exclaimed Sulina.

'I'm very sorry to interrupt your meeting but I am on direct orders from the Commissioner to speak to Secretary Galati,' said Bell firmly.

'So what is so important about this private matter that it cannot wait?' asked Galati angrily.

'It concerns Madam Galati, sir,' replied Bell.

'You may state whatever you wish about my wife, Chief Inspector, as I have no secrets from my Ambassador,' said Galati in an unconcerned tone.

'As you wish, sir,' replied Bell before he drew in his breath, paused and said 'it is my duty to inform you that Madam Galati was murdered this afternoon in Harrods department store…'

'My God!' whispered Galati as his face paled with shock whilst Sulina and Bacau looked stunned by the news.

'Where is she now?' asked Galati in faltering tones.

'Your wife's body has been taken to the Marylebone Hospital for a post mortem examination, sir,' replied Bell and Galati shook his head in disbelief.

'Who could have committed this terrible crime?' asked Sulina.

'We do not know precisely at present, your Excellency,' replied Bell.

'But we have reason to believe that the same person or persons who have been responsible for the other Diplomat murders were the culprits behind the murder of Madam Galati,' added Hadley.

'Well this is a tragedy and could have been prevented if you had done your duty Chief Inspector and arrested this maniac!' said Sulina angrily.

Bell waited for a few moments before he replied 'your Excellency, with the greatest of respect for your position, I am at pains to point out to you that my officers here have been working tirelessly day and night to find and arrest the killer and the men behind him ...'

'Killer... men behind him... what are you saying?' interrupted Sulina.

'We believe the killer is a paid assassin from the Balkans, Excellency and my officer's inquiries have been thwarted and obstructed by your staff here...'

'Utter nonsense!'

'As well as by the staff at the Bulgarian and Hungarian Embassies, which has led us to believe that all three Balkan Governments are intent on causing as much murderous mischief as they can to one another, whilst hiding behind the cloak of Diplomatic respectability and immunity in London,' said Bell firmly and Hadley wanted to cheer.

'This allegation of yours is outrageous, Chief Inspector!' shouted Sulina as he stood up and pointed menacingly at Bell.

'You may think so, Excellency but unfortunately it is the truth and now it is my duty to arrest you, Vlad Bacau, on suspicion of conspiracy to murder Igor Plovdiv and Rossi Hatvan....'

Bacau's jaw dropped before he screamed 'you're mad!'

'And anything you say will be taken down and used in evidence against you... take him away Hadley!'

'Very good, sir... come along now if you please, sir,' said Hadley as he attempted to take Bacau's arm.

'Take your hands of me!' shouted Bacau as he stepped back, drew a small revolver from his jacket and aimed it at Hadley.

'Now give that to me!' said Hadley as he held out his hand.

Bell shouted 'my officers are armed and will not hesitate to shoot if you resist arrest Bacau!' as Cooper immediately stepped forward, drew his revolver and pulled back the hammer ready to fire. A moment of silence followed before Sulina said 'give me your weapon Bacau and go with these fools... I will soon have you free from their ridiculous charges!'

Bacau nodded and placed the small revolver on Sulina's desk. Cooper snatched it up and Bell said to Bacau 'now you will also face a charge of threatening a Police Officer with a dangerous weapon!'

'My God! You British with your rules and regulations!' exclaimed Sulina.

'Indeed your Excellency... and by observing our righteous laws and acting with due diligence we have built an Empire that stretches around the world,' said Bell.

'It will soon come to an end, Chief Inspector,' said Sulina.

'Possibly, sir, but I'll wager not in our lifetime!'

'You are very sure of yourself,' said Sulina with a sneer.

'I am... because I have done my duty and advised Secretary Galati of his wife's cruel murder and arrested Vlad Bacau on suspicion of conspiracy to murder, your Excellency.'

'Well I trust that you are satisfied!'

Bell ignored the remark and said 'Sir George West, our Home Secretary, will be in touch with you in due course... so good afternoon to you, sir,' then added 'take him away Hadley.'

The prisoner, escorted by the detectives, left the room, Galati and Sulina looked on open mouthed with surprise.

Once they were all aboard the waiting Police coach, the Chief ordered the driver to take them to the Hungarian Embassy in Portman Square.

'Now for Vadim Osijek, let's see what he has to say for himself when we arrest him,' said Bell.

'I hope he won't be foolish enough to resist, sir,' said Hadley.

'No matter, Hadley, you heard the Commissioner's strict instruction to shoot the suspects down if they resisted,' replied Bell in a nonchalant tone before he glanced at Bacau.

'I did, sir.'

'And it would save the British taxpayer the cost of an expensive trial,' said Bell as he calmly looked out of the open window at the passing traffic.

'Indeed it would, sir.'

The rest of the journey was completed in silence and when the coach pulled up outside the Hungarian Embassy, Bell said 'Sergeant Cooper, pleases stay here while we are in the Embassy and don't hesitate to shoot Mr Bacau if he makes any false move.'

'Very good, sir,' replied Cooper as he drew his revolver and pulled back the hammer. Bacau's pale face registered fear that he could be shot at any moment, he sat motionless on the seat opposite Cooper.

'Come along Hadley, let's get this damned business over and done with!' said Bell as he opened the door and climbed down from the coach.

Minutes later they were admitted to the Embassy and Bell asked to see Secretary Osijek immediately.

'Do you have an appointment, sir?' inquired the receptionist.

'No, and I don't need one, so just tell him that we want to see him now,' replied Bell.

'I'm afraid he may not see you, sir, as he's very busy.'

'Tell him that Chief Inspector Bell and Inspector Hadley from Scotland Yard are here on urgent business... I'm sure that will clarify his thinking and allow him to re-arrange his priorities,' said Bell. The receptionist nodded and hurried away returning minutes later saying 'Secretary Osijek will see you now, gentlemen, so please follow me.'

Vadim Osijek looked up from his desk when the detectives entered his office and were announced by the receptionist. He stood up and with a contemptuous smile said 'good afternoon, gentlemen, please take a seat and tell me how I can help you.'

'Vadim Osijek, I have a warrant for your arrest on suspicion of the murder of Sergei Brasov...'

'This is utter nonsense!' shouted Osijek angrily.

'And anything you do say will be taken down and given in evidence, do you understand?'

'You're mad!'

'Take him away, Inspector.'

'Very good, sir,' said Hadley as he moved towards Osijek.

'I'm a Diplomat and claim immunity so I'm not going anywhere with you two useless bumbling fools!' shouted Osijek.

'Is that your final answer, sir?'

'Yes it is!'

'Then shoot him, Hadley.'

'Very good, sir,' replied Hadley calmly as he produced his revolver and pulled back the hammer ready to fire. He raised the weapon and pointed it at the pale faced Secretary who whimpered 'my God, you really do mean to kill me.'

'You have a choice, sir... and we will certainly shoot you if you don't come quietly,' said Bell in a matter of fact tone.

'You bastards!'

'Now, now, sir, there's no cause for bad language,' said Bell.

'I can't believe this is happening to me,' said Osijek in a half whisper.

'Well I'm afraid it is... so are you coming or shall I give Inspector Hadley the order to fire?'

The Secretary raised his hands for a moment then dropped them down, shook his head and said 'this mistake will cost you your careers as Policemen.'

'If I had Guinea for every time that's been said to me I could retire now and live in luxury by the sea,' said Bell as Osijek left his desk and accompanied them out of the office. When they reached the hallway downstairs, Osijek called out to the receptionist 'tell the Ambassador that I've been arrested and charged with murder!'

The receptionist stood up from his desk in wide eyed amazement and stammered 'yes, yes, sir... I will.'

When they boarded the coach, Osijek was surprised to see Bacau sitting there with Cooper pointing his revolver at him, he shook his head and said 'you British are mad, absolutely mad!'

'That's your opinion, sir, but others who know us well don't agree with you, because they respect our determination to live within the law and punish those who choose to commit murder,' replied Bell as the coach pulled away and headed back to the Yard.

The two men were booked into Custody then taken to the holding cells to await interviews, legal representation and official charging. Whilst Cooper remained behind to deal with the paperwork, Hadley and Bell made their way up to the Commissioner's office.

The great one looked up and asked 'well?'

'Madam Galati was the victim of the fatal attack in Harrods, sir.'

'Dear God... have you informed her husband?'

'We have, sir.'

'And did you get witnesses to this killing?'

'Not really, sir, only the shop...'

'Are you telling me Chief Inspector, that no one saw this brutal attack in a busy department store?' interrupted the Commissioner.

'It appears not, sir.'

'Good God Almighty...anything else?'

'We have arrested Bacau, the Rumanian and Osijek, the Hungarian, sir,' replied Bell.

'And did they resist?'

'Only slightly, sir.'

'What do you mean only slightly?' asked the Commissioner testily with a frown.

'Bacau pulled a revolver on Hadley, sir...'

'Did he now... and what was your response?' interrupted the great one.

'Cooper drew his weapon immediately and waited for my order to fire, sir,' replied Bell.

'That's what I like to hear!'

'Yes, sir, and after that Bacau came quietly.'

'Excellent... now, tell me about Osijek, the Hungarian.'

'He only blustered and told us that it would be the end of our Police careers, sir,' replied Bell.

'Ah,... the old threat that every guilty suspect makes when he's caught, Chief Inspector.'

'Indeed, sir and I told him as much.'

'Very good, but from now on we must expect a torrent of political pressure from all quarters so I hope that you have all the facts that will lead to the certain convictions of these two.'

'I am confident, sir,' said Bell.

'That's good to hear, Chief Inspector, and I think we should keep Karpov, the Russian suspect in protective custody until things are a little clearer,' said the great one.

'I agree, sir, it makes good sense,' said Bell.

'So, gentlemen, is this the end of the investigation?'

'I believe it is, sir,' replied Bell with a smile.

'We still have to arrest the assassin who carried out the murders of Hatvan and Plovdiv, sir,' said Hadley and Bell glanced disapprovingly at him.

'Well I thought this fellow Bacau committed those crimes,'

said the Commissioner in a surprised tone.

'We think he's the mastermind behind those murders, sir, but the actual killer who stabbed them and Madam Galati is still at large,' replied Hadley.

'Well then catch the blighter as quick as you like!' roared the Commissioner.

'Yes, yes, sir, we will,' stuttered Bell.

'I'm very disappointed in what I've just heard and it seems to me that the case against these two in Custody is far from conclusive, gentlemen.'

'I think we have most of the evidence that will convict them, sir,' said Bell in a positive tone.

'You must hope that is true, Chief Inspector, otherwise it really could mean the end of your careers if you're mistaken,' said the Commissioner as his side whiskers bristled.

'Yes, sir,' whispered Bell.

'I suggest you question this fellow Bacau intently to find out who the assassin is and where we can find him,' said the Commissioner.

'It will be our top priority, I assure you, sir,' said Bell.

'Good... meanwhile I'll inform Sir George of our progress so far and tell him to expect serious diplomatic repercussions from the Embassies.'

'Very well, sir.'

'You both concentrate on finding this maniac who is still at large for heaven's sake.'

'We will, sir.'

'Keep me well informed, gentlemen... and now bloody well get on with it!'

As the detectives descended the stairs Bell said 'we'll question Bacau together, Hadley.'

'Very good, sir.'

'Then you must see Princess 'what's her name' and arrange for her informants to come forward and make their statements so we have a watertight case against the suspects.'

'I will see her immediately after we have finished interviewing Bacau, sir.'

'Good... then while I interview this Osijek fella, you get over

170

to the Marylebone and find out from Doctor Evans if the same weapon was used to kill the Galati woman as the others.'

'Right, sir.'

'Now get your clerk organised to take notes and meet me in Custody as quick as you can.'

'Very good, sir.'

'We'll see what Bacau has to say about his assassin with the Bowler hat!'

'We will, sir.'

'It's our top priority to find this killer before he strikes again!'

CHAPTER 19

Chief Inspector Bell was outside the interview room talking to Cooper when Hadley arrived with George. Bacau had been brought from his cell and was already seated at the table waiting for the detectives.

'I've sent for our duty solicitor, Mr Berkeley, to sit in with us until Bacau's legal representative arrives, Hadley,' said Bell.

'Very good, sir.'

'And I expect Bacau's nauseating legal worm will request Police bail... which I will oppose vigorously,' said Bell firmly.

'That's quite understandable in the circumstances, sir.'

'I think so... I mean these Johnny foreigners are not like us, Hadley.'

'No they are certainly not, sir.'

'They're not men of their word.'

'I tend to agree, sir.'

'In my experience they'll promise the earth then do a bunk abroad as soon as your back's turned,' said Bell as Mr Berkeley arrived.

'Chief Inspector... Inspector,' said Berkeley with a nod to them.

'Mr Berkeley... I think we can go in now, gentlemen and begin,' said Bell before Cooper opened the door for them to enter the interview room.

Despite intense and fierce questioning from the Chief Inspector, Bacau remained defiant and very angry about his arrest and the allegation of his conspiracy to murder. He denied all knowledge of a limping assassin with a Bowler hat and remained steadfast in his refusal to accept any of the charges levelled against him. Half way through the lengthy interrogation Mr Bracewell, his solicitor appointed by the Embassy, arrived and after hearing what had transpired demanded the immediate release of his client on Police bail. The Chief Inspector refused categorically and a fierce argument ensued. It was finally agreed that Bacau would appear before the Bow Street magistrates in the morning where Mr Bracewell would insist on his client being released pending any trial.

After Bacau had been taken back to his cell, Hadley told George to stay with the Chief and take the notes during the interview with Osijek whilst he and Cooper left for the Marylebone and then on to visit Princess Helena. The detectives were just about to leave the Yard when Mr Morton Barrymore of Olivier and Barrymore, the distinguished solicitors in Holborn, arrived to represent Vadim Osijek. Barrymore was accompanied by two officials from the Hungarian Embassy who looked decidedly menacing. After meeting them in Custody, Hadley went back to the interview room and asked Bell if he wanted him to remain and assist at the interview with Osijek.

'That will not be necessary, Hadley, because I think I can handle these people without much difficulty,' replied Bell.

'I'm sure you can, sir.'

'You get over to the Marylebone and talk to Doctor Evans and make sure you call on the Princess afterwards, get her informants in here as soon as possible, we need their statements to convict these foreigners,' said Bell.

'Very good, sir,' replied Hadley before he and Cooper left the Chief in the interview room. Moments later Bell went along to Custody to meet Mr Barrymore and the Hungarian officials while Osijek was brought up from his cell.

Big Ben was striking six o'clock when the detectives left the Yard in a Police coach bound for the Marylebone Hospital. During the journey they discussed the events of the day and Hadley shared his doubts and misgivings about Bacau's guilt with Cooper.

'He's adamant that he knows nothing, Sergeant, so I'm not sure about anything now.'

'I must admit it is all very confusing at the moment, sir, but perhaps after we've spoken to the Princess's informants we will have a clearer picture.'

'Oh I do hope so, Sergeant,' said Hadley wistfully as he glanced out of the open window at the traffic.

On arrival at the Marylebone the detectives hurried through to the mortuary and found Doctor Evans examining the naked body of Madam Galati with his assistant Smythe.

Evans looked up and said 'I was hoping for an early night, Jim, but when I was informed that you were on the case I thought I'd better get on with examining this latest victim of yours.'

'I'm glad you did, Doctor, because it is urgent,' replied Hadley with a smile before he looked down at the pale, lifeless body on the marble slab.

'It always is with you, Jim.'

'That's because the Commissioner is involved, Doctor.'

'Ah, the great one strikes again... why can't he spend his time doing paperwork like then rest of us instead of poking his nose into every investigation?'

'I'm sure I don't know... now tell me, was the same weapon used to kill Madam Galati as the others?'

'The short answer is 'yes', Jim, but this time the killer had to make two attempts because when we undressed her we found that her whalebone corset had deflected the first blow causing only a slight wound, but the second passed through it and up into her chest cavity from the back, piercing her heart,' replied Evans.

'She would have died instantly then.'

'Without a doubt, Jim... and I must add that this assassin certainly knows how to kill with ease... have a look at the smooth entry into the body,' replied Evans as he and Smythe turned the pale, lifeless form on to its side so the entry wound in the back was exposed for Hadley and Cooper to examine.

'It's the mark of a true professional, Doctor.'

'I would say so, Jim, and the measurements for depth penetration and width fit exactly to the others,' said Evans as he lowered her body to the slab.

'Right, Doctor... please let me have your report as soon as possible for the Commissioner.'

'I will, Jim,' replied Evans with a sigh.

The detectives arrived outside the Princess's home in Berkeley Square just before seven thirty and were admitted by the maid. After waiting for a few moments in the hallway while the maid informed the Princess of their arrival, they were conducted upstairs and announced to her.

'Oh, James I'm so glad you've called,' she said with a smile as she stood to greet them.

'May I ask why, Helena?'

'The evening papers say that Madam Galati has been murdered in Harrods, is it true?' she replied as she waved them to sit.

'Indeed it is,' replied Hadley.

'May God help us... so are we all in danger from this maniac, James?'

'I don't think so Helena, but please be cautious when you leave your residence until we have caught this killer,' replied Hadley.

'I will, James... but it is all so frightening for a woman on her own in London.'

'I'm sure... but we're here to protect you, Helena.'

'Thank heavens for that.'

'Tell me, how is the Countess?'

'She is a little better I'm pleased to say, the Doctor has given her some strong medicine which he says will calm her fever,' replied the Princess.

'I'm glad to hear it, Helena.'

'Yes it is a relief.'

'Now the purpose of my visit is to ask you to make arrangements for me to interview your informants now that we have arrested Bacau and Osijek.'

'Yes, of course.'

'And I would like to do that before you leave London on Saturday, Helena.'

'Oh, I've decided to stay at least another month to assist you with your investigations, James,' she replied with a smile.

'Well I am delighted with that good news, Helena,' said Hadley brightly while Cooper grinned and raised his eyebrows.

'It's my duty to help you all I can, James,' she said in a quiet soothing tone.

'Thank you, Helena,' he replied in a whisper and blushed slightly.

'And I've written to my cousin, the Prince, and informed him that I am staying on in London to assist you.'

'Ah, how very wise of you, Helena... now would you please arrange for your people to be at Scotland Yard tomorrow?'

'I will, James.'

'How many of them are there?'

'Four all told, James and I will send them in my carriage at shall we say... eleven o'clock?'

'That will be most acceptable, Helena... it will give me time to get organised,' said Hadley with a smile.

'I understand, now I won't be coming with them, but they all speak good English and will be happy to tell you all they know about those evil criminals Bacau and Osijek.'

'That's very helpful... may I know their names and where they work?' asked Hadley as Cooper took out his notebook for the details.

'Of course, there's Stefan Molovich and Greta Narnia, they work at the Rumanian Embassy, then Jan Rigor and Esther Romanov, from the Hungarian Embassy,' she replied.

'Ah, so there are two men and two women.'

'Yes, James... they are all very loyal to me and I trust them completely.'

'I'm sure you do, Helena.'

As Cooper finished writing, she asked 'will you stay for something to eat, James?'

'Thank you, but no, Helena, we have much to do this evening before we can go home... I'm sure you understand,' replied Hadley with a smile.

'Of course I do, James.'

The detectives left the Princess and made their way back to the Yard in the coach.

'If these spies tell us what they know about the suspects and are prepared to back it up in court then I'm sure that we'll get convictions, Sergeant.'

'Yes, sir, and it all should be straight forward from now on.'

'Let's hope so.'

As soon as they arrived at the Yard Hadley went up to see if the Chief was still in his office whilst Cooper started writing a report on the informants.

Bell looked up from the paperwork as Hadley entered his office and asked abruptly 'well, Inspector?'

'I'm glad you're still here, sir... '

'Well I'm not!'

'Quite so, sir,' replied Hadley with a sigh.

'You'd better sit down and tell me what you've discovered this evening,' said Bell as he waved Hadley to the creaking chair.

'Yes, sir... Doctor Evans confirms that the weapon used to kill Madam Galati was identical to the one used to murder the others, sir.'

'Well, I think we all knew that, Hadley.'

'Yes, sir... but it's good to have it confirmed.'

'I suppose so... and what did Princess... what's her name... have to say for herself?'

'She gave us the names of four witnesses who are coming in tomorrow at eleven to make statements about the suspects, sir,' replied Hadley.

'Well I hope that they bring some positive information we can work with because Osijek insists he is totally innocent of the murder of Brasov in Hyde Park,' said Bell angrily.

'I didn't expect he'd confess, sir.'

'Bloody foreigners... you can't trust any of them, Hadley.'

'You can't, sir.'

'The fella had the cheek to threaten me with dismissal from the Force when I told him and his legal worm that I opposed bail and he'd face the Bow Street magistrates in the morning, Hadley!'

'But they all do that, sir... as you well know.'

'I know... but this time he said that his Ambassador would issue an ultimatum to Sir Jason and the Prime Minister stating that unless all charges were dropped against him then Hungary would break off diplomatic relations with us... may God preserve me from these bloody foreigners!'

'It won't happen, sir.'

'This is serious, Hadley... and it could mean the end of my career... my pension, everything would be in disgrace!' said Bell and Hadley felt genuinely sorry for his Chief.

'It's the slings and arrows of outrageous fortune, sir... and part of our job.'

'I should have gone into the army as my father advised,' said Bell in a defeated tone.

'But you didn't, sir, and I might say that I think you have been a good and professional officer who has served the Police Force very well indeed and coped with all sorts of difficulties that would have deterred and defeated lesser men.'

Bell smiled and said 'well thank you, Hadley... I'm glad that someone has noticed my modest contributions to the upholding of the law and order in this blessed country of ours.'

'Oh, it's not just me, sir, I assure you.'

'Who else, Hadley?'

'It would not be proper for me to say, sir, but you do have your admirers.'

'Well, that's good to know, Hadley.'

'Yes, sir.'

'And are these admirers in high places?' inquired Bell softly with slightly raised eyebrows.

'Some of them are, sir,' replied Hadley, the Chief beamed and said with a contented smile 'well on that happy note I suggest we call it a day and see what tomorrow brings.'

'Indeed we will, sir... goodnight.'

'Goodnight, Hadley.'

After saying 'goodnight' to Cooper, Hadley sat alone in his office and weighed up the events of the day. He was distinctly unsure of Bacau's guilt and involvement in the murders of Plovdiv and Hatvan but was more comfortable with Osijek's culpability regarding Brasov's death in Hyde Park. The killing of Madam Galati in Harrods was out of keeping with the other murders as she was not a Diplomat only the wife of one. He felt sure that it was one of Bacau's security men who were responsible for the murders and he thought it a possibility that Bacau did not know and someone else was behind the assassin directing his killing spree. He decided to arrest all the security men at the Rumanian Embassy after the appearance of the suspects at Bow Street magistrates. He hoped that the Princess's informants would arrive promptly at eleven o'clock with information which would shed light on the confused situation and mean the arrest of someone in high authority as well as the security men. Hadley was pleased that Karpov was no longer a suspect and when the poor Russian had been informed that all charges against him were being dropped, he cried emotionally with relief. On being told he would stay in protective custody for the time being, he was delighted. Having a dry, comfortable bed to sleep on and regular food in the canteen was like heaven after spending nights cold and hungry in doss houses or the sewer outfall in Mellish Street.

It was ten o'clock when Hadley arrived home to be met by an anxious and concerned Alice.

'Jim dear, you look absolutely exhausted,' she said as she helped off with his coat.

He nodded and replied 'I am dearest.'

'Have you eaten anything this evening?'

'No, but I had a good lunch,' he replied before he made his way into the parlour.

'Oh… where was that?' she asked in a curious tone as she followed him in to the room.

'Cooper and I had lunch with a Princess at her home in Berkeley Square.'

'I see… now tell me, was she a real Princess or a fairy one with a God Mother?'

'She's called Princess Helena Radomir and she is Bulgarian.'

'And what is she doing in London entertaining you for lunch might I ask?'

'The Princess is helping me with the investigation, dear,'

'Are you sure about that?'

'Quite sure, dearest… now have you saved anything for me to eat?'

'There's some game pie left with a little salad.'

'That will do nicely.'

'Good, and while you're eating, you can tell me what you had for lunch with this Princess,' said Alice before she left the room and Hadley sighed before picking up the evening paper. The lurid account in the press of Madam Galati's murder in Harrods did nothing to ease his troubled mind and Alice was less than sympathetic when he told her in detail of the Princesses contribution to the investigation.

He spent a restless night and was glad when the dawn eventually arrived.

CHAPTER 20

As soon as Hadley arrived in his office the next morning he and Cooper prepared the arrest warrants for the Rumanian security men, Simeria, Vaslu and Arud before going up to see the Chief Inspector. He entered the office with a smile and said 'good morning, sir.'

'Morning, Hadley.'

'I've brought the arrest warrants for the Rumanians for your signature, sir,' said Hadley as he placed the documents on Bell's desk.

'And what are we going to charge them with?'

'Conspiracy to murder, sir.'

'All of them?'

'I believe that they are all involved, sir… and I'm sure one of them is our killer in the Bowler hat,' replied Hadley.

'Hmmm… these fellows are all under the direct control of Bacau… is that not so?'

'Yes it is, sir.'

'But he denies all knowledge of the murders and surely he would know if one of his men were the assassin?'

'I've given this some thought, sir, and I believe that, totally unknown to Bacau, someone else in higher authority in the Embassy is controlling the assassin,' replied Hadley.

'Who do you suspect?'

'I'm not sure, sir, but it could be Galati.'

'And so he took the opportunity to murder his wife as part of the whole conspiracy?'

'Possibly, sir, her death would save him from further ridicule over her promiscuous behaviour, which was well known by all,' replied Hadley.

'Do you think he is ruthless enough to murder his own wife?'

'Plenty of men do, sir.'

'Quite so, Hadley… and usually with good reason,' said Bell in a firm tone before he picked up his pen, dipped it in the inkwell and signed the warrants.

'Thank you, sir.'

'When do you propose to arrest them?'

'As soon as I've finished interviewing the Princess's informants, sir.'

'Very well, Hadley... but don't forget we have to be at Bow Street at ten for the committal of Bacau and Osijek.'

'I hadn't forgotten, sir.'

'And if the hearing is delayed for any reason, you'll have to leave me there whilst you come back to question these witnesses.'

'I will, sir.'

'Good, and hopefully they'll be able to give you some useful information that will finally close the investigation into this sorry mess,' said Bell.

As Big Ben struck the half hour at nine thirty, Hadley and Cooper joined Bell in the Police coach for the short journey to Bow Street Magistrates court. Bacau and Osijek followed on in a Police prisoner wagon, much to their disgust. When the coaches arrived in the yard behind the austere building, the prisoners were escorted down to the cells whilst the detectives took their seats in the courtroom. They nodded at Mr Bracewell and Mr Morton Barrymore, who were there to ensure that their respective clients were freed on bail. After the prisoners were brought up to the bar, the court rose when Mr Crossley Milton and his two dour, aloof, colleagues entered. The hearing began and the clerk asked the prisoners their names and addresses, which surprised the magistrates. The charges were read out and the public gallery, which was full of reporters and security men from the two Embassies, waited eagerly for the outcome. Hadley noticed the three Rumanians who he planned to arrest later and was pleased that they were there and had not left the country.

The Chief outlined the case against the two suspects and asked that, pending further Police inquiries, they should be held on remand until a later date. Mr Bracewell and Mr Morton Barrymore put the case for their respective clients to be released on bail as they were respected and reliable persons who would vigorously contest any charges brought against them regarding the conspiracy to murder the three Diplomats. Mr Crossley Milton looked severe and spoke to his two colleagues, who kept glancing at the suspects in the dock before whispering to each other. Eventually Mr

Crossley Milton nodded and then declared that the suspects would be released on bail for a surety of ten thousand pounds in the case of Vadim Osijek and fifteen thousand pounds in the case of Vlad Bacau as he was not a Diplomat and more likely to abscond. The sums of money demanded raised gasps of incredulity from the court and the reporters in the public gallery started talking so loudly that Mr Crossley Milton had to call for order.

Hadley glanced at Bell who raised his eyebrows, shook his head and said 'they'll do a bunk abroad and we'll never get them.'

'If they do then we'll have to catch them before they get away, sir.'

'I don't share your optimism, Hadley,' said Bell before Mr Crossley Milton announced the date of the next hearing would be in one week and made the comment that he hoped it would be sufficient time for the Police to conclude their inquiries. Bell thanked Mr Crossley Milton and confirmed that it would be sufficient while Hadley crossed his fingers. The court rose and the three, dour magistrates left to a hubbub of noise.

The detectives hurried back to the Yard and arrived as Big Ben was striking eleven o'clock. Hadley and Cooper made their way up to their office where a Constable was talking to George.

'Ah, glad you're back, sir, apparently your visitors have just arrived and are down in Reception,' said George.

'Good, follow us down with pens, ink and plenty of paper, George, we've work to do and you'll be typing it all up for the Chief,' said Hadley before he left the office with Cooper as George sighed and shook his head.

Hadley decided to have all the informants in the interview room and question them together. Hadley made himself and Cooper known to the anxious looking people sitting on a long bench and asked them to follow him into the room. The two men were quite young, the women were attractive and they were all well dressed. They settled down around the table as George arrived with his writing implements.

Hadley said with a smile 'now ladies and gentlemen, thank you for coming today and for the record would you please state your names and where you work?'

'Yes, sir, I am Stefan Molovich, I work at the Rumanian Embassy with Greta Narnia here,' said Molovich as he pointed at the pretty woman sitting next to him.

'And what do you do at the Embassy?'

'I am a translator, sir, I speak several languages fluently,' replied Molovich.

'And you Miss Narnia?'

'I look after some of the receptions and organise dinner parties, sir,' she replied with a smile. Hadley nodded and looked at the other man who said 'I'm Jan Rigor, sir, and I work at the Hungarian Embassy with Esther Romanov.' Esther smiled and glanced at Hadley then Cooper before fluttering her eyelashes at him.

'And what do you do, Mr Rigor?'

'I am a clerk to the Charges d'Affairs, sir,' he replied.

'And you, Miss Romanov?'

'I am responsible for seeing that Embassy guests have everything they need, sir,' she replied with a smile.

'Very good... now as you know Princess Radomir has asked you all to come here and assist us in our investigations into the murders of the three Diplomats.'

'Yes, sir, and we will do everything we can to help,' said Molovich.

'Thank you, so please take your time and tell us everything you know about Vlad Bacau and Vadim Osijek... we'll start with you Mr Molovich,' said Hadley.

'Yes sir, I know a lot about Bacau and I can tell you he is a ruthless man without pity and he only strives to please Secretary Galati.'

'Go on if you please.'

'He has been engaged with his men in following Madam Galati everywhere she goes and reporting back to her husband... I am sure that one of them murdered her in Harrods, sir.'

'Do you know which one?' asked Hadley is blue eyes bright with anticipation.

'I believe it was Dacau Simeria, sir,' replied Molovich.

'Have you any proof?'

'He was absent all afternoon, sir, and when he came back at about four o'clock I noticed he had some blood on his shirt cuff.'

'Did you say anything to him?'

'Yes, sir, and he said he'd had an accident getting into a coach.'

'I see… anything else?'

'Yes, Simeria always carries a knife,' replied Molovich.

'Please describe it.'

'It's a thin stiletto and he boasts that his Uncle gave it to him after he'd been a soldier in the Crimean war, sir.'

'What motive did Simeria have for killing Madam Galati?'

'He didn't have any, in fact he quite liked Madam… but I am sure he was told to do it by someone in authority,' replied Molovich.

'Who do you suspect ordered the murder?'

'I don't know, sir, but it would not surprise me if Secretary Galati ordered it.'

'Why?'

'Because his wife was unfaithful and had many lovers, her behaviour was well known by everybody but he always took no notice despite the rumours,' replied Molovich.

'So if he tolerated her behaviour why should he suddenly decide to murder her?'

'Because her affairs had reached such an embarrassing point t the situation could not continue without jeopardising his position in the Embassy and he would be forced to leave in disgrace,' replied Molovich.

'Do you think Bacau knew of this order to kill Madam Galati?'

'Probably not… I know that Secretary Galati often kept certain things from him.'

'I see, well it appears that Bacau was not trusted.'

'I'm sure he wasn't, sir and that was why he tried so hard to be in favour with Secretary Galati but he was not trusted as he had Hungarian parents and Galati despises Hungarians,' said Molovich and there followed a few moments silence while Hadley gathered his thoughts about Balkan politics.

'Do you suspect that Simeria murdered Igor Plovdiv and Rossi Hatvan?' he asked.

'Yes I do, sir, because he was out both nights when the murders were committed and came back very late… he looked anxious before he went in to see Secretary Galati.'

'Does he walk with a limp?'

'Yes he does, he said it was the result of an accident when he fell from his horse several years ago,' replied Molovich and Hadley glanced at Cooper who raised his eyebrows.

'Does he wear a Bowler hat?'

'Yes, he has several, sir.'

'Why did Simeria murder the two Diplomats?'

'I think he was ordered to by Galati as both were lovers of Madam Galati,' replied Molovich.

'Surely Bacau would have known about this?'

'I think he did, sir... but kept quiet in case he offended Galati.'

'Thank you Mr Molovich... now Miss Narnia, what can you tell us about Vlad Bacau?' asked Hadley.

She gave her poor opinion of Bacau and his men but failed to say anything that could be used in evidence in their prosecution, except she had asked the scullery maid about Simeria's bloodstained shirt and was informed he recently had two that had to be washed with blood on them.

'Did the maid say where the shirts were bloodstained?' asked Hadley.

'Only on the cuffs, sir,' she replied.

'Thank you, Miss Narnia... now Mr Rigor, please tell us about Secretary Osijek.'

'Yes, sir, in my experience Osijek is a cunning man only interested in making Hungary the most powerful state in the Balkans and he will do anything to ensure that happens.'

'Do you suspect he murdered Sergei Brasov in Hyde Park?' asked Hadley.

'I'm sure of it, sir.'

'Tell me why you are so certain.'

'He went out that afternoon and did not arrive back until late and he admitted to me he was in Hyde Park at the time of the murder, sir.'

'But many people were in the Park, so his being there doesn't make him guilty.'

'I realise that, sir, but he had motives.'

'Then please tell us what they were.'

'Sergei Brasov was an accomplished and dedicated Diplomat who was well respected by everyone who had dealings with him and he often outwitted Osijek, which had caused much embarrassment to the Hungarians but the overriding motive was jealousy, sir.'

'Please explain.'

'He was in love with Madam Galati and after a brief affair she had thrown him over in favour of Brasov and Osijek's pride had to be avenged... you have to come from our part of Europe to really understand, sir,' Rigor said and Hadley sighed before glancing at Cooper who raised his eyebrows.

'Now Miss Romanov, please tell us what you know about Secretary Osijek,' said Hadley.

'I believe that he murdered Brasov, sir, because it was common knowledge that he hated him after Madam Galati started her affair with Brasov,' she said.

'Please continue.'

'Well, he often raged about it and one of the maids overheard him say he would kill him as soon as he got the chance,' she replied.

'Do you know if this maid would testify to that in court?'

'I'm not sure, sir, because it would mean she would have to leave her job without any references and she could end up on the streets,' she replied.

'That's a shame but I'm sure we could assist her if it came to that,' said Hadley with a smile.

'Thank you, sir... I will ask her and let you know.'

'Good, now of course once you all come to the trial and give your statements to the court then obviously your positions will be untenable at the Embassies,' said Hadley.

'We realise that, sir, but Princess Radomir has discussed this with us and she will see that we return to Sofia and are employed by her or the Prince,' replied Molovich with a smile.

'Well it seems the gracious lady has thought of everything,' said Hadley.

'She has, sir, and I have to say that the Princess is a very clever woman, who always gets what she wants,' said Molovich and Cooper looked at Hadley and gently nodded.

'I believe you... now when the statements are typed up by my clerk, I would like you to read and sign them before you leave,' said Hadley and George raised his eyebrows as he finished writing.

'Yes, of course, sir,' said Molovich and the others nodded.

'Thank you all very much for coming in and assisting us with our inquiries,' said Hadley.

'It's our duty to help you, sir, and our Princess insists on it,' said Molovich.

'Thank you, my clerk will organise some tea for you while you're waiting,' said Hadley before he stood up.

'Princess Radomir asked me to give this note to you, sir,' said Molovich as he produced an envelope from his jacket pocket and gave it to Hadley.

'Thank you, Mr Molovich,' said Hadley as he glanced at the envelope addressed to him and marked 'private and confidential' before he left the room followed by Cooper.

Outside in the corridor, Cooper said 'I bet she's inviting you to dinner or something, sir, so she can get… '

'Thank you, Sergeant, that will be all,' interrupted Hadley as they strode along.

'Yes, sir.'

'May I remind you, Sergeant, that we have three Rumanian security men to arrest before the day is out?'

'No, I don't need reminding, sir.'

'Good… then let's get to it!'

CHAPTER 21

The detectives left the Yard in a Police coach as Big Ben struck twelve noon. Following them was a Police wagon with four Constables on board to assist in the arrest of the Rumanians. During the journey Hadley opened the letter from the Princess, it read: *'Dear James, please come and have dinner with me tomorrow evening at eight as I have something to discuss with you that is very private and I can only tell a dear friend, yours truly, Helena.'*

Hadley gathered his thoughts and said 'the Princess wants me to have dinner with her tomorrow evening, Sergeant.'

'Ah, then I was quite right, sir, it was an invitation.'

'Indeed you were.'

'Are you going to go, sir?'

'Yes, I think so, but I'll give it some more thought before I make a final decision.'

'That's very sensible, sir, as I'm sure she has designs on you and will try to lead you astray…'

'Nonsense, Sergeant, she sees what professional men we are and reacts favourably to us with confidential information,' interrupted Hadley.

'Then has she invited me, sir?'

'Er, no, Sergeant, she hasn't.'

'Ah, thereby hangs the tale, sir, she wants to have you all to herself' said Cooper with a knowing grin.

'You have an over active imagination, Sergeant.'

'Somehow I don't think so, sir.'

'Oh, yes you do.'

'Not where the Princess is concerned, sir, you mark my words.'

'Time will tell,' said Hadley with a sigh before he gazed out of the open window.

'And you'll know soon enough if you have dinner with her, sir,' said Cooper, Hadley shook his head and they remained silent for the rest of the journey.

The detectives and the Constables were admitted to the Embassy and Hadley asked to see Ambassador Sulina immediately. They were asked to wait while the receptionist informed Sulina that they wished to see him. Returning minutes later he told Hadley that the Ambassador would see him now. The Constables were told to wait in the entrance hall and the detectives followed the receptionist up the stairs and along the corridor to Sulina's office. When they entered and were announced, the Ambassador stood up from his desk, looked angrily at them before he asked 'what's the meaning of this intrusion, Inspector?'

'Your Excellency, I have warrants for the arrest of your three security men, Simeria, Vaslu and Arud…'

'On what charge?' interrupted Sulina.

'Conspiracy to murder, sir,' replied Hadley.

'This is preposterous!'

'Nevertheless, sir…'

'You have already arrested Bacau on the same charge and next you'll be arresting me!' interrupted Sulina.

'I don't think so, sir.'

'Well I'm not so sure, Inspector, and I must warn you that I will be making representations to your Prime Minister to stop this arrant nonsense otherwise there will be serious repercussions between our two countries at the highest level.'

'Sir, with respect…'

'Inspector Hadley, I believe that you have no idea who murdered these Diplomats and Madam Galati, so you are just casting about hoping to catch someone and anybody will do!' Sulina shouted angrily. Hadley waited for a few moments for Sulina to calm down and was just about to speak when the door opened and Bacau entered the room. The Ambassador smiled and said 'ah, you've arrived just in time, Bacau.'

'Yes your Excellency.'

'These misguided Police officers now have warrants for the arrests of Simeria, Vaslu and Arud,' said Sulina.

Bacau looked hard at Hadley before asking 'on what charge, your Excellency?'

'The same as you… conspiracy to murder,' replied Sulina.

'Then once again they are gravely mistaken!' said Bacau.

'Indeed they are!'

Hadley cleared his throat and said firmly 'sir, I have my duty to perform so I would be obliged if you would summon these security men so I may arrest them.'

'You are making a mistake, Inspector and I can promise you the consequences that will follow your actions will destroy your career as a Police Officer,' said Sulina.

'I'm prepared to take that chance, sir,' replied Hadley.

Sulina shook his head and said 'very well, Inspector… Bacau, please go and bring our people here.'

'Yes your Excellency.'

After Bacau had left the office, Sulina said 'I believe that you are an honest man but you are hopelessly misguided and it will lead to your inevitable downfall.'

'I am following lines of inquiry into four murders, sir, and three lead directly to this Embassy and your security men,' replied Hadley.

'And what proof do you have to make such a ludicrous allegation, Inspector?'

'We have witnesses to your security men's culpability, sir.'

Sulina shook his head and said 'then we shall find out who these so called witnesses are and deal with them,' as Bacau returned with the three men. Sulina spoke at length to them in Rumanian and finished by saying to Hadley 'I have told them that their imprisonment will be only a matter of hours, Inspector.'

'Don't be too sure about that, sir.'

'I am confident that after I have spoken to your Home Secretary their release will be as quick as your dismissal from the Police Force.'

Hadley ignored the remark and asked 'have you told them to come quietly, sir?'

'Indeed I have, Inspector.'

'Thank you, sir, now do they speak and understand English?'

'They do.'

'Good,' said Hadley before he charged each of them by name with conspiracy to murder and they all remained absolutely silent.

The detectives escorted the prisoners down to the hallway and the Constables took charge of them before leading them out to the Police wagon.

On the return journey to the Yard Hadley said 'we'll question Simeria first as he's the prime suspect for the murders, Sergeant.'

'Very good, sir, and he looks like a cold hearted assassin to me.'

'He does indeed, and it will be interesting what he has to say for himself when we present him with the allegations made by our witnesses about his bloodstained shirts.'

'I think he's the killer all right.'

'I believe he is, Sergeant.'

'And it would save a lot of time if he confesses, sir.'

'I agree... but I doubt if he will,' replied Hadley as the coach pulled into the Yard.

The three men were escorted to Custody where they were booked in and taken to a cell to await their interviews. The detectives went up to their office and Hadley asked George to make some tea and get sandwiches from the canteen.

'Very good, sir, will ham and cheese suit you?'

'Yes, George, but before you do anything tell me about our witnesses.'

'Well, sir, I typed up the statements and took them down and after reading them they all signed,' replied the clerk.

'Well done, George.'

'Thank you, sir... they are all in a folder on your desk.'

'Excellent... now please make some tea as I am gasping!'

George made the tea and then went off to buy sandwiches while the detectives read the statements as they sipped the hot reviver.

'This should put the final nails in the coffins of Bacau, Simeria and Osijek, Sergeant.'

'I'm sure it will, sir.'

'After we've had lunch, I'll report our success to the Chief while you go down and arrange the interview with Simeria and I will join you.'

'Very good, sir.'

Half an hour later Hadley made his way up to the Chief's office, knocked and entered.

'What news, Hadley?' asked Bell as he waved him to the creaking chair.

'We've interviewed the Princess's witnesses, sir, and they've made statements which I've brought for your perusal,' replied Hadley as he placed the buff folder on Bell's desk.

'Excellent, and do they categorically identify Osijek and Bacau as the killers?' asked Bell his eyes ablaze with excitement.

'Indeed they do, sir.'

'Thank heavens for that, Hadley.'

'Quite so, sir.'

'Now we can hang them after the trial, which should be over and done with in record time, provided the legal worms representing them don't prevaricate.'

'Yes sir, and in Bacau's case, it appears he is implicated in the conspiracy but one of his men, named Simeria, did the actual killing of Plovdiv, Hatvan and Madam Galati.'

'We can hang him as well then, Hadley.'

'Yes, sir.' sighed Hadley.

'This is all good news and I know the Commissioner will be pleased when I tell him.'

'I'm sure, sir.'

'So... have you arrested this Simeria fella and the others yet?'

'I have, sir, they are all in custody and I'm just about to go down and question them now,' replied Hadley.

'What a splendid days work, Hadley, you have done very well!'

'Thank you, sir, it has been a giddy experience up until now but I'm sure the end is in sight.'

'Yes, thank God... I'll read the statements before I tell the Commissioner the good news and you'd better stay in your office in case he wants you to clarify anything,' said Bell.

'I will, sir.'

'And let me have a report on what Simeria and the other foreigners say.'

'Of course, sir.'

'And see if you can get a confession out of them, Hadley, it'll speed things up and save court time and money.'

'I'll try, sir.'

When Hadley arrived in the interview room, Cooper and George were already there and seated across the table from Simeria. After Hadley had sat down, he looked hard at the Rumanian and tried to understand if this man was a professional assassin or just a mindless killer who obeyed orders. He waited for a few moments and kept eye contact with the swarthy, rebellious looking man before he said 'Mr Simeria, you have been arrested and charged with conspiracy to murder but I...'

'I am innocent of this nonsense!' interrupted Simeria loudly as he thumped his fist on the table which shook George's ink pot causing a splash of black ink to land on his paper. The clerk tut-tutted and blotted the offending blob then glared at Simeria.

Hadley continued 'but I believe that actually you carried out the fatal attacks on Igor Plovdiv in Whitechapel, Rossi Hatvan at the Opera House and Madam Galati in Harrods.'

'I did not kill these people, why should I?'

'Because you were ordered to, Mr Simeria.'

'Who by?'

'That is what we intend to discover,' replied Hadley.

'You are mistaken, sir, nobody ordered me to do anything like this and I did not kill these people!'

'Then how can you account for bloodstains on your shirts after the murders?' asked Hadley and Simeria smiled, replying 'I caught my hand on a buckle on the Ambassador's coach.'

'What were you doing in the coach?'

'Nothing, the buckle is outside at the back where the luggage is carried and I was placing the Ambassador's case there and strapping it down,' he replied.

'You did this three times?'

'No, only once.'

'But we have information that you had three bloodstained shirts washed by the scullery maid.'

'Then you have been misled, sir, because there was only one shirt that had some slight bloodstain on the cuff,' replied Simeria firmly.

Hadley gathered his thoughts and asked 'where were you last Wednesday evening when Igor Plovdiv was murdered in Whitechapel?'

'I was with Vlad Bacau at the Embassy writing a report on Madam Galati until after ten o'clock then we went out to a pub with the others,' he replied.

'What others?'

'Vaslu and Arud, you've just arrested them... surely you remember?' said Simeria with a grin.

'I am not sure that you realise the seriousness of your situation, Mr Simeria...'

'You're the one who faces a serious situation, Inspector, because my Ambassador will have me out of here within a few hours and you will be blamed for my wrongful arrest,' he interrupted.

'Somehow I don't think so... where were you last Friday night when Rossi Hatvan was killed?'

'I was with my colleagues guarding our Ambassador at a function in the Italian Embassy,' replied Simeria and Hadley was taken aback.

'Did you leave the Embassy during the evening?'

'No, we were all there until after midnight.'

'I suppose your Ambassador will vouch that you were with him?'

'Of course, Inspector, so you see, your allegations are without any foundation because I can prove where I was when the murders were committed... I think it would be sensible for you to release me now.'

Hadley ignored the remark and asked 'where were you when Madam Galati was murdered?'

'Outside Harrods,' Simeria replied.

'Were you indeed... and what were you doing there?'

'Waiting for her to leave the shop before following her,' he replied.

'Were you with anyone?'

'Yes, Vaslu was with me.'

'Were you following her before she entered Harrods?'

'We were.'

'I presume on Secretary Galati's orders?'

'Yes.'

'Did you or Vaslu go into the shop at any time?'

'No we didn't.'

'When did you realise that's something had happened to her?'

'After the Police arrived we asked a woman coming out what had happened and she told us that a foreign lady had been stabbed in the Millinery department, I guessed it was Madam Galati so we left and returned to the Embassy and reported it to Secretary Galati.'

'So he knew his wife was dead before we officially informed him?'

'I can't comment on that because I've just told you that I guessed it was her but he obviously had to wait for confirmation from the Police,' replied Simeria.

Hadley remained silent gathering his thoughts as he was now uncertain about Simeria's culpability.

'Thank you, Mr Simeria, I have no more questions for you at the moment, you'll be returned to your cell whilst I question your colleagues,' said Hadley.

Despite intense questioning, Vaslu and Arud denied they were implicated in the murders and had alibi's for the times and dates when the crimes were committed. They were returned to their cells while the detectives made their way up to the office where Hadley asked George to make some tea.

After Hadley slumped into his chair he said with a sigh 'it seems as if we're going round in giddy circles with this investigation, Sergeant.'

'I agree, sir, they all seem to have watertight alibis which leaves us floundering once again.

'Heaven only knows what the Chief will say when I tell I him because he was expecting a confession,' said Hadley.

'He certainly won't be pleased, sir,'

'That's an understatement, Sergeant,' said Hadley with a grin as George arrived with the tea.

Big Ben was striking five o'clock when Hadley slowly climbed the stairs to the Chief's office. He knew that he was in for a difficult time with Bell and so he breathed deeply before he knocked and entered.

'Ah, Hadley, you've arrived just in time, the Commissioner wants to see us and hear your report before he releases a Press statement.'

'I'm afraid it's not good news, sir.'

'Whatever do you mean?'

'I have questioned these Rumanians closely and they all have watertight alibis for the times of the murders, sir.'

'Good God! What are you telling me, Hadley?'

'I believe that they are all innocent of the crimes, sir.'

'But what about the limping fella 'what's his name' with the Bowler hat? I mean, surely he's our man and we can hang him without too much bother,' said Bell now wide eyed with disappointment.

'Simeria has a cast iron alibi, sir, he was with Bacau on the night when Plovdiv was killed and guarding his Ambassador at the Italian Embassy when Hatvan was murdered,' said Hadley.

'Well I think they're all bloody liars and we should hang the lot of them!'

Hadley shook his head slowly and after a few moments Bell said 'well let's go and tell the Commissioner the bad news, Hadley.'

'Very good, sir.'

'He'll want to know what you're going to do next to sort out this mess... so you'd better think of something pretty quick!' said Bell as he stood up from his desk and strode towards the door.

The Commissioner listened carefully to Hadley and when he had finished speaking the great one said calmly 'whatever they deny, gentlemen, I think we should proceed with the charges against them and let the Barristers argue it out in court in front of a judge and jury.'

'That's what I think, sir,' said Bell.

'I'm glad you agree, Chief Inspector.'

'Oh I do, sir.'

'In my experience these foreigners are all liars and they will be exposed as such when cross examined by Prosecuting Counsel,' said the Commissioner.

'That's exactly what I said to Hadley not a moment ago, sir,' said Bell with a smile.

'Then you were quite right to say as much, Chief Inspector.'

'Thank you, sir.'

'We have the witness statements along with the admission from Simeria that he was at Harrods when Madam Galati was murdered and that alone will take some explaining away in court,' said the Commissioner.

'Indeed it will, sir,' said Hadley.

'So don't be discouraged but go to it with firm resolve, Hadley, and I'm sure that we will get convictions out of this in due course.'

As Hadley returned to his office he felt uplifted by the Commissioner's comments to proceed and he decided to accept the Princess's invitation to dinner in the hope that she might add more useful information to his investigation. Once at his desk he wrote a short note to her, sealed it in an envelope and asked George to place it in the outgoing mail.

CHAPTER 22

At nine thirty the next morning Hadley and Cooper joined the Chief Inspector in a Police coach to take them to Bow Street Magistrates court. The three Rumanians followed on in a Police prisoner wagon. After arriving at the austere building, the detectives sat in the courtroom, nodded to Mr Bracewell, who was representing the prisoners, and waited for the magistrates. The public gallery was full of noisy reporters and Hadley wondered what would appear in the midday editions of the London papers. He glanced at Bell who must have read his mind because he said 'the press dogs are having a field day with all these foreign murders.'

'Indeed they are, sir,' replied Hadley.

'God only knows what lies and misinformed opinions they'll print next,' said Bell.

'I expect it will be anything that takes their fancy, sir.'

'True… and mark my words, Hadley, someday they'll take a step too far and the Government will have to act to curb their excesses when public opinion riles up against them,' said Bell as the clerk of the court called them to order and rise.

Mr Crossley Milton entered the courtroom with his two colleagues and glanced around before he took his seat followed by all attending the court. The clerk called for the prisoners to stand whilst the charges were read out. Afterwards the Chief Inspector made application for them to remain on remand as further Police investigations were ongoing.

Mr Bracewell then launched into a firm but well reasoned argument for the prisoners to be released on bail on surety from the Rumanian Embassy. After very careful and lengthy consideration with his colleagues, Mr Crossley Milton roundly denied Bracewell's application for bail and nodded at Bell, who smiled.

Mr Crossley Milton looked hard at Bracewell and continued 'these prisoners are accused of conspiracy to murder and as foreign nationals may well abscond abroad to escape British justice and the court cannot allow that to happen.'

The next hearing was set for a week on Monday and the court

adjourned as the prisoners were taken down.

The detectives returned to the Yard to begin the paperwork which would be passed to the Crown Prosecution Service for Bacau, his security men and Osijek. Cooper returned their revolvers to the armoury as they were no longer needed whilst Hadley began writing up his notes. Other than stopping for a lunch of canteen sandwiches and endless cups of tea, Hadley and Cooper worked tirelessly throughout the afternoon with George typing up all they had written. As Big Ben struck six o'clock, Hadley called it a day and told his colleagues to go home for the weekend.

'We can start again on Monday morning, gentlemen, refreshed and ready to finally close this investigation,' said Hadley with a smile.

'Yes, sir, goodnight,' said George as he left the office.

'Goodnight, George,' replied Hadley as Cooper came over to his desk and asked 'are you going to have dinner with the Princess this evening, sir?'

'Yes, I've decided to accept her invitation, Sergeant.'

Cooper looked concerned and said 'please be very careful, sir.'

'Surely you don't believe I can come to any harm having dinner with the Princess?'

'I'm just concerned and have an uneasy feeling about tonight, sir.'

Hadley smiled and said 'don't worry, Sergeant, you have a good rest this weekend... take your wife shopping then perhaps to a music hall to make up for the time you've had to work late recently.'

Cooper grinned and replied 'yes, I will, sir... and you watch out this evening... just in case!'

'I will... goodnight, Sergeant.'

'Good night, sir.'

It was just before eight o'clock when Hadley knocked at 10 Berkeley Square and was admitted by the maid. He followed her up to the drawing room and was greeted by the smiling Princess, who was wearing a deep purple velvet dress with pearls sewn onto the bodice. She wore a matching velvet choker with a large pearl suspended from the centre and her pearl and diamond earrings glinted and sparkled in the candlelight. Her complexion was flawless, her lips were ruby red and her dark, lustrous hair was drawn back and up into a French pleat then surmounted by a diamond studded tiara. Her soft, gentle brown eyes mesmerised him for a few moments.

'My word, Helena, you look absolutely radiant this evening,' he said breathlessly as he took her outstretched hand.

'Why thank you for such an elegant compliment made with sincerity.'

'Oh, you are most welcome.'

'Please do sit down, James… may I offer you some of my special Bulgarian wine before dinner?'

'Thank you, Helena that would be most agreeable.'

She smiled, rang the small hand bell and when the maid appeared she ordered the wine.

'It was very kind of you to invite me to dine with you this evening, Helena.'

'It is my pleasure James, I assure you.'

'And of course I am very curious to hear what you wish to discuss with me and …'

'May we leave that until after dinner?' she interrupted.

'Yes by all means,' he replied with a smile, as the maid entered with the wine in two crystal glasses on a silver tray.

They wished each other good health and sipped the smooth red wine before Hadley asked 'and how is the Countess?'

'She is much better thank you, James… and she hopes to be up from her sick bed quite soon.'

'Well, that's a relief.'

'It is… now please tell me how your investigation is proceeding at the moment.'

'It's going very well and we hope to secure convictions of all the suspects. The statements that your people have made will certainly help our prosecution no end,' he replied with a smile.

'I'm so glad that we've been able to help you, James.'

'It is appreciated, Helena, I assure you.'

She sighed and said wistfully 'I only want to…' she faltered.

'Yes, Helena?'

'I'll tell you after dinner,' she whispered, Hadley smiled at her and said 'it must be important.'

'It is to me, James,' she replied as the maid entered and announced that dinner was served.

Hadley escorted the Princess into the dining room and her closeness to him along with the scent of her perfume made his senses reel. He knew he was now under the spell of this beautiful woman and felt he could not escape from her attentions this evening. She waved him to sit at the far end of the ornately furnished table and took her place at the head. The silver cutlery gleamed along with the glistening wine glasses in the light from the flickering candles.

'It is a shame we're so far apart, James,' Helena said with a smile.

'It is,' he whispered.

'I like us to be close... now I hope you will enjoy the meal I have chosen this evening.'

'I'm sure I will if it is as good as the lunch we had recently.'

'Oh it is, I assure you,' she replied as the maid brought in the first course on a silver tray. She served the Princess before Hadley and he looked at the profusion of salad wondering what was in it. Helena noticed his furrowed brow and said 'its Shopska Salata, James... made of cucumbers, tomatoes with spices and topped with cheese.'

'It looks delicious,' he said before picking up his knife and fork.

It was indeed tasty and as they ate the maid poured more wine into their crystal glasses and after curtsying to the Princess, left the room. Hadley sipped the wine and relaxed a little whilst remaining curious about the Princess's motive for inviting him to a private dinner. He wondered whether she had some vital information about the case which her informants had not told him or whether there was some other reason behind the invitation.

When Hadley had finished the salad, she asked 'did you enjoy that, James?'

'I did, Helena, it was delicious, thank you.'

'Good... now we have Kyuvech, which is a favourite of mine...its tender lamb with mixed vegetables and spices... I know you'll like it.'

'I'm sure I will,' he replied with a smile as the maid entered with another young woman to clear the plates. More wine was poured and the main course was presented in a large silver tureen and placed on the table before being dished out by the maid. The aroma was mouth-watering and Hadley could hardly wait to try the food. After the maid had left the room, they toasted each other with the heavy red wine and having now drunk a good amount, Hadley began to feel a little light headed.

During the meal the Princess talked lovingly about Sofia and its social life, assuring Hadley that he would be very happy if he visited the city and remained there for any length of time.

'And you'd be very welcome to stay with me, James,' she said with a knowing smile.

'Thank you, I'd like that, Helena but for the moment I do have my duties to attend to,' he replied.

'Yes, of course, but I meant in the future when you have some holiday.'

'I will certainly give your kind invitation some considerable thought,' he replied thinking that Alice and the children would not relish staying in a distant foreign country with this Princess.

The dessert consisted of Garash cake, which was full of walnuts, followed by Kashkaval cheese with more wine and when Hadley finished the meal his head was swimming and he was teetering on the edge of drunkenness.

'Let's have our coffee in the drawing room where we can talk,' said Helena and Hadley nodded.

After they returned to the room and sat opposite each other, the maid arrived with the coffee and two goblets of brandy on a silver tray. The Princess spoke to her in Bulgarian and she nodded, curtsied then left the room.

'Nobody will disturb us now, James,' Helena said in a whisper as she poured the coffee into two bone china cups.

'Good,' he replied and then to his surprise she came over, sat beside him and handed him his cup.

'This is so much nicer, don't you agree, James?' she asked before sipping her coffee. Hadley was lost for words but remembered what Cooper had said about the Princess and he felt decidedly uncomfortable.

'Yes... yes,' he replied falteringly before taking a large sip of his coffee while she stared relentlessly at him for a few moments.

He began to blush and she eventually leaned towards him, saying in a soft seductive tone 'I think you are a very brave and intriguing man, James, so tell me about your most dangerous case.' Hadley was surprised by the compliment and tried to think of a suitable answer.

He cleared his throat and replied 'I believe it was my last investigation into the Holy Grail murders, but before I tell you anything about that little escapade, Helena, please tell me why you invited me here this evening.'

'I wanted to see you and let you into my secret, James, but it is not yet time,' she replied with a curious smile. Hadley remained silent and finished his coffee in the hope that it would help him sober up a little. She then handed him a brandy as he decided to tell her about the Grail investigation - he would keep it very brief as he was anxious to know her secret and whether it had any bearing on the present murder case. He gave a succinct account of what had happened in the Scottish castles, the wounding of Cooper and the brave actions of Talbot in apprehending the gunman. The Princess gasped, held her hand to her heaving breast as her beautiful eyes opened wide in horror at the dangers Hadley and his officers had faced.

When he had finished the epic tale and his brandy, she whispered 'I'm so glad that you were not hurt, James.'

'So am I, but it was more by luck than judgement.'

'I don't believe that for a moment,' she whispered before she lunged at him and gave him a kiss on his cheek. He blushed and said 'Helena, you shouldn't have done that.'

'Why not? I think you are very brave and I do admire you so much.'

'Thank you, you're very kind,' he said as she lunged at him again and kissed him passionately on his lips. He tried to move back but he was unable to stop her powerful advance so he surrendered and yielded to her desire. When their lips parted she said in a whisper 'there, that was wonderful, James.'

'It was, Helena.'

She sighed and asked 'do you think I'm beautiful?'

'Absolutely staggeringly so,' he replied.

'Then kiss me again, James,' she whispered and he did not hesitate. When she eventually pulled away from him she said 'you are a wonderful man and I need you to stay with me tonight, James.' He did not know how to reply to her obvious demand for intimacy and he suddenly felt very alarmed.

'Helena…'

'Yes my darling James?'

'I care for you very much indeed… but I cannot surrender to your wishes,' he said as gently as he could.

'Why not, James?'

'Because I have a dear wife and family who are all very precious to me and I could not…'

'But surely our true love must come before anything else!' she interrupted.

'I am not in love with you…'

'But I am in love with you!'

'Helena, please…'

'Don't 'please' me, James!'

'Helena, do calm yourself…'

'I have within me a burning passion for you… you are my chosen one and I will have you to myself before this night is out!'

'I think I'd better leave…'

'No you will not leave James!' she interrupted as her eyes burned fiercely with emotion.

'Helena…'

'If you leave me you will regret it for the rest of your life!'

'That may be so… but I must leave you because I think you've become overwrought with drink, Helena.'

'I want you to be with me always…'

'That's just impossible!' he interrupted.

'I would give you anything you wanted, James, money, position, a title… anything your heart desired,' she said with tears in her eyes.

'I have no doubt about that Helena, but I have told you, that tempting as it may be, I am a happily married man with a loving wife and family and I could not betray their trust with you.'

'You're a fool, James!'

'I may be, Helena… and so many have said that to me in the past but I hold to my beliefs in family values and loyalty to those closest to me.'

'We could have had a wonderful life together James… every

city in Europe would be at our feet.'

'I am sure, Helena.'

She remained silent as the tears coursed down her cheeks before she said in a whisper between little sobs 'you must go then.'

'Before I leave, please tell me your secret, Helena.'

She looked up at his face and slowly shook her head, replying 'I have already told you my secret, James, I am in love with you… that is my secret.'

Hadley felt genuinely sorry for this beautiful, unhappy woman and he had mixed emotions as he gave a quick kiss on her cheek before he stood up.

'Goodnight, Princess,' he said softly and she whispered 'goodnight.'

Hadley left the house as quickly as he could in his unsteady state and stood outside on the pavement breathing in the cool night air gathering his thoughts. He was still struggling with his emotions when the sound of a Hansom entering the quiet Square attracted his attention. It pulled up on the far side of the shrubbery garden that is in the centre of the spacious Square. A passenger alighted, paid the driver and Hadley strode towards the entrance to the garden in the expectation of reaching the Hansom before it trotted off towards Piccadilly. He was almost half way through the garden and was about to call out to the cab driver when he sensed someone close behind him. As he was more intent on reaching the cab before it disappeared, he brushed away any notion that there was someone there. Suddenly he felt a hand on his shoulder and he whirled round to see silhouetted in the gas light, a Bowler hat, then the glint of a stiletto blade as it travelled up towards his chest. He parried the blow with his left arm and gasped at the agonising pain when the stiletto pierced his forearm and grated on the bone. With his right fist he lashed out at his assailant's face but he moved his head instinctively so Hadley's punch missed completely. The assailant drew the blade back for another attempt and Hadley saw the stiletto as it moved at lightning speed up towards his chest so he grabbed the blade and felt it cut deeply into his hand. Hadley, while still holding the stiletto, swung his right arm around the assailant's neck and tried to choke him as he attempted to twist him down to the ground. The Bowler hat came off and they struggled violently before they lost their balance and toppled over into the bushes. Hadley was now on top of the kicking and struggling assailant and he let go of the blade. He was about to land a heavy blow to the man's jaw beneath his large moustache when he was aware of someone else above him. He heard a shout before two sickening, heavy blows to his head caused him to spiral down into a whirlpool of black unconsciousness.

CHAPTER 23

As Hadley returned to semi consciousness he opened his eyes and tried to focus, but his head was racked with an intense pain, which blurred his vision. Slowly, a face came into hazy view and he was relieved to see it was Cooper.

'What the bloody hell happened to me, Sergeant?' he asked in a whisper.

'You were attacked last night, sir.'

'Was I?'

'But you're safe in hospital now, sir,' interrupted Cooper.

'Don't try to speak, sir, just rest,' said another voice and Hadley turned his bandaged head slightly to see a nurse by his bedside.

'Oh dear God,' he whispered as the Doctor arrived. The nurse moved aside to allow the Doctor to examine him. He peered down at Hadley then looked closely into his eyes and said 'the patient is still heavily concussed, nurse, so keep him under constant observation for any signs of deterioration in his condition and let Matron Kelley know immediately if there is any change.'

'Yes, Doctor.'

'I will see him again in another hour or so,' said Doctor Morris before he hurried out of the little side ward.

Hadley looked down at his heavily bandaged left hand and arm then said in a whisper 'oh what a bloody mess.'

'Please don't try to speak, sir,' said the nurse.

'Alright, alright… can I have something to drink?'

'Yes of course, but I'm afraid it's only water until the Doctor says otherwise,' she replied with a smile.

'That'll do,' he whispered as the ward Matron appeared in her white, crackling starched uniform.

'How is the patient, nurse?' she asked.

'He is conscious, Matron.'

'Good… so we'll see what progress he makes now.'

'Yes, Matron.'

'Has he had any fluids yet?'

'I'm just about to get him some water, Matron.'

'Then hurry up Nurse Thompson, we don't want him to suffer

with dehydration on top of everything else!'

'No, Matron,' she replied as she hurried from the room.

'And I'm afraid you can't stay here any longer, Sergeant,' said Matron Kelley firmly.

'But…'

'There are no 'buts' on my ward, Sergeant, so out you go!'

'May I please have just a minute more with my Inspector?' asked Cooper with a smile.

'Very well then… but only one minute,' she replied.

Cooper bent down close to Hadley and whispered 'it was a patrolling Constable who knocked you and your assailant out cold with his truncheon because he thought you were two drunks fighting…'

'Did he by God?'

'Yes, and he battered your attacker senseless because he struggled so violently that he is still unconscious, sir.'

'Have we got him under Police guard?'

'Indeed we have, sir.'

'Good, do we know who he is?'

'No, sir, we don't… but he's heavily bandaged and in a side ward… I've not been allowed to see him yet,' replied Cooper.

'Then we've got him at last.'

'We have indeed, sir.'

'Was the knife recovered?'

'We found it this morning, sir and it's been taken to Doctor Evans for examination,' replied Cooper.

'Good… will you please let my wife know where I am, Sergeant?'

'When we knew what had happened to you the Chief sent a message to her first thing this morning and organised a coach for her, sir… so I'm sure she'll be here at any moment,' replied Cooper with a smile and Hadley gave a slight nod.

'Your minute is up, Sergeant,' said Matron as the nurse arrived with a glass and a jug of water.

'Yes, Matron… I'll see you later, sir.'

'Only if I say so, Sergeant,' said Matron Kelley firmly.

'Yes of course, Matron,' said Cooper with a grin before he left the room.

Hadley sipped the water then laid his aching head back on the soft pillow and fell asleep. When he awoke he saw Alice sitting at his bedside.

'How are you feeling, dearest?' she asked with her eyes moist with tears.

'Better for seeing you,' he replied in a whisper.

'That's good.'

'I think I'll be in here for a few days,' he said.

She nodded and replied 'the Doctor says you'll be here for at least a week, dearest.'

'A week?'

'Yes...'

'I can't stay in here for a week... I've got important things to do.'

'Then Cooper will have to attend to them... and I'm sure he can manage without you because you're not going anywhere until the Doctor says so,' Alice said firmly and he sighed.

'What time is it?' he asked.

'I'm not sure now, but it was well after two o'clock this afternoon when I arrived here.'

'Afternoon?'

'Yes, it's Saturday afternoon,' she replied.

'Good heavens,' he whispered.

'I was worried sick when you didn't come home last night and when I was told that you were in hospital after being attacked in Berkeley Square by some madman with a knife... I thought, well Alice Hadley, you could be a Police widow before the day is out.'

'I am so sorry, dear.'

They sat in silence whilst Hadley tried to think of what had happened when he was attacked but it was all still very hazy and unclear to him. He wondered what would happen next but his aching head made any coherent thought impossible. After a short while the Doctor entered and smiled at his patient.

'How are you feeling now, Inspector?'

'Better I think, Doctor... but why do I feel so weak?'

'It's because you've lost a lot of blood and it will take time for you to recover from that heavy loss,' he replied.

'Was it from my head?'

'No, Inspector, you sustained a deep, penetrating cut to your left arm and severe cuts to your left hand. In the darkness the

Constable who struck you did not see your wounds, only when he and the cab driver carried you out of the garden did he notice your condition, by then you'd lost a lot of blood,' replied Doctor Morris.

'I see… now what about my attacker, how is he?'

'Your attacker is still unconscious Inspector… and you will be surprised to learn that it was a woman who attempted to kill you.'

'A woman!' Hadley exclaimed as he tried to sit up in bed with his mind reeling at the disturbing news.

'Yes, Inspector.'

'Are you sure?'

'Absolutely sure and I must admit it was a surprise to us as we thought it was man because of the moustache… but that proved to be false.'

'Good heavens… do you know who she is?'

'No, she had nothing about her person which could identify her but do you have any idea who she might be, Inspector?' asked the Doctor and Hadley thought for a moment before replying 'I'm not sure, but it could be someone I've met recently.' Alice gave her husband an old fashioned look and asked 'and who might that be?'

'You don't know her, dear… but Doctor, my Sergeant would recognise the person who I think it may be.'

'That would be helpful, he's still outside so I will allow him to see the woman, provided he does it quietly and he can tell us if he recognises her,' said the Doctor.

'Thank you.'

After the Doctor had left the side ward, Alice asked firmly 'and who is this woman, dearest?'

'I'm not sure, so we'll have to wait and see if Cooper recognises her,' he replied.

'Were you with her last night?'

'I don't know if it was her on not.'

'But you were with a woman, isn't that so?'

'Yes, I'm afraid it is true, dear,' he whispered.

'And who was this hussy may I ask?'

'Princess Radomir.'

'Oh no, not her again!' Alice exclaimed as Cooper came in looking stunned followed by the Doctor and Matron.

'Well, Sergeant?'

'You'll never believe this, sir.'

'I think I will.'

'It's the Princess's cousin… the Countess, sir.'

'I was right then,' whispered Hadley.

'So who is this person, Inspector?' asked the Doctor.

'She is Countess Helga Somovit, a cousin of Princess Radomir and she lives in Berkeley Square,' replied Hadley.

'We must advise her next of kin and…' began the Doctor.

'Sergeant,' interrupted Hadley.

'Yes, sir?'

'Take six Constables and arrest the Princess and everyone else at the house because they are all complicit in the conspiracy to murder me!'

'Very good, sir.'

'And come back and let me know once they are all in custody and charged.'

'Right, sir.'

'And tell the Chief Inspector who my assailant is so he can report it to the Commissioner.'

'Yes, sir,' said Cooper.

'I think we now have our assassin and know who was the mastermind behind this killing spree,' said Hadley.

'Indeed we do, sir,' replied Cooper before he strode purposefully from the ward.

There followed a few moments of stunned silence before Alice said 'I never liked the sound of this Princess.'

'I am aware of that, dear.'

'And what were you doing at her home last night may I ask?'

'She sent a note inviting me there saying she had some secret information and I assumed it would help in the case,' replied Hadley.

'And what was this information?'

'Nothing that I didn't already know, dear,' he replied diplomatically.

'So it was a waste of your time then.'

'Of course and it was obviously a ruse to lure me into a deadly trap,' replied Hadley but before Alice could say anything else, the Doctor said 'I think that's enough now… I suggest that you try and rest, Inspector… and Mrs Hadley, would you please leave your husband for a little while?'

'Of course, Doctor.'

'Thank you… and Matron…'

'Yes Doctor?'

'Please see that the patient has no more visitors until I say so.'

'Very good, Doctor,' replied Matron Kelley in a firm tone.

Hadley fell into a deep sleep for several hours and when he awoke he saw Nurse Thompson sitting at his bedside.

She smiled and asked 'would you like a drink, sir?'

He nodded and she poured some water from the jug into a glass then gave it to him. After a few sips he asked 'what time is it?'

'It's just after eight o'clock.'

'Has my Sergeant returned yet?'

'Yes, he's waiting outside with another gentleman who I think is your Chief Inspector, sir.'

'And where's my wife?'

'Mrs Hadley has gone home, sir, but told Matron that she would return later this evening,' she replied and Hadley nodded and closed his eyes.

A quarter of an hour later the Doctor arrived and spoke softly to the nurse but it disturbed Hadley and he awoke. The Doctor gazed down at him and asked 'how are you feeling now?'

'A bit better, thank you, Doctor… but still tired.'

'That's to be expected.'

'Can I see my Chief and Sergeant for a moment?'

'Yes if you must… but only for a few minutes,' replied the Doctor.

'Thank you… please ask them to come in,' said Hadley, the Doctor nodded at Nurse Thompson who left to find them.

Chief Inspector Bell entered the room with Cooper and Bell looked very concerned when he saw Hadley.

'My God, you are in a state, Hadley.'

'Just a bit of a one, but I'm on the mend, sir.'

'You must stay here until you have fully recovered from this cowardly attack by this mad Countess then take some leave to recuperate,' said Bell firmly.

'Indeed I will, sir.'

'So don't you worry about a thing, Cooper and I will take the case forward, Hadley.'

'Thank you, sir... now... what news of the arrests, Sergeant?'

'I'm very sorry to tell you, sir, that when I arrived at the house, the Princess had left with all her Bulgarian staff and there were only two scullery maids on the premises who knew nothing so were not much help,' replied Cooper.

'The bloody woman has done a bunk, Hadley!' exclaimed Bell indignantly.

'I feared as much,' whispered Hadley.

'You can never trust women... especially foreign ones.'

'In this instance I think you may be right, sir.'

'Of course I'm right, Hadley.'

'Yes, sir.'

'Now I've telegraphed Inspector Bagley at Dover, in case she tries to leave the country, and ordered an immediate search of the Bulgarian Embassy,' said Bell.

'I just hope you can find her, sir.'

'We will... Inspector Hanson is leading the investigation into her disappearance,' said Bell firmly.

'Then you've done all you could, sir.'

'Indeed, but if she left her house at the time you were attacked, then she's had at least eighteen hours head start, so she could have easily escaped across the Channel,' said Bell.

'That's possible sir and what about her spies who gave witness statements?'

'Hanson is following that up as his first priority and he will arrest them all without hesitation,' replied Bell.

'They may know where she is, sir, but don't be too surprised if they have also disappeared,' said Hadley.

'I won't... and if they have gone, it will cause ructions between the Embassies when the Ambassadors find out that they've had Bulgarian spies in their midst,' said Bell.

'Indeed it will, sir.'

'The Commissioner has already prepared himself for this eventuality and will have an urgent meeting with Sir George to deal with any violent responses from the Hungarians or Rumanians.'

Hadley sighed, closed his eyes and whispered 'oh dear... what a bloody mess this is.'

'Indeed it is, Hadley, because now we have to consider releasing our suspects and dropping all charges if this mad Countess proves to be the killer,' said Bell angrily.

'We will, sir.'

'I can tell you that it'll be insufferable if our Government has to apologise to these foreigners!'

'I think that's enough now, gentlemen, so would you please leave,' said the Doctor. Bell replied 'yes of course,' before they nodded and left the ward.

Hadley slept soundly and only awoke when Alice arrived at his bedside.

'How are you feeling now, dearest?'

'I think a little better.'

'Good,' she said with a smile as Nurse Thompson entered and asked 'now you're awake, sir... would you like something to eat?'

'Yes, please.'

'I'll bring you some beef soup then,' she said with a smile before leaving.

Alice spoke gently to her husband and told him that the children were worried but being very good and she would bring them to see him tomorrow. He smiled and relaxed knowing that he could do nothing but try to recover as quickly as possible. He felt better after he had eaten the hot soup and as soon as Alice left he fell into a deep sleep. The Doctor and Matron came to see him at intervals throughout the night and were satisfied that his condition was improving.

The next morning Hadley awoke to find another nurse by his bedside.

'Good morning, sir, how are you feeling today?' she asked.

'Much better thank you.'

'Good, would you like some breakfast now?'

'Please.'

She smiled, left the ward and returned with scrambled eggs on toast and a mug of tea.

Hadley had to be helped to eat as his left hand was useless, heavily bandaged and still painful. He quite enjoyed having the pretty nurse feed him and managed to drink the mug of tea using his right hand. He noticed that his hand trembled slightly as he held the mug and his vision blurred when he glanced down. He realised that the blows to his head must have been quite severe. He had just finished his breakfast and thanked the nurse when Matron entered.

'So how are you today?' she asked.

'Much better thank you.'

'Good, I'm going off duty now so Nurse Carter here will look after you and Matron Brodie is in charge of the ward.'

'Thank you, Matron.'

'And I've told Brodie that you are to have no visitors until the Doctor says so.'

'Very well, Matron... now tell me, how is the Countess?'

'Her condition is causing some concern at the moment,' she replied.

'Oh really... how serious is it?'

'She is not responding as well as we expected after surgery...'

'Surgery?'

'Yes, she has a fractured skull and Doctor Morris decided it was necessary to operate last night to relieve the pressure on her brain,' replied Matron.

'Dear God,' whispered Hadley.

'So we must hope that she improves as time passes.'

'Of course,' replied Hadley, Matron Kelley gave a nod and left.

Alice and the children arrived at midday and, after permission from the Doctor, were admitted by Matron Brodie. His daughter, Anne, cried and his son, Arthur, looked concerned at seeing their father heavily bandaged in bed. Hadley assured his family that he was on the mend and would soon be discharged from hospital after which he would take them for another holiday at Bognor where he would recuperate. The news delighted the family and they were busy talking about the holiday when Cooper arrived with Matron Brodie.

'The Doctor has given your Sergeant permission to see you for just a few minutes,' said Matron.

'Thank you,' replied Hadley. Cooper greeted Alice and the children then asked 'how are you feeling today, sir?'

'Much better thank you.'

'That's very good, sir... but I'm afraid I've some more bad news.'

'Let's hear it.'

'All the witnesses have absconded from their Embassies so the Chief Inspector has issued arrest warrants and ordered all London stations to search for them and he has alerted Inspector Bagley at Dover if they attempt to leave the country.'

Hadley sighed and said 'I'm not surprised, Sergeant, and thank you for letting me know.'

'I'm sorry about this latest setback, sir.'

'It can't be helped, Sergeant,' said Hadley as Doctor Morris entered.

'Inspector, the Countess has regained consciousness and is demanding to see a Policeman and a priest, so would your Sergeant like to follow me and find out what she wants?' asked the puzzled Doctor.

.

CHAPTER 24

Cooper followed the Doctor and Matron into the side ward where the Countess lay propped up in bed. Her head was heavily bandaged, she was pale faced and her eyes were half closed. The Doctor moved to the bedside, looked into her eyes for a moment and said gently, 'the Policeman you asked for is here, Countess.'

She turned her head slightly as she focused her gaze on Cooper before he moved towards her bedside.

'How can I help you, Countess?' he asked.

After a few moments she asked in a barely audible voice, 'where's Helena?'

'I don't know, Countess, she's no longer at your house in Berkeley Square,' replied Cooper.

'Thank God she's got away,' the Countess mumbled.

'Do you know where she's gone?'

'Back to Sofia.'

'Will she return to London?'

'Never... because our work here is done,' whispered the Countess.

'What work is that?' asked Cooper hoping for a confession.

'We have settled all the matters close to her heart and I can pass to the next world in peace,' she sighed and closed her eyes.

'Do these 'matters' concern the murdered Diplomats?' asked Cooper. After a moment, the Countess gave a slight nod then whispered, 'and the Galati woman.'

'What reason did you have for murdering them?' asked Cooper gently.

'They all betrayed Helena... so they had to die... it is a matter of honour,' she whispered.

'How did they betray her?'

The Countess remained silent for a minute then replied, 'they all rejected Helena when she offered her undying love to them while they deceived her by having affairs with other women.'

'I'm sad to hear it.'

'All men are deceivers and deserve to die,' she whispered in a vicious tone..

'Not all men.'

217

'Those who are not deceivers are just blind fools.'

Cooper remained silent for a moment before asking, 'why did you kill Madam Galati?'

'She was a whore who deserved to die... she knew no shame with men who thought she was beautiful.'

'And why did you attack Inspector Hadley?'

'Because he turned Helena's love away when she offered it to him, the same as all the other deceivers did,' she replied.

'He is an honourable man, Countess.'

'Helena loved him... he was her only hope for her future happiness.'

Cooper was about to ask another question when a priest entered and the Countess smiled.

'I can now make my peace with God,' she whispered.

'Indeed you can try, Countess,' said Cooper.

'And tell Inspector Hadley that I enjoyed masquerading as a man to fool you both... I watched your pathetic attempts to catch me with much amusement,' she said as she closed her eyes.

'I will tell him, Countess.'

Cooper returned to Hadley's bedside and told him what the Countess had said.

'I'm not surprised... it's a pity that she will die and won't face trial,' said Hadley as the Doctor entered with Matron.

'Well Inspector, it was quite astonishing to hear what she had to say,' said Doctor Morris.

'It was a full confession without a doubt,' said Cooper.

'Indeed it was... and what a wicked woman she is,' said the Doctor.

'She gives all women a bad name,' said Matron.

'It'll be interesting to hear what she says at her trial,' said Morris.

'But isn't she going to die soon, Doctor?' asked Cooper.

'I don't think so... not after she had the surgical procedure to remove the pressure on her brain.'

'Really, Doctor?' asked Hadley.

'I am quite confident that she will make a full recovery in time and although I told her so, she firmly believes she is at death's door and that's why she asked for a priest,' he replied.

Hadley smiled and said, 'that's very good news, Doctor.'

'Indeed it is,' he replied.

'We have a lot to discuss, Doctor, so may my Sergeant remain for a while?'

'He can stay for half an hour then I want you to get some rest, Inspector.'

'Thank you, Doctor.'

'And Matron... please make sure that the Sergeant leaves promptly.'

'Oh I certainly will, Doctor,' she replied as she looked at the watch pinned to her starched uniform and noted the time.

After their discussion, Cooper left and Hadley fell into a deep sleep remaining so under the watchful eye of Matron Brodie and Nurse Carter until the next morning. When he awoke, Nurse Thompson was by his bedside and asked with a smile, 'how are you feeling today, sir?'

'Very much better, thank you nurse.'

'Good... now would you like some breakfast?'

'Please.'

It was mid-morning when Matron Brodie finally left the ward and handed over responsibility to Matron Kelley who resumed her duties and appeared in Hadley's room saying with a smile, 'you have two distinguished visitors, sir.'

'Have I now,' he replied in surprise as the Commissioner strode in followed by the Chief Inspector.

'Morning, Hadley.'

'Good morning, sir... Chief Inspector.'

'How are you feeling now?' asked the Commissioner.

'I'm much better thank you, sir, and recovering well.'

'Are they taking good care of you?'

'Yes indeed they are, sir.'

'Good, and when you're discharged from hospital I want you to take extended leave until you feel ready to resume your duties,' said the Commissioner.

'Thank you very much, sir.'

'You've done well Hadley and I commend your bravery.'

'Thank you, sir.'

'Now, after discussing the political ramifications of the case with Sir George and Sir Jason, I've released a press statement which is printed in 'The Times' this morning... it informs the public of all the known facts, Hadley. The Chief Inspector has brought you a copy,' said the great one as Bell produced the paper and placed it on the bedside table.

'Very good, sir.'

'The initial reaction from the Balkan Embassy's is one of shock and disbelief that this mad Countess has been responsible for the murders of their Diplomats,' said the Commissioner.

'I'm sure they are as surprised as I was when I discovered who my attacker was, sir.'

'Quite so, Hadley... I've seen the woman myself this morning and to me she looks completely insane.'

Bell nodded and said, 'I agree with you, sir, and if we can't hang her because of her insanity then she'll be committed to a secure lunatic asylum for the rest of her life.'

'You're quite correct, Chief Inspector.'

'Thank you, sir.'

'So... I'm pleased to hear that you're on the mend, Hadley and I look forward to seeing you back on duty when you return from your leave,' said the Commissioner.

'Thank you, sir.'

'Oh, and by the way, I've given Constable Davis permission to see you later when he has finished his duty rota,' said the great one with a smile.

'Thank you, sir.'

'Well, good day to you, Hadley,' he said with a nod before he turned and made for the door.

'Good day, sir, and thank you for coming to see me.'

Hadley glanced at Bell and asked, 'I suppose Davis was the Constable who knocked me senseless?'

'He was the one, Hadley,' replied Bell with a grin before he followed the Commissioner out into the general ward.

Hadley sighed, picked up the paper and was surprised to see that the report was at the top of the front page. It read in large capital letters:

"*FOREIGN ASSASSIN ARRESTED IN BERKELEY SQUARE*
Inspector James Hadley of Scotland Yard, who was leading the

investigation into the recent murders of three Diplomats, arrested the knife wielding killer, in a death defying struggle in the bushes of the Square's shrubbery garden. Inspector Hadley was repeatedly stabbed and seriously injured in the struggle before he was assisted by Constable Davis who helped him bring the violent incident to a satisfactory conclusion. Inspector Hadley and the assassin were taken to the Marylebone Hospital for treatment. The violent assailant has been positively identified by senior Police Officers as Countess Helga Somovit, a Bulgarian woman of considerable strength and cunning, who is alleged to have committed these dreadful crimes in London. The Countess is under constant Police guard at the hospital where her condition is giving cause for concern. Further details of the case will be released by Scotland Yard in due course."

Hadley sighed again, slowly shook his head and put the paper down as the door opened and Doctor Evans entered.

'Morning, Jim.'

'Ah, good morning, Doctor,' said Hadley with a smile.

'I heard you were in here and had to see for myself,' said Evans as he sat at the bedside.

'Well it's kind of you to come and it certainly makes a change to see you out of the mortuary,' said Hadley with a grin.

'Yes, all my colleagues say I look quite different in daylight,' said Evans with a chuckle.

'Indeed you do.'

'So, how are they treating you, Jim?'

'Very well I must say.'

'Good… Matron Kelley has a fearsome reputation but I'm sure she has a soft spot for brave Policemen.'

'Yes she seems to have.'

'Now… what about this mad Bulgarian woman who attacked you?'

Hadley told the Doctor in detail of the attack and the confession of the Countess and when he finished, Evans looked amazed.

'What a dreadful, callous woman, Jim.'

'Indeed… she fooled us all and is quite proud of it.'

'And fancy masquerading as a man like some music hall comedy act to commit murder,' said Evans.

'I think that was a very clever ploy as she knew she would inevitably be seen by someone near the crime scenes.'

'Quite so, Jim, and of course the stiletto that she used to attack you fits exactly the stab wounds to all the victims,' said Evans.

'I had no doubt,' said Hadley as Matron Kelley entered.

'Sorry to disturb you Inspector, but two lady visitors have arrived and wish to see you, they say they are your cousins but I have my doubts,' she said firmly as she put her hands on her hips.

'Please show them in, Matron,' replied Hadley with a smile knowing full well who they were.

'Are you absolutely sure, sir?' persisted Matron.

'Yes I am… and thank you for your concern, Matron,' said Hadley and Evans grinned.

'Oh very well then… but they can't stay for long you know,' she said before she left the ward.

Hadley looked at Evans and said with a smile, 'you must stay and meet these two… they are my colourful streetwalkers who keep me well informed.'

'Well I look forward to meeting live ones because usually I see only dead ones when sadly they appear on my marble slabs,' said Evans as Agnes and Florrie waltzed in.

'Oh, Jim, how are you?' asked Agnes as she hurried to his bedside.

'I'm much better for seeing you both, thank you Agnes.'

'Oh, Jim we were so worried about you,' she said before she bent down and kissed his cheek followed by Florrie who, after giving him a longer kiss, said, 'yes we were and old blimmin bossy boots out there wasn't going to let us in to see you!'

'Matron has her duties to perform Florrie and she is only protecting me,' said Hadley with a smile.

'Well we told her straight that we were going to see you even if we had to wait 'til she retired,' said Agnes.

'Or dropped blimmin dead!' added Florrie and Evans laughed.

'I'm sure… now ladies, I'd like you to meet Doctor Evans, he's our pathologist here at the hospital… so Doctor… may I introduce Agnes Cartwright and Florrie Dean?'

'Charmed I'm sure,' said Evans with a smile as he stood and shook hands with them.

'Are you taking care of our Jim?' asked Agnes.

'No I'm not, young lady.'

'Ohh… young lady… I've not been called that for awhile I must say,' said Agnes coyly.

'You've never been called that in your blimmin life,' said Florrie with a grin.

Agnes ignored the remark and said, 'when we read about you in the papers…'

'You're in all of them,' interrupted Florrie.

'We were so worried that we had to come and see you, Jim,' said Agnes.

'Thank you.'

'Molly sends her love…' began Florrie.

'And Vera and her girls hope you are getting on alright and are on the mend,' interrupted Agnes.

Evans raised his eyebrows and said with a smile, 'I think I should leave you to your 'cousins' and the good wishes from your army of female admirers, Jim.'

'Perhaps you should, Doctor,' replied Hadley with a grin, Evans nodded and said 'goodbye' to them all before he left.

The women chatted nonstop for almost twenty minutes before Matron appeared and asked them to leave so her patient could rest. Agnes nodded while Florrie pulled a face at Matron who ignored the gesture. They left the room after kissing him and saying firmly that they would be back to visit him soon.

It was after five o'clock when Hadley's dressings were changed again and his wounds inspected by the Doctor, who declared that he was satisfied with their continued healing. Tea was served and when Hadley had finished the light meal, Matron informed him that he had three visitors. He was pleased to see Cooper and George accompanied by a young man, who he assumed was Constable Davis.

'Good afternoon, sir,' said Cooper as he sat at the bedside.

'Afternoon, Sergeant.'

'Hello, sir, and how are you feeling now?' asked George in a concerned tone.

'I'm much better, thank you, George.'

'That's very good to hear, sir, and I've taken the liberty of buying some dainties to help your recovery,' said George as he handed a brown paper bag full of iced cakes to Hadley.

'Why thank you, George I shall enjoy them with my afternoon cup of tea.'

'My pleasure, sir.'

'And I presume you are Constable Davis?' asked Hadley.

'Yes, I am, sir,' replied Davis anxiously.

'Ah... you're the Officer who knocked me senseless and....'

'I am so very sorry, sir,' interrupted Davis as Hadley smiled then continued, 'and probably saved my life.'

Davis blushed slightly and replied, 'oh, I don't know about that, sir.'

'I do...so how long have you been a Policeman?'

'Only a month, sir,' replied Davis.

'Well I think you'll go far in your police career, Davis, as you're now famous and mentioned in The Times for assisting me with the arrest of the mad assassin before knocking me out in the process, although that is not mentioned in the paper... I'm glad to say,' said Hadley with a grin.

'My fame is not deserved, sir, because I didn't know who you were at the time and I honestly thought that you were a couple of drunks fighting because when I approached I could definitely smell alcohol.'

'Quite so, Davis,' said Hadley as he cleared his throat and Cooper grinned.

'And when the cabbie helped me carry you and the other person out into the gas light, I saw all the blood and realised you both needed medical attention, so the driver helped me put both of you in his cab and drove you here.'

'Well thank God he did,' said Hadley.

'Yes, sir.'

'I'm told that the other person is a woman... is that really true, sir?'

'It is, Constable, she's a Bulgarian Countess.'

'Well, I never... I thought he was a bit of a strange fella with such long hair,' whispered Davis.

The detectives talked about the investigation and the cunning duplicity of the Countess and Princess Radomir while Davis listened in wide-eyed amazement. They were in full flow when Matron entered and told them that it was now time to leave. As he left, Davis apologised profusely to Hadley for injuring him and the Inspector smiled, thanking the young man again for his quick action, which probably saved his life.

Alice arrived soon afterwards and spent over an hour with her husband before leaving him, feeling greatly relieved that he was making good progress and would be home in a few days time.

CHAPTER 25

It was on Friday morning that Doctor Morris examined Hadley's wounds and being satisfied they were healing without any infection, discharged him from the hospital. Arrangements were made for a Police coach to take him to his home in Camden where Alice and the children greeted him affectionately. Hadley enjoyed a restful weekend with his family and felt better by the hour.

On the following Monday the Hadley family journeyed by train down to Bognor Regis where they stayed once again at the Esplanade Hotel. It was a moderate establishment where the food was good, the beds comfortable and the sea views wonderful. The manager was delighted to have them back again and welcomed them warmly. The family relaxed, enjoyed the sunshine and had a wonderful week's rest before leaving Bognor on the next Saturday morning. Hadley was impatient to return to the Yard to find out what had happened whilst he had been on leave.

When Hadley arrived in his office early on the Monday morning, George was already there and looked surprised to see his Inspector.

'Good morning, sir, I didn't expect to see you back so soon.'

'I'm sure you didn't, George, but here I am… fit and ready to find out what's been going on in my absence,' replied Hadley with a smile as he sat at his desk.

'In that case, I'll make a pot of tea and tell you, sir,' said George as Cooper arrived.

The clerk glanced at him and said, 'ah, now the Sergeant's here, I'm sure he'll oblige you with all the details, sir, while I make the tea.'

'Thank you, George… so, what's been happening, Sergeant?'

'Morning, sir, I'm surprised to see you, I thought you'd stay on leave for at least another week,' said Cooper.

'Well I was impatient to return, Sergeant and as I felt much better I could see no good reason for staying at home.'

'Right you are, sir,' said Cooper as he sat at his desk.

'So tell me everything.'

226

'Very well, sir... when the Countess had recovered sufficiently from her injuries, the Chief and I visited her in hospital where he managed to persuade her to confess to the murders of the Diplomats and Madam Galati.'

'Did he now,' said Hadley in surprise.

'The Chief found it relatively easy, sir and once she started he couldn't stop her going on about how all men were deceivers and should die.'

'I'm sure.'

'She seemed quite proud of the fact that she managed to fool us by masquerading as a man and of course she planned all the killings with the Princess,' said Cooper.

'Well we were certainly fooled by all the lies, Sergeant.'

'We were, sir and to think while we were having lunch with the Princess, the Countess wasn't ill in bed but was at Harrods attacking Madam Galati.'

'It was shameful deception in the extreme... did she give a reason for her murder?'

'Not really, sir, but I got the impression that the Princess was very jealous of Madam Galati.'

'I'm not surprised because she was very lovely and attracted all the men.'

'She certainly did, sir.'

'So I presume that the murdered Diplomats were lovers of the Princess but they all deceived her one way or another.'

'You're quite right, sir... she met them when they were Diplomats in Sofia and according to the Countess, they all refused to marry her when she proposed to them, which I understand is the correct way that is done by Royalty.'

'Indeed it is, Sergeant, our beloved Queen had to propose to Prince Albert you know,' said Hadley.

'I didn't know that,' said Cooper as George brought in the tea.

'Ah... you're a life saver, George.'

'Thank you, sir, I do my best,' he replied as he put the cup on Hadley's desk.

Big Ben was striking ten o'clock when Hadley went up to the Chief' office. Bell looked up from his paperwork, smiled and said, 'ah, Hadley you're back I see.'

'I am indeed, sir.'

'Fully recovered I trust?' he asked as he waved him to the creaking chair.

'More or less… thank you, sir.'

'Excellent … well I'm pleased to inform you that I managed to get the mad Countess to sign a confession to all her crimes, Hadley.'

'So I understand, sir.'

'And the case against her will now be an open and shut affair, so if her defence doesn't plead insanity, then we'll be able to hang her in double quick time,' said Bell with a contented smile.

'Without a doubt, sir.'

'The Commissioner is very pleased and so is Sir George… and Sir Jason has managed to quieten the Balkan foreigners down without an apology, so we'll not expect any more trouble from them,' said Bell.

'Thank goodness for that, sir.'

'I agree, Hadley… now the Countess has been discharged from the Marylebone and is being held in solitary confinement in Holloway awaiting a trial date.'

'I'm pleased we've got her under lock and key, sir.'

'So am I, Hadley, but it's a shame the Princess and her spies managed to escape across the Channel… it would have been quite a court appearance if we'd got her in front of a judge!'

'Indeed it would, sir.'

'And the Press would have had another field day!'

'Very true, sir.'

'So there's nothing for you to do now, Hadley... it's all done, so you should have stayed on leave.'

'I was impatient to return, sir.'

'Well I understand that and must admit it's good to have you back.'

'Thank you, sir.'

At the trial of the Countess at the Old Bailey, Sir Digby Frobisher led the Prosecution and as she had confessed to the murders he was just obliged to make a statement of the facts to the court. Her defence counsel, Mr Oswald Dingle-Smith, made a plea of her insanity, which was corroborated by Doctor Morris and Doctor

Wainwright from the Marylebone Hospital. They both agreed that her mental state was far beyond any normality and her pathological hatred of men was the cause of her unmitigated violence towards them.

The judge, Lord Manningham, looked severe when he sentenced her to be kept for the rest of her natural life in Broadmoor, the prison for criminally insane and violent women. The Countess looked at Bell, Hadley and Cooper, who were sitting behind the Barristers, and gave them a curious smile before she was taken down by two Constables.

Cooper leaned towards Hadley and whispered, 'I think you had a very lucky escape in Berkeley Square, sir.'

'I did indeed, Sergeant.'

'It's a shame the bloody woman escaped the hangman,' said Bell in a frustrated tone.

'I believe it's better that she is locked away for life than dead, sir,' said Hadley and Bell shook his head.

After behind the scenes activity by Sir Jason, Secretary Galati, Bacau and his men along with Osijek were all recalled by their Governments and returned to the Balkans. Their replacements at the Embassies appeared as distant and aloof as their predecessors.

A week later, the Commissioner sent for Hadley and the Chief Inspector. He waved them to sit and said, 'I have received some disturbing news from Sir George who has just returned from a meeting with Sir Jason. The British Ambassador in Sofia has reported in his confidential mail that Princess Radomir has been found dead in the Palace.'

Hadley went pale and Bell asked, 'was she murdered, sir?'

'Apparently there are considerable doubts about the circumstances, Chief Inspector.'

'Really, sir?'

'Yes, it appears that she was found in her boudoir by her maid late at night, there were no signs of any violence and after rumours of a fierce argument with a certain Count on the day she died, our Ambassador believes that she took her own life,' said the Commissioner.

'Oh dear God,' whispered Hadley.

'The official line put out by the Bulgarian Government is that she died of a sudden heart seizure,' said the Commissioner.

'And of course we'll never know for certain will we, sir?' asked Bell.

'No, Chief Inspector, but it is a sad ending to a very troubled woman.'

'Indeed it is, sir,' said Hadley.

They remained silent for a few moments before the Commissioner said 'well, gentlemen, you know what the dramatist William Congreve said about women?'

'Yes sir... Hell hath no fury like a woman scorned,' whispered Hadley as he glanced down at his scarred hand.

'You're quite right, Inspector.'

Hadley returned to his office and asked George to make some tea while he told Cooper the sad news of the Princess's death.

'I'm not surprised that she met an untimely end, sir.'

'Neither am I, Sergeant, she was dangerous and passionate woman who courted un-requited love, which always ends in disaster and should be avoided at all costs,' said Hadley with a sigh.

'Not like the mad, man hating cousin who attacked you, sir.'

'Indeed... she was very well suited to be the Princess's instrument of death.'

'What a terrible world we live in, sir, when jealous women kill,' said Cooper with a shake of his head as George brought in their tea.

'Shall I get some sandwiches from the canteen, sir, or will you have lunch out?' he asked as he put the cup on Hadley's desk.

'I think we'll have an early lunch at the Kings Head today and relax for an hour or so, thank you, George,' replied Hadley with a smile.

'Very good, sir.'

**Follow Hadley and Cooper in the gruesome case of
The Macabre Murder**